THE
SILENCE

THE
SILENCE

DAISY
PEARCE

THOMAS & MERCER

Published by Thomas & Mercer, Seattle

www.apub.com

Amazon, the Amazon logo, and Thomas & Mercer are trademarks of Amazon.com, Inc., or its affiliates.

ISBN-13: 9781542017824
ISBN-10: 1542017823

Cover design by Tom Sanderson

Printed in the United States of America

For my mum, who always believed

Prologue

The pill is small and round and grey. It is unbranded, like the bottle, and almost entirely unremarkable. I am used to swallowing them now. At first they left a metallic taste in my throat, like pennies. Now I barely taste a thing. Sometimes I drink them with juice or coffee. I used to take them with wine, but all that's changed now. It's all changed.

And so. I'm standing in the bathroom, water puddling at my feet. I look down at myself, noticing that I'm dressed but no shoes. The light coming through the window is the dirty grey of smog or a ruptured exhaust. It's early, and I am at home. The heating hasn't come on yet, and I can see my breath. Winter frost on the windows. I am shivering with cold. And I must take this pill.

There is someone at the door. I can see the shape of the figure through the patterned glass. I swallow the pill dry. My hair is wet, and he is knocking against the glass, saying, 'Are you done yet?', and he is saying, 'Stella, we need to get going', but I can tell by the set of his shoulders that what he means is I will swallow you, I will swallow you whole, and I am afraid.

Chapter 1

The moon is rising, the sky lavender-coloured. Carmel and I have walked to the end of our road, enjoying the twilight and the open windows of the houses through which can be heard the clinking of cutlery, soft music, laughter. When we draw near to the bus stop Carmel sees the poster and she nudges me, grinning.

'Go on, Stella,' she says, 'go and stand beside it. Please, please, please. Just one photo. We'll do it quickly. Give it a double thumbs up.'

'Can I give it the finger?' I ask, and if she hears the tremor in my voice she doesn't comment on it. I stand beside the poster, smiling weakly, uncomfortable. My skin tingles with anxiety and something a little like revulsion. *Hurry up*, I think. The bus is drawing nearer. Carmel clicks the camera and then frowns down at the image.

'Huh,' she says, 'wasn't as funny as I thought it would be.'

Later, we are in Soho. I've got a mildly pleasant buzz on from the beer we drank before we left the flat and the warmth baking from the pavements. We're laughing, Carmel and I, and I don't see it coming, not then. I don't know the bar we're going to but Carmel does. She tells me she's been there with a previous boyfriend, but – as I tell her – that doesn't narrow it down. Inside it is dark and low-ceilinged. There is the thump and hiss of loud music, the wall dank with condensation. I press my hand against it and leave an almost perfect wet print. I order cocktails from a menu chalked on the wall and struggle through the crowd, where I find Carmel talking to a tall man with a neat haircut, tattoos crawling up his neck. His face is pressed close to her ear, and she is smiling.

I hand her a drink and look around. It is busy. The cocktail is exotic, with a dark kick of rum in the back of my throat. Inside, curled up like a milk-fed cat, is the part of me which would much rather be in bed. It's a sour sort of homesickness. I swallow my drink and head back to the bar. Carmel has snaked her arms around the man's waist; they lean into each other, like dancers, like drunks. I smile. I'm happy for her. She deserves her pleasure.

At the bar I order something else, mispronouncing the name. The barman makes me repeat it until I get it right, having to speak louder and louder into his ear. I feel stupid and tiny and too old for all this. As he hands me my drink I thank him and tip him because, absurdly, I want him to like me and think I am cool. I've always been needy, even as a kid. At nine years old I would make myself sick worrying about my parents separating and as a result spent a lot of time needling them for attention, sandwiching myself between the two of them on the sofa, small grabby hands at their hems. *Where are you going? Don't leave me.* There were no child psychologists in those days and the doctor didn't know what was wrong with me. On bad days I overheard them talking about me. I didn't have enough friends, my mother was saying, and my father said well whose fault is that, and my mother replied I just want the best for her, and my father said she should be in school for God's sake, and on and on. What it all came back to was one or both of them saying, 'It isn't normal.' And that scared me most of all. I wanted to be normal. I wanted to be just like everyone else.

I look into my glass, surprised to see it empty. Carmel and the man with the tattoos have found a booth in a darkened corner, sitting in it pressed close together, his hand reaching around her back possessively. I think it's time I leave or I'll miss the last tube. I turn when he touches me. It was enough, that deft sweep of his fingers against my bare arm, to make me turn around.

'Excuse me, are you—'

The question hangs in the air, creating a vacuum. I turn to face him, this dark-haired man, tall and strong-featured. He has the thick, heavy nose and jaw of a caveman. This is the first word I think of when I see him: Jurassic.

'You are, aren't you? You're her.' He's smiling, looking me over. 'I don't – I don't believe it. It is you, isn't it? Katie Marigold.'

◆ ◆ ◆

I nod. It was my name, or rather, it was her name: the little girl with the ringlets and the gap between her front teeth. Katie Marigold. That was me, from ages four to twelve. A halo of blonde curls, frilly little dresses like clouds orbiting my waist, my dimpled, chunky legs. I was adorable. I even had my own teatime television show in the eighties. It ran for eight years: *Marigold!* The exclamation mark was important, as was my catchphrase, which I was contractually obliged to say at least once per episode – *I fink we'd better ask Daddy.* Awful, right? It got applause every time, the audience awwww-ing and bleating like lambs. The programme was syrupy-sweet, a fictional family living in a cottage called Honeypot with a golden Labrador called Frisky and the same storyline regurgitated every week: mild family problem, implausible complication, catchphrase, resolution doled out thickly like wedding cake, audience reacts, credits. 'A sitcom for simpletons', it was described as once by some unwed bitter old hack who predicted my future thus: dead of an overdose at thirty. Nice woman. My mother wrote to her. I didn't see the letter, but I remember her mouth pressed tightly together as she was writing, lips as thin as a fishing hook.

Little Katie Marigold. Obviously, Carmel thought it was hilarious. Sometimes she would make me do the voice, that cutesy little lisp through the gap in my teeth. When I got them fixed she was gutted I couldn't do it anymore. I would catch her looking up the old episodes on the Internet and quoting me my lines or singing the theme song to me when I walked into a room, creasing herself up into giggles. I did adverts too, everything from Dentabrite toothpaste to Patches dogfood ('*I fink we'd better ask Doggy!*'). By the late eighties we were pushed further and further out into the scheduling wilderness. The show had become dated, unfunny, and borderline racist. ('*Keith, there's a man squinting at me in the garden!*', '*That's Ho Ching, honey, he's Chinese.*') I'd outgrown the dress, the shoes, the buttery voice. My career was over just as puberty hit me like a truck. No one wanted to see Katie Marigold with tits and acne. I did a couple of interviews and a TV special just before my twelfth birthday, and then I shed Katie Marigold like a skin. I made the papers just once more, a year later, when my mother died. They had a long-lens photographer on the day of the funeral, capturing my face hovering over my black peacoat like a haunted white balloon. I had just turned thirteen.

◆　◆　◆

'You're not going to make me do the voice, are you?' I say. My words are blurry. The cocktail was stronger than I thought.

'No! God, no. It's just – wow. You know, I watched that show all the time as a kid. We all did, the whole family. I used to love that dog, all the tricks he could do.'

'We had nine of them.'

'What, dogs?'

'Yes. We had to keep replacing them because they kept dying.'

I'm a little too drunk, I think. I'm being morbid. Need to snap out of it. I smile, show some teeth.

'Sorry. Have I ruined the magic for you?'

He laughs at that, smooths his hand down the front of his shirt. I'm getting a good look at him now as his lips draw back into a long, languorous smile. His eyes are dark like twin pools of ink. I don't like him at all. Too old, too clean-looking. He looks like a sleazy dad jettisoning his marriage. Wedding ring in his jacket pocket, condom in his wallet.

'Listen, can I, uh' – he scratches his cheek with his thumbnail, looking uncomfortable – 'can I buy you a drink, Katie?'

I look over my shoulder but I can't see Carmel anymore, so I turn back to the man and smile brightly. 'Sure, why not.'

'Great!' He seems genuinely pleased, and I'm weirdly flattered by his attention. I never get recognised anymore. *Marigold!* didn't achieve cult status; no one wants to see reruns of it, and it's never been out on video or DVD. It sank, a rusty anchor tolling off the fathoms, without trace.

Later, we leave the bar, both of us staggering against each other a little. It has started to rain, and the air has that sticky, urgent feel of a summer storm. He gives me another one of those lupine grins and makes a show of looking at my shoes.

'You can't walk in those. We'll need to get a cab.'

'Has that line ever got you laid?'

'You tell me.'

I stiffen and turn towards him. To my surprise he doesn't pull away and now our faces are very close, his mouth just inches from my cheek. The intimacy is almost unbearable. This close I can smell him; smoke and whisky and bright white tropical heat. His skin is clear and his cheekbones high, flat blades severing his features. Dark hair wavy, as though combed by fingers.

'I have a boyfriend.'

'Liar.'

My mouth drops open. He closes it with gentle pressure, just the pads of his fingers, laughing. My pulse flutters in my neck, my wrists, where the skin is transparent and thickly veined.

'Come on, I'm serious.'

'So am I. Piss off.'

He laughs again. 'Okay, let's make a deal. Okay? Little deal. Humour me. I'm going to take you for one more drink. One drink. That's all I'm asking for. If you still think I'm an idiot after one drink, then . . .' He shrugs.

'One drink?'

'Yup. Back at mine.'

He is still looking around for a taxi. When he sees my expression he laughs.

'One drink, I said. I didn't say where.'

The next morning I wake with a throbbing head and an oily taste in my mouth like rancid butter. Another hangover, a blinder. Beside me, in a bed I do not immediately recognise, in an unfamiliar room, a man is sleeping with his back to me. His broad shoulders are decorated with freckles like an unknown galaxy. I move slowly, so as not to wake him. Inside my head bells are ringing, clamouring. I wonder if it is possible to die from a hangover, and I think then as I always do: I am off the booze for the rest of the month. Lips that touch liquor shall not touch mine. Lord, my head.

My phone shows me that Carmel has been calling and calling. Wondering where I had gone, I suppose. If I was safe. I should have told her I was leaving, I think as I gather my clothes into my arms. I shouldn't have just left the way I did. I look back at the sleeping figure in the bed and suppress an involuntary shudder. What had I been thinking? I know what Carmel will say. She'll tell me I have 'daddy issues'. She's probably right. God.

On the train, early Sunday morning; the tube is full of black-eyed revellers with sour morning breath, ravaged and blinking in the sunlight like released hostages. On the platform at London Bridge, I spot another of those posters, the one for the new film coming out that Carmel had taken my picture in front of. It's called *Bossman*. An action film. I walk past it quickly, feeling my heart and my head throbbing. My memories from last night coming back to me. They feel feverish, a cartoon. After leaving the cocktail bar, the man and I had taken a taxi to another dive with candles burning in gothic-looking sconces. A kiss on the bank of the Thames beneath a line of fairy lights, gently swaying, the smell of the river, brackish greasy. A passionate embrace inside the hallway of his building which had left the ghostly imprints of our bodies on the glass panels.

But in the morning, asleep, one hand thrown over the covers, he had looked old. There were threads of silver in his hair, long lines about his mouth. Thank God, I think, as I finally reach our rented flat and fumble for my keys, that I never have to see him again.

◆ ◆ ◆

Three days later I see him again. It's lunchtime and I am not at work. I'm in a pub just round the corner, sitting facing the wall so that no one can see my tears. I wish I could smoke. I've ordered a gin and tonic with a whisky chaser, but the thought of food makes my stomach shrivel. I left work half an hour ago, and I don't think I'm going back this afternoon.

'Katie?'

I don't recognise his voice, and I don't turn around at the unfamiliar name. He approaches the table and says it again, tapping me delicately on my shoulder. I can hear the rustle of paper as he moves, and I wipe my fingers under my eyes carefully. Still, his smile rapidly fades as he sees my expression, dissolving into a look of concern. I note he is holding flowers. Peonies the colour of antique silk, hand-tied. They're beautiful. My throat swells with emotion at them: how fragile they are, how short their brief lives. I can't speak and so he sits opposite me. I'm embarrassed to admit it, but I don't remember his name. He pats my hand with awkward familiarity. 'I was on my way to your work but then I saw you through the window. I'm sorry. I didn't realise . . .' He falls silent. I smile weakly.

'These are for you.' He indicates the flowers. 'Uh – I'm not normally this clumsy, I promise. I had a better speech than this planned out.'

'I'm sorry I ruined it.' I press the heels of my palms into my eye sockets until white flashes appear behind my lids. 'I've had some bad news.'

He doesn't ask. Instead he asks if I want another drink. Yes, I tell him, something strong. He comes back with a gin and tonic – a double measure, he tells me – thick slices of lime, ice chattering in the glass. I take a sip.

'How did you find out where I worked?'

'The hotel on Pelham Street, you said. I only went into three before I found the one you worked in. Don't you remember? You told me.'

'Did I?'

He laughs. 'Not very memorable, then?' he asks, and I have the decency to blush. 'You know who I am, at least. That's something, right?'

He waits, tapping his fingernails against the table. There is a smile lurking behind his frankness, a carefully disguised tease.

I nod. 'Sure I do.'

'Go on.'

I take another sip. I am thinking desperately. He watches me with those imperious dark eyes, and then I see he is mouthing something at me. Mark. Mark-o.

'Marco!'

'Well done.'

'Oh, Marco, I'm so sorry. I'm giving you a terrible impression. Thank you for the flowers, they're beautiful. Today is just an awful, awful day.'

'Do you want me to call someone for you?'

He speaks quietly, and his kindness makes me feel like crying again.

'No, I think I'm just going to go home. It's my dad. He's had a stroke.'

'Oh, Katie, how awful. I'm sorry. Is it serious? Do you need to go to him?'

I shake my head. The shock is wearing off now, and I am starting to shiver. A haemorrhagic stroke, his sister said in the phone call I'd received at my desk, her voice trembling. I've never heard her sound so afraid. A bleed on the brain; according to the doctor, it's lucky we got to him when we did.

'You stay where you are, love,' Aunt Jackie said when I'd offered to take a train up that afternoon. 'Nothing you can do at the moment. Your father's not going anywhere and me and Darren are driving up this evening.'

I miss my mum. We lost her, my dad and I, when I was nine days a teenager. She jumped from the roof of the multi-storey car park just outside town, near the industrial estate. She was found on a patch of waste ground where weeds sprouted through the cracks in the earth like exclamation marks. A pointless, violent death, I heard my dad say. His voice was raw from crying. I was silent for two months, a mute. I couldn't take it in. She hadn't left us a note or given anything away. The last time I saw her she'd given me five pounds for my seventy-pence bus fare and told me to keep the change. I still have it, the change. I've put it in a jar, sealed it. It is airless in there, and the rattling sound it makes is like old bones. I've taken it to every house I've ever lived in. I don't know what else to do with it. Here's the thing about being an only child. One day it all falls to you to keep everyone going.

'Katie,' Marco was saying, looking concerned, 'I have my car outside. Let me take you home.'

He drops me at the flat in his smooth, expensive car. It is built like a sleek, dark bullet and as well maintained as a racehorse. It even has a name. Sadie. Marco puts the radio on quietly and other than asking me where to turn off barely speaks on the journey to Lewisham. I ask him if he wants to come inside. He tells me no and kisses me softly on my head. 'Call me when it gets better,' he says, and watches me walk into the house. Afterwards Carmel comes home from work and finds me on the sofa beneath a duvet. I've started myself on a crying jag which lasts nearly half an hour.

She rocks me and soothes me and tells me over and over again it's all right, it's all right, Stella. I like the feeling of being cosseted again: it makes me feel plump and indulged, just like I was as a little girl.

Marc-o. Marc-oh. I need to remember that. He'd shown me such kindness.

Chapter 2

In the early evening the city light is the colour of sucked toffee, still warm. Carmel and I are laughing, squeezed onto the tiny metal balcony which creaks beneath our feet. We won't die if we fall, Carmel tells me, only break our backs. It'll be fine, it'll be fine. Traction could be fun, it'll be fine. We're laughing at our mortality and drinking beers, the windows open wide behind us to let in the last of the daylight. The view from up here on the second floor is municipal: the patch of littered concrete which serves as parking for all the tenants, the back of a Lebanese restaurant, a line of bins. Further ahead, we can just make out the tower of St Saviour's Church on Lewisham High Street. We're talking idly, bare legs pressing warmly together, when Carmel suddenly pitches forward, hissing as though in pain.

'It's them! It's them!'

I lean over the railing, beneath us that sound of grinding metal as the balcony groans. I hear Carmel telling me to be careful. I'm clinging to the wrought iron until my knuckles turn white. The cyclists are back. Our neighbours from upstairs, shiny with sweat, muscular bodies packed into taut Lycra, slick and glossy as seals.

'I need my glasses,' I'm saying.

Carmel says, 'Look at those calf muscles. Thank you, Jesus.'

They haven't seen us although I'm sure they know we're here. We heard them leave and came straight out here, and we haven't moved since. They are locking up their bikes, wiping the backs of their necks, which are deeply tanned from a summer bent over the handlebars.

I turn to Carmel. 'Say something.'

'Hello!' she calls out, unfolding herself. She is all legs, glistening conker-coloured thighs. That gets their attention. They look up, shielding their eyes.

'Good ride?' She is smiling down at them; strong white teeth. One of them steps forward, the blond one, although really they are interchangeable: all hardened muscle and sweeping jaws. They're almost Grecian, as though carved from marble and somehow animated.

'Yeah – great, thanks.' He lifts the hem of his cycling top and scratches at his flat stomach idly. I wonder if Carmel is going to collapse. 'Listen. Uh – you girls haven't seen anyone hanging around here in the evenings, have you? Noticed anything like that?'

Carmel and I look at each other and shake our heads.

'Okay. Keep an eye out. Been a lot of break-ins round here recently. Good idea to double-lock the doors when you go out.'

'Thanks,' Carmel says, sliding an arm around my waist. 'But the only thing I have of value is her.'

'Shut up!' I hiss, but I'm laughing and it feels good. The warm sun on my skin, the last heat of the day. It's been a week since my dad went into hospital and he's being released soon. Aunt Jackie sounded upbeat when she called me earlier, her voice high and happy. Carmel and I went out for food and ended up by the river eating chips greasy and crusted with salt. Her eyes were kohl-lined electric blue, her skin a soft dark shimmer.

'I got the email today,' she told me shyly, failing to hide her smile behind her napkin.

'And?'

'I got an interview. Listen to this. They're flying me to Paris. Oh, Stella!'

'Oh my God, that's amazing! Well done!'

She couldn't conceal her excitement, wriggling on the bench. I felt, briefly, a flare of envy as sharp as a needle puncturing my chest. Then it was gone. Carmel has been after this job – a buyer for a very prestigious lingerie company – for a year, more or less. Twelve months of networking and being in the right place, being introduced to the top people, her smile as broad and gleaming as a chrome grille.

I drew in a deep breath and smiled. Well done, I heard myself say. She told me we were going to cautiously celebrate so as not to jinx her chances but I could see it in her eyes. She knows this job is hers. Everything else is a formality. The idea of her moving away – moving on – filled me with cold. She saw, because that is how she is, and slid an arm around my shoulders.

'We'll work on your job next, Stell. Promise.'

I leaned against her shoulder. I took on the job at the hotel as a tide-over, a way to pay the rent while I ingratiated myself with the local galleries. Nine years later I'm still there on front of house, checking guests in, answering the phones, smiling, always smiling. Nine years of treading water.

The wall behind us was spilling over with honeysuckle. The smell of it drowsy, heavy. Carmel is so beautiful, even in her jeans and an old T-shirt. Next to her I happily evaporate, ghost-like. Short hair, thin face. I always look tired, always cross. People are often surprised by my warmth. I wasn't expecting you to be nice, they tell me; you look so cold. I saw myself once, reflected in the dark glass of an empty shop window. A woman with hunched shoulders, as though braced for impact.

◆ ◆ ◆

A week later, and my dad is out of hospital. I am able to go and see him, staying on a rusting camp bed in the sitting room of his tiny flat with its comforting smells of tobacco and leather. Dad's voice is only slightly slurred at the edges.

I grip his hand until Aunt Jackie says, 'Stell, I think you're hurting him.'

I don't think about Marco at all until I arrive back at King's Cross. I'm crossing the platform towards the exit, thinking about dinner, and then, boom, I see him. He is standing outside the newsagent's with a woman. I slow and stop and feel a pinch in my chest, a cold needle beneath the skin. They are talking, her head craned to look up at him. She has blonde hair cut in a severe bob and delicate pink lips like a little doll. She is petite and pulled together, smiling at him with a row of perfect teeth. He touches her on the arm, saying something, and they both laugh, and when he lifts his suitcases and leans towards her as though for a kiss I turn away, ducking behind a coffee stand and out through the side exit, to where the taxis are. I am crying, and I don't know why.

I'm not going to call him, I tell Carmel and Martha the following week at the opening of a new gallery in Brixton, in fact I'm going to delete his number off my phone. But I don't delete it and I do call him, leaving drunk, slurry voicemails on his answerphone at two o'clock in the morning until I pass out with my face buried in my pillow. My lipstick leaves a red smear on the cotton like a strange kiss.

◆ ◆ ◆

Two days later I am in the shower and Carmel is knocking on the door.

'Your phone has rung like a million times,' she barks as we pass each other in the corridor, 'and leave your hair like that, it suits you.'

I pull a face at her and reach for my phone. An unknown number, nine missed calls. While I am holding the phone it rings again. This time I answer. The line is fuzzy and chaotic with traffic.

'Hello? Hello?'

'Katie? Do you know who this is?'

'I think so.'

'Go on.'

I laugh. This time I have remembered his name. 'Marc-oh.'

'Very good.' He sounds like a cat, smug and contented with himself. 'Now tell me yours.'

'It's Stella. I'm sorry – I know I should have told you right at the start.'

To my surprise he laughs. 'You think I didn't know?' There is a beat. 'I got your messages.'

'I'm sorry. I'm so sorry. I was drunk.'

'I noticed.'

Another beat. I feel awkward and prickly.

I open my mouth to apologise again when he says, 'Now, can you guess where I am?'

I hesitate. 'Piccadilly Circus.'

'Wrong country. I'm in Lisbon. I came here for a meeting and it's ended early.'

'That's a shame.' I pick at the nail polish on my toes.

'Yes. I'm due to stay here for another two nights but I'm bored.'

'Uh-huh.'

'Well?'

'Well what?' I am frustrated, mildly waspish. I remember the look of the woman with her pastel-coloured dress and gleaming blonde hair, slippery like water. I am not in the mood for games.

'Do you want to keep me company?'

'Sure, what do you want to talk about?'

'No, honey.' Patient. 'I mean here. Come here and keep me company.'

'Okay, well. No. I mean, there are lots of reasons.'

'Hold on—' He holds the phone away from him for a moment and I hear him briefly speaking in Portuguese. 'Sorry. You come here. I'll have Alice book you a flight this afternoon.'

'Who's Alice?'

'My girl Friday. And my girl Monday, Tuesday and so on. She's my personal assistant. She'll sort it for you. All you need to do is pack.'

'Is she blonde?'

'What?'

'Alice. Is she blonde? Quite small?'

'I suppose so, yes. Why?'

'What about work?'

'Skip work. Forget work. Come here; it's beautiful. Do you have a passport?'

'Yes – uh – somewhere. In the tin in the kitchen drawer, I think.'

'Tell you what, Stella. If you find it, call me back and I'll book a flight. If you can't find it, don't call me, and I'll never bother you again. There's your get-out. All right?'

I hesitate. I can hear him breathing down the line. I imagine him smiling, standing in the sunshine, bigger than I remembered, broader in the chest.

'Okay,' I tell him. 'Okay.'

I find my passport.

◆ ◆ ◆

A month later my dad has another stroke. This time an intracerebral haemorrhage in the brain tissue itself; a pointless, violent death, he had said about my mother, and now those words come back to me as I leave London on the 17:26 towards Cambridge. At school I had learned the word haemorrhage came from the Greek, 'blood bursting forth'. I write that phrase down in my notebook, pressing the pen into the paper so hard it leaves indentations on the pages beneath like braille. I want to print it onto my skin, carve it with sharp edges; blood bursting forth. I get into Aunt Jackie's car and see her pale and morbid-looking, unable to stop crying. I swallow against a lump building in my throat. She is saying, 'I'm sorry, honey. I'm sorry, Stella. I'm sorry. He's gone.'

The bureaucracy of death is daunting. A steep-sided, slate-grey pit without handholds. Death certificates and probate and government departments and utility companies and creditors. The council need to know, and so do friends. Aunt Jackie takes out an obituary in the local paper. The man on the phone asks her if she wants it with an ornamental font and a filigree frame and she says yes, ending up spending nearly fifty pounds.

'I don't know how we're going to afford the funeral, Stella,' she tells me as we stand outside the front door to his block of flats. It's windy and cold, the clouds thick and low and white. 'It's not like we can sell the house – it goes back to the council. And he has so many debts. I don't know if we'll even be able to afford a plaque for him.'

And she dissolves into fresh tears, opening the door to his little flat – the one with the kitchenette in the sitting room and the shared bathroom down the hall, the one that smells of tobacco and fried food. There's his old chair with the high back and the place where his head faded the pattern in the fabric, his television with the taped-over remote, a lamp, the bookshelves. Tins of food piled into the plywood cupboards. The remains of his life. I find his last betting slip on the fridge – the horse is called the 'Rose of Jericho'. When I take his suit out of the wardrobe – old and cheap and faded to grey, this will be his mortcloth, his funeral clothes – I tuck the betting slip into the pocket.

That night I travel back to London, and Marco collects me from the train station. He pulls me into him with a long exhale of breath and briefly the grief which has been permeating everything, black and heavy like tar, lifts. He raises my hand and inspects my nails, which I have been biting in quick, birdlike pecks. The skin there is ragged painful. I like the pain. I can focus on the pain. He kisses them gently, one after the other.

'I don't know what we'll do.' Later I'm talking to Marco and Carmel around our table, drinking wine. Their faces are twin moons of concern. 'Have you any idea how expensive funerals are? I've been looking all week. The cheapest we found is nearly two grand. Two grand!'

'Didn't he have anything at all? No secret stash of money squirrelled away? They usually do, gamblers.' Carmel lights another cigarette.

I shake my head. 'We've been through everything. Nothing but final demands and overdrafts. Aunt Jackie is beside herself. And we've still got to clear out the flat.'

Marco leans forward in his seat. 'Give me her number.'

'Aunt Jackie? Why?'

'Just give it to me. I'll talk to her. Neither of you should be worrying about this, not now. When my dad died I remember my mum had to deal with all this shit on her own. It's horrible.'

Carmel is looking at him askance. I don't think she's drunk – not yet – but she is glassy-eyed, overly emotional. She was fond of my dad. Told him he looked like Cary Grant. It hadn't been true, but he had puffed up with pride all the same.

'That's good of you, Marco,' she tells him, and he smiles at her, pats her on the knee clumsily. She responds by placing her hand atop his and squeezing. 'You're a good man.'

My man. My good man. I'm thinking about him a lot, two weeks later. Of how he had called Jackie the next day and arranged to pay for the funeral my father would have wanted; a quiet and simple ceremony and an uproarious wake, a stack of money behind the bar and drunken toasts shouted over the music. Of how Marco had travelled to Cambridge and helped Jackie to clear out the flat when I hadn't been able to face it, hiring a van to take everything to charity that couldn't be sold. He'd even managed to find a home for the ageing cat my dad had insisted on feeding and calling Skipper even though it did not belong to him, or anyone else. Marco did all of these things because the grief had folded me double, like decompression sickness, the bends. Agony in my joints, trouble breathing. I have surfaced too far and too fast.

The night Marco returns from Cambridge he comes to my flat. He looks tired, and as I slide my arms around his middle I can smell sweat on him, and dust. He kisses the crown of my head and tells me, 'I have something for you. I found them today. They belonged to your parents.'

I open the small box. It is their wedding rings. I stare at them for what seems like a long time, a rushing sound building in my ears. It makes it hard to hear Marco telling me how they'd found a large block of ice at the very back of my father's freezer, how he'd chipped it out and left it to defrost in the kitchen sink. And encased inside, prehistoric: the rings. He and Aunt Jackie had dug them out with teaspoons.

'He must have been given your mother's ring by the coroner all those years ago. Your dad put his in the freezer with your mum's so he couldn't get to it, at least not quickly.'

I nod, understanding. I've seen Carmel do similar with her credit cards. If you can't get to them, you can't spend them. My dad hadn't wanted to pawn the only thing he had left of her, of them.

'Jackie wanted you to have these. She thought you might – I don't know – maybe you'd want them, to remember.'

'Thank you. Thank you, Marco.' I press them to my chest, to the ache there. 'You didn't need to do that. You've already done so much.'

He shrugs, looking worn out. I kiss him, long and lingering, and he circles my waist with his arms. My heart throbs, engorged with something. Love, I tell myself. You love this man.

'It's good to see those dimples again,' he tells me when he pulls away. 'That famous smile.'

I smile wider, and he ducks his head and kisses me again. I let him. As he follows me into the kitchen to get a beer from the fridge he shows me the newspaper he is carrying tucked under his arm. He spreads it on the table, and I peer down at it. The article is about *Bossman*. It stars Joey Fraser, the boy who played my brother in *Marigold!* although of course he is a man now, older than me. Since *Marigold!* ended he has been in Hollywood action movies – always the quirky sidekick, the nerdy engineer, the third murder victim, never the starring role. The article mentions that following a sexual harassment claim Fraser has returned to England and gone into hiding. That won't last long, I think. I've never met a man who craves the limelight more. There is a photo of him accompanying the piece. He has barely aged, despite being in his forties at

23

least. The same wide, adoring eyes, the same treacle-coloured hair. He's had work done, I am sure. There are no tell-tale frown lines, no crow's feet around the eyes. He looks polished and buffed and tanned. I realise my hands are shaking. It's his photograph, I think. It has been a long time since I have seen him, and I don't like the way it makes my heart quicken, the queasy distaste in my throat.

'Are you all right, baby?' Marco asks me, a hand on my shoulder. 'I thought you'd be interested, that's all.'

'Oh yeah, it's fine. I'm fine,' I tell him, smiling. But still. I'm thinking about Carmel making me stand in front of his poster to take a photo, the way it had made my insides feel like ice. By the time Marco leaves that evening, I have blacked out Joey Fraser's picture with a pen, going over and over the same lines until the paper becomes shiny and black as tar. My jaw aches as though I have been grinding my teeth.

Chapter 3

I begin sleepwalking again. I haven't done this since I was a kid, when my parents would find me wandering the garden or slowly descending the stairs like a little ghost. Most nights since the funeral I have been sleeping at Marco's flat and tonight I jolt awake with a feeling of horror. I am in the lift facing the mirrored wall. I can see my fingers are tangled in my hair and it looks like I am snarling. The lift shudders. How did I get here? I don't remember. We'd been drinking, and we'd laughed as he'd insisted on carrying me to bed like a little girl. Now the doors slide silently open, and the concierge in the lobby is looking at me with something like horror, and I am pulling the hem of the T-shirt down over my nakedness and trying to tell him to stay away from me. I bite.

'Here.' Marco presses something into my mouth. It is a small pill, chalky-tasting. I crush it between my teeth and ask for water. He is wiping the blood from around my mouth with a wet tissue.

'What is it?'

'It'll help you sleep. What the hell were you doing?'

'I'm sorry. I must have been sleepwalking. I didn't mean to scare him.'

'You didn't scare him, but he rightly thinks you're a fruitcake. You must have looked like a vampire. Christ, honey, this looks sore.'

He tilts my face up towards the light. I have bitten my lip and made it bleed. He presses the tissue against it tentatively.

'I must have been dreaming. I don't remember.'

My flesh prickles with shame. I take the water and gulp it. Marco is watching me, leaning against the sink. The look on his face frightens me.

The next day I wake in the pale morning light. Marco is dressing and I watch him silently. I slept full and deep with no dreams. His hands cross as he knots his tie. There are worry lines on his forehead, more at the corners of his mouth, drawn down in concentration. He sees me watching him, one leg curled outside the duvet. He smiles.

'I'm sorry, Marco,' I tell him. I say his name the way I said it the first time, Marc-oh. A delicious sound with an almost exotic lilt, like Vietnamese or Thai. I say it again. 'I'm sorry,' I say. 'I'm sorry for making your life complicated.'

He sits on the edge of the bed, stroking my hair from my face with the flat of his hand. He tells me it is okay, and he tells me not to worry and beneath it all is a wariness he thinks I don't see. As he leaves the room I prop myself up on my elbows, look at him over my shoulder. It's coquettish by design. I want something.

'Honey,' I say. He looks over at me. 'Can you leave me another one of those little pills?'

For a second I think he might say no. I know Carmel has some Valium at home because her mother eats them like sweets, like ripe cherries one after the other, because of her nerves. I know Carmel keeps them in her dresser drawer with her Pill and bottles of lube and a pin badge of Smurfette she's had since college. I know this because I've been taking one a day since the funeral, just to keep the edge off. But I can't keep taking them. She will start to notice. Besides, I'm due back at work next week and the thought of it fills me with a dread as cold as bright-blue water.

'Sure,' he says finally, and closes the door.

The café we go to for lunch is small and busy, and Carmel and I are lucky to get a table. The walls are pine-clad, except in the places where cracked Victorian tiles still cling grimly to the walls.

'Sorry I'm late.'

Martha, who is never late, puts her bag on the table and starts ferociously unwinding the scarf from her neck. Carmel and I exchange a glance. We have known Martha eight years, since a New Year we spent in Berlin. There had been a party on a rooftop and fireworks at midnight, and I'd forgotten to bring a coat so I was shivering in my dress, face tilted up to the sky. Martha had given me hers, a thick camel-coloured trench which hung heavy on my shoulders. We'd introduced her to our friend James and only saw him again three days later, rushing to the airport to catch our plane. He looked like he'd been sleeping in a hedge.

'I love her,' he'd said simply, as we checked our luggage in. Carmel had oversized sunglasses on, her manicure chipped and fractured. She had laughed – hah! – and James had turned to her earnestly. 'I love her and I'm going to marry her.'

He had, of course, and now three years later here she was, her pretty round face looking uncharacteristically flustered, a brick-red colour building in her cheeks. She looked from me to Carmel and back again.

'What?'

'Is everything all right?' Carmel asked her.

'Yes, fine.'

'You look pale,' I said. She did. Tired too, I could see purple smears beneath her eyes.

'I'm fine.'

'You look like shit,' Carmel said. 'Are you ill?'

I saw Martha take a breath and then another, swallowing as though she might cry. The soft flare of her nostrils. Her hand strayed to her stomach. It was not tears she was trying to hold back. I realised before Carmel did, but only just.

'Holy shit, you're pregnant.'

Carmel's mouth fell open.

Martha put her head on the table and groaned. 'I can't stop being sick. It's like a wave, one after another. I didn't know it was this hard. I'd never have done it otherwise.'

'Done what?'

'Had sex!' she said loudly. I saw a few heads turn to our table and I couldn't help smiling. Martha took my hand. Hers was cool and soft, gentle.

'I was sick on the bus on the way here,' she told us as Carmel poured her some water. 'Then again just down the road. A man asked me if I was all right, and when I turned around I thought I would faint. Oh God. Perhaps I will die. I hope so. Dying would be better than this.'

I see Carmel make a slicing motion across her neck with her finger – shut up, shut up – and Martha looks at me, her pale eyes big and round. 'I'm sorry. Stella, I'm sorry. So clumsy!'

'It's okay.'

'It's not, it's not. *Was für ein Arschloch*, I'm sorry. How are you? How was the funeral?'

'Terrible,' I answer honestly.

'It must be very hard,' Martha tells me, squeezing my wrist. I feel tears prickle at her kindness, the balm of it.

Carmel rolls her eyes. 'Listen. I've got her puking on one side of me, and you crying on the other. I've nothing against body fluids but for now, can we not?'

We laugh. It is the first spontaneous laugh I think I've had in weeks, wholly organic. It feels good. Martha tells us that she is worried that she will start swearing during labour.

'I hope I do not make the midwives blush!' she says. 'I found out that your cervix expands to ten centimetres!'

Carmel and I exchange a look. 'Oh no,' I mouth. She shakes her head.

'That's the worst thing I've ever heard.'

Carmel is looking at her hands, measuring.

'That's the same size as a box of Dairylea,' Martha tells us wonderingly. 'It's a melon being squeezed through a straw.'

'Jesus Christ, Martha, you're a hell of a woman.'

'Do you think it will hurt too much?'

Carmel and I exchange another look. I mutter something about the joy of children transcending the agony, and then I start laughing. I can't help it.

Carmel snorts. '"The joy of children"?' she repeats. 'Your fanny is going to look like roadkill.'

And then she and Martha both begin to giggle, only for a minute we aren't sure because Martha also has her head in her hands and could be crying. We laugh and laugh until tears spring to our eyes. It's good. I feel light and untethered as though an anchor has been weighing me down.

Chapter 4

I book a weekend break in a B&B in Cumbria for me and Marco.

Carmel laughs at me. 'You're turning into one of those couples,' she says.

'What couples?'

We're sitting on the sofa together. I have a bag of crisps on my lap, and now I press one against my tongue, enjoying the tingle of salt.

'You know.' She puts on a syrupy voice. '"Two weeks today!! Love my little koala bear", "Can't wait to see my boo-boo, a whole hour apart!" All that shit. You know. On Facebook.'

'You jealous?'

'Of Marco? Hardly.'

I'm used to her acerbic tongue, of course. But even this shakes me, a little.

'He looks after me.'

'You don't need looking after. What are you, a toddler?'

I nudge her with my foot, and she breaks into a smile. 'Sorry. Maybe you're right. Maybe I am jealous. You used to have more time for me. Remember that time at the Red Lion, when we did the pub quiz?'

'That was ages ago.'

'Yup, and it was the last time we hung out. Without Marco, I mean.'

'Next weekend. No – no, I can't – the weekend after. We'll do something fun. I promise.'

'You promise?'

'Cross my heart and hope to die.'

Marco and I drive to Ullswater on the Friday evening and heavy rainclouds follow us along the M6, thickening as we approach the tiny guesthouse we are staying in. Just as we leave the car the downpour begins, and we run into the warmth with our hands over our heads, giggling. Marco is convivial and smiling, teasing me and calling me kitten, running his hands down the curve of my spine. We fall into bed and do not leave for two days and the rain pounds against the windows like tiny fists. Marco feeds me in bed – fruit slippery from his fingers, plump chocolate truffles, buttered toast – and I feel loved and safe. We have escaped, I think, feeling warm beneath the covers, we have escaped and we are happy.

When it happens it is like a huge silver bell tolling, once. Only once. We are eating Chinese takeaway from cardboard boxes, making a mess. I am sitting in a chair by the window where I can look out over the view of the lake, the mountains in the distance, shrouded in drifts of dark cloud like lace, like Italian widows. Marco is watching me from the bed, where he lies imperious against the cushions. He rests the box in his lap, chewing, looking at me thoughtfully.

'That show you did—'

'Oh God, Marco—'

I'm groaning but it is good-natured, feigned. Still, he holds up his hand, palm turned out. Stop.

'Just listen, just listen. That show, *Marigold!*. How long did it run?'

'Eight years. Seven series, seventy-four episodes including the pilot.'

'Huh. And nine Labrador dogs, is that right?'

'That's right.'

'I read about Joey Fraser in the paper again today. It said he was working in Hollywood.'

'Oh yeah?'

'Yeah.' He digs with his chopsticks to the bottom of the carton. 'I think it was something with Samuel L. Jackson. Did you know about this?'

It's Will Smith, I think, but my voice says, 'No.' It shakes just a little, a shimmer of sound, wind across glass. I don't think he hears it.

Joey Fraser was cast from a stage school and even at eight already had a theatre background. He talked a lot about voice projection and establishing space. Once, when I came down with a bout of tonsillitis, he offered to put on a wig and fill my role and no one knew if he was joking or not. He was the only one of the original cast to achieve anything close to a career.

'Yeah,' Marco continues, chewing thoughtfully, 'I thought it was funny, that's all. I mean, meeting you like that and then seeing his name in the paper. What do they call it, when things happen like that, like one after another and all joined together?'

'Synchronicity.'

'That's it. That's the one. Like that.'

We are silent for a moment. I can see his shape in the dim light, the hard rope of his muscles. Marco had told me his personal trainer was an ex-marine, bullying, close-shaven. Kicked him out of bed in the pearly light of dawn.

'He said in the interview that the show – your show – had been exploitative. To the kids, I mean. Would you agree with that?'

When I don't answer immediately he nudges me with his foot against my thigh, repeating the question.

'He's full of shit. He's just trying to get attention for himself and his failing career. They didn't exploit us. We filmed, what, three times a week? I had a tutor on set – we all did – and a nurse and an assistant and God knows what else. Exploitative. Shit.'

'Are you mad?'

'Do I sound it?'

He see-saws his hand. A little bit, he seems to be saying. I squeeze his foot beneath the covers.

'Sorry. Joey Fraser was always a prick, even at eight years old. I have a lot of bad memories from those days and he features in most of them. I just – he'll say anything, you know? Don't believe it. We were treated well; we were looked after. We were just kids.'

'It must have made you a lot of money. The show was named after you, wasn't it?'

'No. "Marigold" was the family surname.'

'Yeah, but you – you were the star.'

His toes press into me again. I favour him with a weary smile.

'I made some money, sure.'

'Did your parents put it in a trust fund?'

'Why are you even asking me about this?'

He leans forward, running his palms up my bare arms, making me shiver.

'Because' – another kiss and another – 'I'm interested. You made a lot of money at a young age. It kind of makes you a freak.'

'Thanks a lot!'

'You know what I mean. How many kids do you know under the age of ten worth a million pounds?'

I laugh scornfully.

'First, that estimate is way off. Second, the big money was in advertising and public appearances – I could make the same money as I did on a whole series in one thirty-second ad for baked beans.'

Marco is looking at me with interest. 'You haven't answered my question.'

I study him. He has a day's worth of stubble peppering his jaw, shocks of grey in his hair. We've been together just two months and are still at the stage of our relationship when we want to devour each other, sinking our teeth into each other's names, the details, the rich smell of him in the crook of his neck. Perhaps that's why I can't tell him where the money went. Perhaps that's why the lie slips from my mouth like ribbon being pulled from between my lips.

'I don't know. I just tapped into it when I needed it. I couldn't tell you how much.'

I lift his feet into my lap.

'Did you spend it all?'

'Every penny.'

Liar. *I fink we'd better ask Daddy.*

Later Marco is naked, his arm beneath me, leg curled around my thigh. He is sleepy. I am watching his eyelids flicker, the way his lips part slightly. He shifts a little onto his elbow, kisses me lightly on the tip of my nose.

'What happened to your teeth?' he asks drowsily. I am close to drifting off myself and for a moment I struggle to understand what he means.

'The gap,' he says. 'Katie Marigold has a gap between her teeth.'

'Oh, that. I had it fixed. You can get it filled in.'

'It's a shame.'

'I hated it.'

'It's meant to be lucky.'

I don't know what to say. From the outside, my life must look charmed. I had been a star, in a show named after the character I played. My face had been on magazines and TV screens and there had even been a range of biscuits called *Marigolds!*. They had been buttery-soft with my face stencilled on the underside. The weirdest thing. Dad had hated them.

'Goodnight, baby,' I say.

'Goodnight, little orphan Annie,' he murmurs. I am instantly cold, as if my internal organs are covered with frost. I stiffen and he opens his eyes wide.

'What's wrong?'

'Why did you call me that?'

'It's a joke.'

'It's a joke that my parents are dead?'

'Oh, Stella.' He switches on the lamp beside the bed. I am quivering, flush with anger. My cheeks boil, red as though slapped.

He shakes his head, draws breath. 'It was a joke. It was misjudged. I meant – you know, a child actress. I'm sorry. I'm tired, I'm not thinking straight.'

'It was cruel.'

'It was. Yes.'

We look at each other, and he plants another dry kiss on my forehead before reaching over and turning off the light. I lie in the darkness, arrow-straight, my hands clenched into fists. My enraged blood floods my system. He apologises again, but his voice is slurred, gluey. In moments he is asleep. I lie awake a long, long time. Finally, I get up and walk across the room. The thick carpet muffles my movements but still I creep. I can hear Marco's deep, regular breathing, the watery gurgle in the back of his throat as though he has a cold. I drag his suitcase over to the window. If I open the curtains just a little some of the streetlight comes through.

I unzip his washbag and empty it into my lap. Razors and deodorant and aftershave, a blister pack of painkillers. And at the bottom, tucked away into the pocket, are the pills in a small plastic baggie. I recognise them even though they are unmarked, rough to the touch. I swallow one and fold them back into the bag, stashing it deep in his holdall. The pill will help me sleep but most of all it will rob me of this feeling of loneliness and abandonment.

Chapter 5

I meet Alice on the same day I lose my purse and can't get home. I am one of those woman who crams everything they need into one place – Oyster card, cash, credit cards, ID – and now I'm standing on the street in a thin rain, outside my bank who have refused to give me any money without identification. I'm in South Kensington and although I am fairly sure I left my purse on the Overground, I am also quite certain it could be at home. Maybe. Carmel is not answering her phone, and home is a ten-mile walk. So I end up walking half an hour or so to Marco's office. It is a big Georgian property in Bedford Square with a brass plaque on the door. 'Nilsen, Swann & Partners'.

The first time I'd introduced Carmel to him she'd smiled and said, 'Nilsen? Like Dennis Nilsen? The mass murderer?'

'Only nicer,' Marco had said, smiling.

She had nodded. 'Uh-huh. His victims thought that too.'

It is Alice who buzzes me in. The woman from the train station. Thin and aristocratic-looking with pink sugared-almond fingernails.

'Mr Nilsen – Marco – isn't available,' she tells me, when I ask. 'He won't be back till this evening and not at work till tomorrow.'

I tell her what has happened, and she looks at me flintily, as though she doesn't believe me. I must admit I probably look a state – I have been taking Marco's pills almost daily, at least four or five a day, sometimes more. I like the feeling they give me of drifting, as though my feet float above the ground. She asks me if I would like her to call a cab. Tells me they can put it on the company account. I nod, relieved.

'I'm so grateful,' I tell her. 'My dad died, you see – it was very sudden, and, and—' *Oh God, am I crying?* I swipe angrily at my eyes. *What is happening to me?*

Alice smiles stiffly. 'I heard. I'm very sorry, Stella. For your loss.'

We are both silent for a moment. She looks at the phone, perhaps hoping it will ring. Behind her is a bright contemporary painting.

I point at it. 'That's a David Hockney.'

'Yes. It's called "Amaryllis In Vase". I think it was bought at auction.'

'It's an original? That must have cost a fortune.'

'Oh, yes. We have a number of them from the same collection. You're the first person to recognise it.'

'I studied art at university. Art history. I wanted to curate galleries. Funny how things turn out.'

'Oh? Marco told me you were an actress.'

'Was. Was an actress. I was in *Marigold!*. On the BBC.'

'Sure, I know it.'

She's lying, of course. She's good at it, but I lived half my life with my father, a man who had once told his thirteen-year-old daughter that her mother had not suffered at the end.

'I wrote my thesis on David Hockney,' she continues, turning in her chair to face the picture. 'I went to an exhibition in San Francisco in 2013 – I mean, I made the trip especially. Do you know the first thing Marco said when he saw this piece?'

I shake my head.

'He said he thought flowers in a vase was a bit unimaginative. "*Unimaginative*".'

'He's a heathen,' I say. Alice looks up at me with those cool, grey eyes and chances a smile, very small and fleeting.

'Would you like to wait in Marco's office, Stella? I'll buzz you when the taxi arrives.'

'Oh, yes. Thank you. I will.'

I go through to a large, airy room with a long window over-looking the street below. Marco's desk is a long block of polished walnut wood behind which sits a large leather chair, intimidating and almost imperious. There are no more paintings on the walls in here, just framed black-and-white photographs and an old map of London, sepia-tinted. I move behind his desk and lean on the chair, running my hands over its worn softness. My fingers move dreamily over the surface of the desk; an ashtray containing a cigar stub, a glass of water smeared with fingerprints, a single, unopened bar of hotel soap. I experience a sudden jolt when I see the picture of Carmel on Marco's computer. In it she's smil-ing, mouth half open, dark eyes fixing the lens. It's impossible to tell where she is and I'm gripping the back of the chair too tight and then suddenly the photo slides to the left and another takes its place, this time of Marco and me in Lisbon at a pave-ment café, both of us grinning and tanned. Frowning, I reach forward to click on the keyboard but then another picture slides into view and I realise what is happening. It's just a slideshow. Pictures from his phone saved to the computer that come up when it's powered down. The one at the hotel does the same. There's another one of me, and then moments later another of Carmel from the same night and this time I'm in it and we're leaning our heads together, laughing. My brain feels soupy as

I watch the shots flick past; a black Labrador that belongs to his parents, a photo of a younger Marco with a woman in the sun, another of me in a café, strap of my dress sliding down my shoulder. I'm looking guilelessly at the camera in this one, the light soft on my face. He took it recently. I remember going to the café. I remember that I ordered French toast but wished I'd had pancakes instead. What I don't remember is that strange, blank expression on my face, my hair fuzzy and unkempt, eyes deeply socketed. *Is that mess me?* I think, staring. *Is that what I look like these days?* Then the phone buzzes so suddenly I feel a flash of heat race through me and Alice's voice on the speaker says, 'Stella, your taxi is here.'

◆　◆　◆

The taxi driver knows me. He keeps stealing glances in his rear-view mirror until we stop at some lights. Then he turns in his seat, eyebrows raised.

'No way. It is you, isn't it? From that show. Years ago.'

I smile tightly.

'I thought it was when I saw you. Do you know what, I wouldn't have recognised you either, only I had your mate in here a couple of weeks ago.'

'Oh, yes?'

'Eddie.'

I stare blankly at him for a second or two until my brain makes the connection.

'You mean Joey Fraser?'

'That's him. He hasn't changed, has he? I told him, I said he hadn't aged a bit. Do you know what he said? He said Hollywood suited him. He was right. He looks twenty if a day.'

I'm grinding my teeth again. I can hear the clicking noise my jaw is making. The taxi driver is still talking but a dull heat is building in my chest. My blood pulses hot.

'He said he was over here for the funeral. I suppose you'll all be going, won't you? Here, when you see him, you tell him Lee says hello? He'll remember me.'

'What— What funeral?'

The taxi driver looks at me in the mirror again and his expression is impossible to read.

'Lesley Patterson.'

Lesley Patterson. I have to think for a minute. Older than me, with long red braids down to her waist. Not now, of course. Then, I mean. She had played my sister Lucy in the show. She'd had freckles and goofy teeth and when she'd had braces fitted at thirteen they'd taken all her lines away. I swallow, clutching hold of the seat for support.

'She's dead?'

'You didn't know? It was in the papers.'

'What happened?'

Suicide. It hadn't made the front page. It was a small story on page eleven, next to a recall advert for baby food. She'd died of carbon monoxide poisoning, the report said. I Google further and discover she'd fed a hosepipe from the exhaust through the window of her car in the little garage attached to the house. Her husband had discovered her nearly seven hours later, when he'd noticed the dogs barking at the garage door.

My phone starts ringing. Marco. I pick up.

'Did you know about this? About Lesley Patterson?' I ask him.

'Hello to you too. Yes, I did.'

'Why didn't you tell me?'

'I did.'

I catch my breath.

'When?'

'When it happened, last week. We talked about it over dinner. Remember?'

I stare at the wall. I don't remember, but that doesn't mean it didn't happen. I'm so hazy on things these days.

'I don't, no. I don't remember.'

'Are you okay? You said at the time it didn't bother you. You and Lesley weren't close, you said.'

That sounds about right, like something I'd say. Because of course we hadn't been close, had we? She barely spoke to me on set, and off set they would all go and play cards together, without telling me. I'd walked in on them all once, all five of them, the Marigold children. Teasing each other, playing with Lego, laughing. Their faces had fallen when they'd seen me. The room had gone horribly quiet. I'd only been seven years old. I'd just wanted to join in.

'No, I suppose we weren't.'

'Listen, this isn't why I called. You've left your purse in my car. Shall I bring it round?'

'Yes. I've been looking for that everywhere. Could've sworn I left it at home.'

'Nope. It's right here. I'll drop it back, I'm only twenty minutes away. There's – uh – there's a lot of money in it, Stella.'

'Is there?'

'Yeah. About three hundred pounds in cash. Is there anything you want to tell me? You're not dealing drugs, are you?'

He laughs nervously. I don't know what to tell him. I don't remember taking that money out, but I suppose I must have done at some point. It seems like a lot, and I wish I could remember what I needed it for. It's not the first time I've done something impulsive with money. I once paid for Carmel and me to go to Ibiza when she'd been so skint she'd been eating ketchup sandwiches with sachets stolen from the local café.

I hang up, drumming my fingers restlessly. I can feel the edges of myself and the anxiety that waits there, sharp as blades. I hope Marco will have some more pills for me. I deserve some more pills.

Chapter 6

'She was unhappy,' Aunt Jackie had told me after my mother's suicide in 1994, the year I turned thirteen. '*She had suffered years of clinical depression*,' the local paper had said, while the report in the *Cambridge Courier* had described her as being '*prone to spells of melancholy*'. It made her sound pre-Raphaelite. My father had said she had never been the same since I was born, a weight I carried with me for almost a decade until my first round of therapy in my twenties. I believed him, you see, believed that my birth – painful and messy and bloody – had somehow triggered this suicidal impulse in my mother, like a switch completing a circuit which lit something in her head.

I didn't find out about the debt we were in until we were forced to sell the house a year after her death, and even then I didn't understand. When I asked my father he simply said they had made some bad financial decisions. He didn't tell me that those decisions had been made with cash in unmarked brown envelopes in a bookie's where the smoke hung in the air like a medieval mist. When my mother had asked him to stop before he ran us into the ground, my father, always convinced of his next big win, had started placing bets in secret. He'd drained my account first, the one my mother had set up for me with the money made from the *Marigold!* series. She'd been clever enough to insist I couldn't touch it before I was eighteen but not clever enough to stop my dad occasionally forging her signature on the account book he used to make the withdrawals. He'd intercepted the statements until all the money was gone, every penny I'd earned, bled away.

Once Mum discovered the extent of it – the overdraft, the remortgage, the loan sharks, the money missing from the emergency kitty she had stored behind the loose bricks of the fireplace – that was the beginning, I think. The long slide down. I would dream of horses, in all my years at college. Pounding hooves, sprays of turf, the smart flat crack of the riding crop. I would dream of my dad and me in the stands and in his hands hundreds and hundreds of betting slips, some stuffed in his pockets, some drifting to his feet like confetti, too many to hold. We were screaming the names of the horses until sweat sprang to our brows and always, always, it would change, and we would be screaming my mother's name until our voices cracked and shook.

I wonder how he felt. That blood clot slowly moving towards the soft, vulnerable part of his brain. How it felt to lie in his tiny rented flat with the slow, mournful buzz of the freezer and inside it, encased in ice, their wedding rings, the two most precious things he owned.

Ten minutes after Marco arrives Carmel is home, her hair damp with the rain. She makes herself tea and stands in the doorway to the kitchen, her hands wrapped around the mug.

'Aren't you going to ask me how my day went?'

'How was your day?'

'You know what today was, don't you?' She lights a cigarette. 'Remember, Stella? It was the day I met Beatrice d'Aramitz from the Paris office.'

'I thought Paris wasn't until next month.'

She smiles, and it looks just a little too forced.

'It *is* next month. Today I met Beatrice at a preliminary interview. Remember?'

'Of course. How did it go?'

'I aced it. I really think I did. She's lovely and, what's more, she really likes me.'

'That's fantastic. Well done.'

'Here,' Marco says. He is holding out my purse to me. 'Before I forget to give it to you. I'd put that money somewhere safe if I was you. God knows where you'll leave it next time.'

'Is that for me?'

I look up at Carmel. Marco has given me the last of his pills and now there are just five left in the little bottle. Already I feel blurry, a smear of Vaseline over the lenses of my eyes.

'That money. The money I asked for.'

I look down at the purse and back up at Carmel again. That jogs something in my memory, a fishhook, tugging. I take it all, all those lovely crisp notes I must have taken out of the bank, and hold them out to her. Marco grabs my arm, not hard, just a little pressure.

'Hang on, Stella. What's going on?'

'Carmel asked to borrow some money. She's short on rent this month. It's fine.'

'How can you afford it on your wages?'

'I have savings,' I say simply, as Carmel takes the money from me. She is smiling but doesn't look happy.

'Three hundred,' I say. It's not a question. 'Is that right?'

'Yes. Thank you. I promise I'll pay you back.'

'New shoes, Carmel?' Marco asks her. She looks down at her feet, we all do. They're beautiful, glossy black leather heels. Expensive. Now I have no difficulty reading her expression. She looks angrily at Marco.

'I needed them for the interview. They're an investment in my future.'

Marco scratches his cheek and looks at me. He plants a hand on my shoulder. The effect is proprietary but I am too cloudy to shrug it off. I am tired, I am tired.

◆　◆　◆

Carmel is excited. We are crowding around the computer, Martha and her and I, leaning into each other, laughing.

'Look, look,' she is saying, scribbling something on the pad beside her. Martha is sipping ginger tea, taking tiny bites of dry crackers.

'I am sick like a dog,' she tells us when she arrives, 'and these' – pointing at her breasts – 'weigh more than baby elephants. This is hell.'

Carmel is looking for venues for her birthday party, somewhere we can dance and drink and look good in photos. We started with stately homes and now we're looking at ballrooms.

'I want glamour. Remember Kate Moss's thirtieth? Faded elegance. The beautiful and the damned.'

'Can't we just open some crisps and go to the Red Lion?' I ask her, only half joking. Carmel looks at me, alarmed. I have told her I will help to pay for this party. Her initial refusal was flimsy, and it did not take long to talk her round. Now her parents are covering the rest and she is excited, making plans. Her guest list is nearly two hundred people. That's the thing with Carmel, everyone wants to know her. She could invite twice that many. Martha sits down carefully, tucking her hair behind her ears. She has perfect hair, almost white-blonde and soft as mouse fur. I always find myself wanting to stroke it.

'You will need staff for a party this size,' Martha says. 'Maybe to serve drinks and take coats?'

'There'll be a bar,' Carmel tells us, 'and for everything else there's you two.'

Martha and I exchange an amused glance. She looks closely at me.

'Stella – have you changed your face?'

I laugh. Carmel turns to look at me over her shoulder.

'I noticed too,' she said. 'You look different. Less make-up. Not just today, either. The last couple of weeks or so.'

'I just fancied a change.'

'But you love make-up! No one can do eyeliner like you.'

'I – I'm just trying something new. You don't like it? Marco thinks it makes me look younger.'

'Marco's hardly Estée bloody Lauder, is he?'

Carmel turns away from me. I can't tell if her anger is real or pretend. I fold my arms.

'I think you look very nice,' Martha says, the peacekeeper, the diplomat. She sips her ginger tea. 'You look like you are healthy.'

'"Healthy". Every woman's dream,' Carmel drawls.

'What's your problem?'

Carmel turns to face me. She likes confrontation, thrives on it. Me, I end up shaking, light-headed. Usually I avoid it, but these days have not been usual.

'Stella. Calm down. I'm just saying it's funny how you've changed.'

'I've changed?' I look at them both, one to the other and back again. 'How have I changed? How?'

'You don't know?'

'Oh, piss off, Carmel.'

I'm so angry. I can feel it like a hot throbbing in my chest. Carmel blinks, shocked. But she is still smiling.

'Well. We hardly see you anymore and when we do—'

'What?'

'You're with Marco.'

'You're annoyed with me for having a boyfriend?'

'No. Not at all. Not with *you*.'

'With Marco then?'

'I don't know. It's hard to describe. Martha agrees with me though, don't you?'

'You've talked about this? With each other?'

'Oh no,' Martha says as Carmel says, 'Yes, of course.' They exchange a knowing glance and I've never felt so lonely. I want to cry. My jaw is clenched so tightly I can feel the pulse like a hard, throbbing percussion.

'So, you don't like my boyfriend, and you don't like the way I look. Anything else?'

'Come on, Stella.'

'No.' I pull away as Carmel reaches for me, grabbing my bag. I am simmering. I have to get away.

Chapter 7

Marco is tracing a figure of eight on the bare skin of my arm. We are lying in his bed on crisp white sheets. His room is twice as big as mine. Bare floorboards and a huge Rococo-style mahogany bed, hand-carved and lavish, almost decadent. He props himself up on an elbow, facing me.

'You're too good to her.'

'We've been friends a long time.'

'Just – be careful, Stella. Okay? With your dad and everything, you're not thinking too clearly. And this money – how much have you given her now?'

'Oh, Marco—'

'Listen. This is my job, kitten. This is what I do, help people make sound investments.'

'God, I love it when you talk finance.' I'm shifting slightly, lifting my hips. He presses them back down gently, shaking his head. Bastard.

'You like that, huh? Like it when I talk about dividends and stock specific risks?'

I groan, and he bites me quickly, urgently, on the tender part of my neck. I gasp at the pain of it, surprised. He is still smiling.

'How much is she asking for? A hundred? More?'

'A bit more.'

'Oh, Stella. How much is a bit?'

'Another two hundred, towards her party.'

'If you give it to her you can kiss it goodbye.'

'She's my friend.'

'When was the last time she did something for you?'

I hesitate.

'It's my money.'

'Uh-huh.'

'I'll do what I want with it. If I want to squander it, I will.'

'Uh-huh, move over a little.'

He moves between my legs, running his tongue over the mound of me, pressing his hot breath into the soft fabric of my knickers.

'I wouldn't dream of telling you what to do, Stella.' Another sharp bite, near my hip. This time I clench my fists. He is smiling, I can hear it in his voice.

'Can we stop talking about this, please?'

'Just promise me.' A soft kiss, another. 'Promise me you'll tell her no if she asks again. Stop enabling her.'

I know what he means. Every time Carmel takes her credit card out she jokes about the smell of burning plastic, about how she hopes to marry someone old and rich with a heart problem. She's always been that way, ever since we were students together at university. I'd once told Marco about how she'd spent her entire grant on an original Seditionaries T-shirt and had to shoplift food for two whole terms.

He takes my hand and kisses my fingers one by one. He is tentative again, almost reverential. If I couldn't feel the throb from the places where he has bitten me I would think he was harmless.

'Did you find out who's been calling you?'

'No,' I say sharply, and don't offer any more.

The phone calls had begun four days ago, in the middle of the night. I'd woken cold and uncomfortable, my neck stiff. My phone had lit up the dark of the room with a pale, eerie glow. Number Withheld, the display said. When I'd answered there had been nothing for a second or two and then a long, low exhale before whoever it was had hung up. Since then it has happened five or six times, always the same. Carmel wants me to go to the police.

'She's worried,' I tell Marco now, who snorts derisively. 'She said *Marigold!* has been in the papers a lot recently with Lesley Patterson's funeral and now this thing with Anne Gregor. It always stirs up the weirdos.'

'Did you hear Anne Gregor didn't make it?' He makes it sound like she'd been running a race. I stare at him open-mouthed.

'You're kidding.'

'I'm not, babe, no. I read it last night on Twitter, of all things. They're calling it the "*Marigold!* Curse".'

'God. God. She was only a bit older than me.'

Anne Gregor had been Bonnie, the second-youngest of the Marigold siblings, with corkscrew hair and a round, moon-like face. She'd originally tried out for the part of Katie Marigold but, as my mother never failed to tell me, she couldn't get the voice right. That soft, waxy lisp.

'Well, I'm just warning you. It'll probably be in the papers again. They're calling it heart failure, but what they mean is coke, surely. She was an addict at fifteen, if I remember right.'

'God,' I said again. I'd read all the stories, of course, when I was a teenager. How Anne Gregor had snorted so much coke her septum had perforated. Five grams a day even while pregnant. But that had been a long time ago, and hadn't I also read, fairly recently, that Anne Gregor had been clean a decade or more? It had been a feature in a Sunday supplement, I was sure of it.

'Joey's back in the news, of course,' Marco says, his hand running over my hip. 'Talking about how hard fame is.'

I laugh out loud.

'Joey Fraser loves a bandwagon. He should have tried walking in my shoes and dealt with some of the shit I had to.'

Marco looks surprised. His hand glides over my stomach, draws me close enough that I can feel the prickle of his stubble.

'Like what, babe?'

I sigh. He kisses me in the place between my ear and collarbone and asks again.

'I used to get weird post. Really weird. My mum couldn't always – what's the word, to get to something first?'

'Intercept.'

'Intercept it, yeah. And it came to my home address, which fan mail didn't, usually it went to the TV studio. And of course when I saw my name, so beautifully written in ink, I opened them.'

Marco is waiting, watching me with his dark eyes. I can remember when we had met thinking he looked sleazy, too old for me. I had been wrong. He presses his mouth against mine for a moment, and I think I feel the faintest stirring of an erection pressing against me. He says, 'Go on.'

'Are you sure?'

He nods. So I tell him about the letters I used to receive containing hair clippings and used tissues, handfuls of dirt and dead flowers. I'd unfold spidery hand-drawn maps with red lines drawn on them to show all the different routes to my house. One afternoon in the spring, just after my tenth birthday, I'd opened an envelope to find a little doll made of wax with pins bristling from its mouth. It had been wrapped in a single frilled sock, the twin to a pair I'd worn and lost on set a week before. The director had been furious because we hadn't been able to find another pair, and he'd said it would ruin continuity. My mother had told him to be a fucking professional and just shoot me from the fucking knees up. I can remember hearing her outburst through the partition wall of my trailer, shocked at her language.

53

Marco looks genuinely shocked, his eyes round and glassy.

'That's awful. I'm so sorry.' He shudders, and there are goose-bumps running up his arms. 'Some people are sick.'

I nod, plucking at the sheet between my thumb and forefinger. Marco lays a hand gently on my arm.

'Did you tell your parents?'

'Yeah. My mum went to the press. Said people like that needed exposing. They came to our house and did a photoshoot in the garden with the two of us in front of the buddleia. She made me hold up one of the letters for the camera. I didn't want to. I didn't want to touch it. It didn't feel good. She said all publicity was good publicity.'

'Did you ever go to the police?'

'Of course. But it wasn't considered a threat unless they did something to physically harm me.'

'This is unbelievable.'

'My mother was furious. She called it voodoo. Said it was someone on the set, someone jealous of me. She wanted to inter-rogate everyone to find out who. The director said no. Probably the only time he ever stood up to her.'

I lie back against the pillows as Marco moves on top of me, and now I can definitely feel his erection, heavy against my leg.

'You must have been frightened.'

'I was.'

He leans over and kisses the inside of my arm. There is a tat-too there; a hummingbird about the size of a coin. He had laughed when he first saw it, surprised. Katie Marigold with a tattoo, he'd said, shaking his head. The good girl gone wild.

Another kiss, moving down. My stomach is flat and empty because I live on my nerves. He plants another kiss on the warm skin there, blows gently on me. He moves inside me with tender urgency and later, when I find I am sleepwalking again, the marks of his teeth are still on my shoulders.

I find myself in the hallway, just outside the door of Marco's apartment. I am crippled with cold, violently shivering. I blink in surprise as I hear Marco's voice saying my name over and over, 'Wake up, Stella, Stella, Stella. Wake up.'

'What's going on?'

'Inside. Come on. You're sleepwalking again, princess.'

My cheeks are wet – am I crying? I press my hands to them. Tears. 'I'm a mess,' I hear myself say. And Marco says, 'No, you are just very sad at the moment.' He offers me a glass of water and presses two pills into my hand.

'I only woke up because you slammed the front door,' he tells me, sitting next to me on the sofa. 'What if I hadn't? What if you end up falling down the stairs? Take these, at least we'll both get some rest that way.'

But I do not sleep for another two hours until the light becomes diffuse and watery with dawn. I lie awake and comfortable, detached from myself, drifting a little. My memory becomes slippery, my thoughts simple flares in some internal darkness. It's a nice feeling, an anaesthetic.

The next day, though, I am foggy-headed, late for work. I have not brushed my hair, and I look terrible, tired and unsteady on my feet. I tell my manager I have taken painkillers for a bad back, but I don't know if she believes me. She gives me a cool look, barely nods. 'Okay, Stella, fine. But you're the first face our guests will see. Next time a bit more effort, yes?'

I nod. 'Yes, sure, fine. I'm sorry. It won't happen again.' But of course it does.

◆ ◆ ◆

The day I get fired is also the day I am taken to hospital. The two aren't necessarily connected, or so I tell myself at the time. It's the pills, you see. Marco has got me some more, and I didn't ask where from, just said thank you. He'd rubbed the tip of my nose as though I had a smudge there, told me I was a good girl. I'd broken one of those pills in half right then and there and swallowed it with cold coffee. Later, when he went to work, I took another, and another. I fell back to sleep, a deep, heavenly sleep, and when I woke I'd missed my alarm. I jolted but there was no fear. The pills, their delicious numbness, saw to that. I didn't even get dressed. When I called the hotel, I was slurring. They asked me not to come back. I don't think I even responded. I fell back to sleep and by the time I wake up the sky is darkening, dull and smoky, and Marco is in the doorway.

'This is a nice surprise. I thought you were at work.'

'Oh God, what time is it?'

'It's gone six. Are you naked under there?'

'Yes.'

He is smiling at me. 'You haven't got up all day?'

'I got fired.'

'Oh, doll.'

'Don't. Don't say anything.'

'Stay there. Don't move.'

He pulls something out of his pocket, his phone I think. For a moment I wonder if he is undressing, getting into bed with me. He steps closer, holding it up.

'Let me take a picture.'

'No!'

'Come on. Just one. Just one little one. Please?'

'No! Absolutely not.'

'It'll just be your body. You won't even be able to see your face. You won't even know it's you.'

'Great, thanks a lot.'

'Come on, you know what I mean. You're sexy. You're a sexy, beautiful woman. Just one photo and I promise I won't show it to anyone.'

He tugs on the covers. I hold them tightly below my chin, laughing.

'No way, Marco. I look like shit.'

'You look great. No make-up. It's sexy.'

I look at him. He is grinning, enthusiastic.

'Oh, for God's sake.'

'Thank you. Come on, this'll be great.'

He pulls the covers off me quickly, and my flesh ripples with goosebumps. I move my hands defensively but he brushes them away, shaking his head.

'No hands. They're covering up the good stuff. Smile.'

I hear the shutter noise on his phone as he takes a few modest pictures, bending towards me. Then I grab the covers again, burying myself beneath them. He pouts childishly.

'No more,' I tell him.

'Fine, fine. Shall we go to the pub?'

'Which one?'

'The Standard?'

'Aw. That's Carmel's favourite.'

'You two have been friends a long time, haven't you?'

'Since college. The first thing she said when she came up to me in class was "I dressed up as you once for Halloween." That's when I knew we'd be friends.'

'When does she leave?'

'Not for another month or so. She's going out at the end of this week to look at a flat, comes back Wednesday, and then it's her big party that weekend. She's horribly stressed, of course, but this is a dream job for her.'

'Funny really.'

'How so?'

'Funny that someone who spends so much time out of her knickers should end up selling them.'

I stare at him for a moment, and when he smiles it is nothing more than a show of teeth. He sits on the end of the bed, holding on to my wrist as if he is checking my pulse.

'Don't you like Carmel?'

'I didn't say that.'

'You didn't need to.'

'I just feel – what I mean to say . . .' He looks at me lucidly, smiling. 'Do you want to hear this?'

'I don't know. Do I?'

'I just think she takes a lot from you but doesn't give anything back.'

'Oh, Marco. Come on.'

'I told you you wouldn't like it.'

'I've known her nearly twenty years. She's my best friend in the world.'

'I know, I know. I'm sure I've put my foot in it. Forget it, forget I said anything. Let's get drunk.'

'Now?'

'Right now, right here. Shall I make us a drink?'

He brings me a Bloody Mary in bed, with a straw and a cocktail stirrer. 'No ice, I'm afraid.'

I take a sip and it burns my throat. 'God, what's in this?'

'Tabasco and grated horseradish. Is it too much?'

'It's fine,' I assure him, and once the vodka kicks in it is. I've never been a fan of Bloody Marys – too close to drinking cold soup in my opinion – but it feels good and decadent leaning back on the pillows in the early evening sipping it, and when he asks if I want another I laugh and tell him yes. Halfway through my second he asks me if he can take another photo, just something for him. Yes, I tell him. Sure. I pose for him with a smile, a drink in my hand. My head is giddy and light and at that moment nothing can bother me. By my fourth drink – this time a strong rum and coke – I am arching my back and bending over the bed and lifting my legs crossed at the ankles, thrilled at his attention, the encouragement.

Afterwards I dream. There is a woman lying on a slab. She is very pale, her skin tinged blue. It is me, and I cannot move. My eyes are open but I can't speak or turn my head. I can sense someone is approaching and even though I summon up all my energy I cannot even blink. Then they are standing over me, and I think, *Oh, it's me*, only it's not. Not quite. Her nose is slightly the wrong shape and her eyebrows are too arched. She looks as though someone has tried to draw me from memory, like there is a vital piece of me missing. The me-woman looks worried and is lacing her hands together, pumping at my chest. *I'm not dead*, I try to say. *Can't you see, I'm not dead?* But no words come out of my mouth and now she is bending over me, pinching my nose closed. I can feel her fingers against me, her breath against my cheek. She smells bad, and when she exhales into my mouth, it tastes like the deep sea; a thick, dark breath. She moves back from me and I can see something hanging from her mouth and I still can't speak, still can't lift my hands. She is searching my face, hands tracing the lines of my nose, and then her hands move to her own face and find her mouth. I watch in immobile horror as her fingers grasp the thing hanging from her mouth and at first I thought it was a slick of brown drool, but now she is closer I can see it is seaweed, a long strand, and she is pulling it from between her lips like a ribbon and it keeps coming, it keeps coming. I can see the sheen of it in the mortuary lights overhead and I want to scream and still she pulls out more and more, clots of it, of seaweed, as though it has been stuffed by the fistful into her mouth and someone is saying my name, over and over, and shaking my shoulders.

When I finally wake, slowly, grudgingly, I see Carmel and Marco standing over me. I am home, in our flat, and Carmel is crying. Marco has his head in his hands. There is a strong, bitter smell, and I cannot move. When I open my mouth I make a thick gurgling sound – *wuh, wuh* – and Carmel tells me not to speak.

'Oh, Stella, oh, Stella,' she is saying. I close my eyes. I don't know what has happened, but all I want to do is sleep. Why won't they let me sleep?

I open my eyes again. There is a paramedic standing over me, handsome and young-looking, clean-shaven. The room is pulsing with a blue light. He is attaching something to the back of my hand, an intravenous line. I stare at it, at Carmel, Marco. My front is sticky and when I put my hand to it my fingers come away red. I feel a needle of fear. I try to sit up.

'Am I dying?' I ask, and the paramedic replies, 'Not now, you're not.'

Later, in the hospital, I lie on my side. I have a dextrose solution being fed into my vein through a cannula on my arm. I am not on the ward: I am in a small curtained-off cubicle in A&E. It is busy, chaotic. When the nurse comes to see me her rubber-soled shoes squeak on the floor. She looks me up and down, briskly. I notice Carmel is in the chair a little to my right. I don't know how long she's been there. She has been crying, I can see. There is a pile of shredded tissue in her lap. Her hands are limp, her complexion dull. It reminds me of the dream I had, that strange woman who had looked so much like me.

'How are we feeling, Stella?' the nurse asks.

I tell her my throat is killing me. She nods, explains that the intubation was necessary to stop me choking on my own vomit. I look over at Carmel but she won't meet my eyes. And where is Marco? I feel like I am dying. I ask for water and the nurse hands me a tiny plastic cup. Tells me to sip.

'There will be some pain for a while in your throat, and maybe in your stomach. You need rest and fluids. You have a good friend here looking after you.' She indicates Carmel, who doesn't smile. 'Make sure you don't drink that too fast. There's a jug here if you need more.'

'What time is it?' I croak.

Carmel looks at her watch. 'Four fifteen.'

'In the morning?'

She nods. Her hands are folded into her lap. They are usually so animated, full of life, gesturing as she speaks. It worries me, this limpness.

As the nurse leaves through the blue curtain I say, 'I don't know what happened, Carmel.'

'You overdosed,' she says simply. 'You overdosed on our sofa and nearly choked to death. When I found you, I couldn't tell if you were breathing or not. You were covered in red, I thought at first it was blood. I thought you'd been stabbed. I've never been so scared.'

It was just tomato juice, I try to tell her. She doesn't listen. She sounds flat, dismissive. I ask where Marco is. She shrugs.

'He went to get coffee and pay for parking. That was, like, an hour ago. I thought you were going to die, Stella.' She starts to cry. It is soundless, and she does not cover her face. I have never understood this. Like my mother, I am horrified by tears. Real tears, the rawness of them. I am not a pretty sight when upset. I sob and snort and wipe my nose with the back of my hand. My eyes burn, rimmed pink like myxomatosis. I pride myself on my stoicism. I hadn't cried when Ben Madison dumped me at college, and I was the only person I knew who hadn't cried at *Watership Down*.

'I came home early from the cinema and there you were on the sofa, and I couldn't wake you,' Carmel tells me, 'and you weren't moving, even when I started shaking you. I said your name. I screamed it.'

The cinema, she'd said. I'd forgotten we were going to the cinema. We'd planned it last week. Some movie about teenagers getting hacked to death in the woods. We love that shit. Pizza and a film, we'd said, and I'd promised to be there. I don't say anything but she looks at me anyway, already nodding because she knows.

'It doesn't matter. You forgot. It happens. It was a shitty film anyway. I walked out before the end.' She wipes her eyes with her fingertips. 'The blonde one got garrotted with a piano wire and the black one was sassy and angry. The usual shit.'

We fall silent for a moment. I think there is some sort of scuffle outside the curtains, I can hear a man, very drunk, shouting, 'I don't want to be here. I want to be home.'

'I lost my job.'

'Is that why you did it?'

'Did what?'

'Took the pills?'

I'm genuinely confused. I blink at her rapidly. My throat is so sore, as though it is being scraped by crushed glass. I take another sip of water; outside the man is still shouting, 'I won't go, I won't go', over and over.

'I didn't—'

'Because that's what Marco said. That you must have taken them while he wasn't around. What are they anyway? God knows you don't need downers.'

I don't know what they are, but I don't want to tell her that. She wouldn't understand. They make me feel good, removed, detached. Carmel thrives on living, on being present. She wouldn't get it.

'Do you want to die, Stella?'

I laugh. It's absurd. Carmel looks at me thoughtfully.

'How come Marco has keys to our flat? That's something you should have discussed with me, don't you think?'

I stare at her. I feel like I've been hollowed out – all that puking, I guess – but also that I've woken up in the middle of a conversation. I have no idea what she is talking about and tell her so.

'Because that's how he got in. I came in and found you on the sofa at about eleven o'clock. I tried to wake you for about five minutes. I was getting hysterical. Then in walks Marco through the front door. Called out your name. He'd got a takeaway for you both. I turned around and he was there, asking me what was going on. He looked angry, Stella. Not upset. Angry. I don't think he expected to see me.'

She rubs her arms as though she is cold, leans forward, elbows resting on her knees.

'I told him to call an ambulance and do you know what happened? I heard sirens. We both did. Pulling up outside the house. Someone had already called them. Was it you? And if it wasn't, who was it?'

Carmel finally looks at me, and I am shocked at how calm she is, how deliberate. I am about to speak when Marco appears, holding coffees. He bends and kisses my brow.

'All right? How's the patient?'

'Sore,' I tell him. He looks tired. They both do. I feel another wave of guilt and bury it. 'Marco, I don't remember a thing.'

He looks over at Carmel then back at me with painful sympathy.

I speak quietly. 'You don't – you don't think I did this deliberately, do you? Carmel?'

'I don't know, Stella,' she says. 'The first thing the paramedic asked me was what you'd taken, and I had to tell him I hadn't a clue. I haven't even seen you with pills unless you count the Valium you think I haven't noticed you taking from my room.'

'You can't possibly think I meant to do this, can you?'

'I think if you're hiding what you're doing – if you're at that point – then you should see someone,' Carmel says quietly, 'and talk about your father.'

She turns to Marco and takes the coffee from his hand. 'I've got to be at work in four hours, and I have to get a taxi. I'm going to need to borrow some money.'

'Again?' I hear him say quietly. I lie back on the starched pillow which rustles about my ears. He takes a note from his wallet, passes it to her. Before she leaves Carmel bends down and strokes my face, a gesture so tender it makes me dizzy. She parts the curtains, pulling her cigarettes from her pocket.

I look at Marco. 'Marco—'

'She's upset. You gave her a scare. You gave us both a scare.'

'What was I doing at home? How did I get there?'

'We had a row.'

'What? Really?'

'Yup. Something stupid. We were both a bit pissed, I think. You don't remember?'

'No, I—'

'You were pretty out of it.'

'What are those scratches on your neck?'

'Ah, Stella.' He rubs his palms along his thighs. I stare at him aghast, feeling nausea building. 'It's okay. We were both drunk and you've – well, you've been through a lot.'

There is a silence for a moment.

'Did I do that? I did, didn't I?'

'Stel—'

'Let me see.'

'I can't.'

'You bloody well can.' I am struggling to sit up but my muscles are weak, shaky. A look passes over his face, almost of distaste.

'I wish you wouldn't swear,' he says quietly. 'You do it more often than you think.'

'Marco, show me.'

He lowers the collar of his dark wool jumper. I clutch at myself, horrified and ashamed. His neck and upper chest are a crosshatching of welts, dotted with blood. I am shaking my head and he takes my hand in his, saying it's all right baby, it's all right. I look down and see his exposed wrist, the tanned skin, the dark and ravenous indentations in his flesh, the small ring of bruising. He sees me looking and laughs but he is nervous.

'You bit me.'

'No. No.'

'It doesn't hurt. Not anymore. You didn't break the skin.'

I cover my mouth with my hand. Bitten him. Something curdles inside me. *Where's your muzzle, Katie Marigold?* Now why am I thinking of that?

'I'm sorry, Marco, I'm sorry, I'm so sorry. I don't remember.'

He smooths my brow. It is nice. I am a little girl again, sickly. I close my eyes, breathe him in. He's been smoking. I can smell the cigar lingering on him, faintly exotic. He keeps them on his mantelpiece in a humidor. When I told Carmel he had them imported from Havana, I thought she was going to roll her eyes right out of her head.

'Carmel said you had a key.'

'Yes, I had *your* key. You insisted that we go back to yours. This was about eleven, I think. I went out to get a takeaway. We hadn't eaten, either of us. Maybe that's why the drink hit us both so hard. You must have taken the pills when I was out.'

'Marco, I didn't – I don't—'

'Ssssh. I know. I know. It's all right now.'

We are quiet for a time. I can feel his pulse beneath the thin skin of his wrist. It's not quite true, what I had been about to say: I don't remember taking the pills. I do. I had taken them out of my bathroom cabinet, the one at home. I can even remember wondering what I was doing there. 'I should be in Marco's place,' I thought as I took the bottle from the cupboard, 'how did I get here', as I shook two, three pills into my hand. I was feeling miserable. It must have been the argument. Fight, I correct myself. Call it what it was. Look at those marks on his neck. I swallowed them dry. I remember that. They made me retch. But I kept them down. But it had only been three pills. Now look at me.

'She told me tonight that she was worried about her party.'

For a moment I am genuinely confused. 'Who?'

'Carmel. While the paramedics were working on you. She said she hoped you wouldn't be in hospital for long because the party was only half paid for.'

'S'right,' I mumble, my eyes closing. I am so tired. 'She put the deposit down last week. We're paying off the rest this week.'

'Clarification. *You're* paying the rest this week. Come on. You need to get some rest. I'm here. I'm here until you get better.'

He hasn't asked me why yet. He hasn't asked why I did it. That is good, because I honestly do not know. I hold his hand. Marc-oh. I am so lucky.

Chapter 8

I am allowed to go home the following evening, a tiny bruise on the back of my hand where the needle went in. I go straight to bed, and I sleep deeply and dreamlessly for nine hours. When I'm jerked awake by my phone my skin feels too tight, and for a second or two I can hear my frantic pulse at my temples. I reach for it just as it stops ringing. My arms tingle with pins and needles.

'Fuc—'

I wish you wouldn't swear, he'd said. I lie back in bed and lift my phone, seeing that the missed call is from Aunt Jackie. That can wait. I begin scrolling through my Facebook, Twitter, Instagram. The Devil makes work for idle hands. I'm on a news site when I see it, beneath a story about free school dinners. The headline: '*Former Child Star Overdose Drama*'. I am throbbing all over with shame as I click it open. There I am, age seven, next to a golden Labrador with my hand on its head, bent at the knee as though I am proposing to it. I am wearing a blue satin dress, which bulges at the arms, making me look distended. There is that gap in my teeth that I had filled in as soon as I left the show. The story is a skeleton; no meat to it.

'*Former child actress and star of* Marigold! *Stella Wiseman was rushed to Lewisham Hospital late on Friday night following a suspected barbiturate overdose. Paramedics were called to a South London address in the early hours of Saturday morning after an alarm was raised about the welfare of a woman. The actress (35) starred in the long-running sitcom from 1985 to 1993 before disappearing from public view.'*

Oh God. A drink. I just need something to take the edge off. I walk into the kitchen and look in the fridge, but there is no wine, no beer. We have vodka in the freezer, and I take a slug of it standing in my pyjamas. There is a clutter of dirty washing-up in the sink, crumbs and stains on the worktop. I can hear my phone ringing and I wander down the hallway carefully, taking the vodka with me cradled beneath one arm.

'Hi, Jackie.'

'Hello, love. Are you all right?'

Since Jackie divorced and remarried her tennis coach she has joined a gym and given up smoking. This means she incessantly chews gum even when working out. Her mouth is in constant motion. I can hear it now, a soft churning sound. She is holding the phone too close to her mouth.

'Why didn't you tell me, Stella? For God's sake. I could have helped you.'

'You've seen the news? It's crap, Jackie, totally out of proportion. Some idiot has sold that story – that non-story, I should remind you – for a few quid.'

'I didn't know it made the news. Marco called me.'

There is a muffled noise, static blown into the mouthpiece. She is sighing.

'I wish he'd called me sooner – I could have been down there in three hours. Honey, don't you know how precious you are? How important? Your parents wouldn't have wanted this.'

I can't take this in. I sit down slowly on the bed.

'Is it drugs? Is that it, honey? God knows what you're taking these days. You don't know what they're putting in it, Stell. They're ruthless, these people.'

'What people?'

'Drug dealers. We had a problem with them here a while ago, hanging round schools and giving it to kiddies. And of course the police aren't doing anything. It's a joke.'

'I'm not on drugs, Jackie.'

'Well, I hardly think you overdosed on Lemsip, did you? Marco is extremely worried about you, we all are.'

'He had no right to call you.'

'Stella, he did the right thing. I'm your family now. I'm all you've got. I couldn't forgive myself if something happened to you too.'

'I'm fine. I'm really, really, really fine.'

'Marco knows a private doctor with his own surgery near Holland Park. We talked about it, and I think you should go and see him. He might be able to help you.'

'Help me with what? There's nothing wrong!'

Silence. I know she's still there though. I can hear her chewing.

'Denial is the first sign of a problem, Stella. You of all people should know that. Your father was the same. Could never admit it.'

'Jackie, I have to go.'

'I'm here. We're all here. Let us help you.'

I hang up and put my head in my hands. Am I losing my mind? Is this how it happens? Slowly, destroying everything, like the descent of lava.

Chapter 9

It is the day of Carmel's party, and the flat is a mess – she is packing for her move to Paris, drinking tea, filling out forms, walking back and forth across the sitting room with her phone tucked beneath her chin.

'Stella, did you hear what I said?'

I look up. I'm reading a book but I'm struggling to concentrate, reading the same line over and over: *There's a large dog loose in the wood.*

'I said will you come and visit me in Paris? You'll have your own room with all your special things in there like a kid with divorced parents. And there is a patisserie just next door so we can get nice and fat on croissants.'

I fold the book onto my lap and look up at Carmel. She is so beautiful – luminous – that I wonder how we can bear it, the glare of her. I know people think I'm jealous. I know that. But I'm not. I could never be. She's never made me feel that way, despite what Marco says.

'Of course I will. I can't wait.'

Carmel looks out of the window. 'My taxi's here. I've got to go the wine merchant with Tia and sort out the boxes of champagne. Will you be okay?'

'Yes. I'm not going to try and hang myself, if that's what you're worried about.'

I laugh, but she doesn't smile. I suppose it wasn't that funny. Tia is Carmel's sister; she arrived last night from New York. We've hired a field just outside London and a huge marquee will be strung with fairy lights and glittering chandeliers. There's going to be a roulette table and a cocktail bar and huge displays of cherry blossom and ferns. I am looking forward to it. And I love Carmel's sister. The last time I saw her, Carmel and I were off our heads the morning after a night out in New York about ten years ago. Her apartment on the East Side had been full of vegetation; mosses and ferns and tiny Tillandsia plants hanging above her bed.

'Stella?'

'Huh?'

'I said maybe you could talk to Tia about work. She knows some great galleries in New York. Could be a big thing for you.'

'Sure, okay.'

She narrows her eyes. 'You won't, will you?'

'I can't move to New York, Carmel.'

'Why not?'

I hesitate and she nods knowingly.

'Marco can't fund you forever. You lost your job over two weeks ago. I move at the end of the month. I just think you should feel—'

'What?'

'I don't know. Urgency? You seem to be ignoring everything; it's not healthy. How will you pay the rent when I'm gone? Where will you live? What will you do for money?'

'I'll manage.'

I can't tell her I haven't thought about it, any of it. It's there the same way all my thoughts are these days: at the back of my skull, muddy and as slow-moving as treacle. Every time I try to focus it slides through my fingers.

'You going to do something with your hair?'

'What do you mean?'

Carmel looks at me flatly. Ever since I came back from the hairdresser earlier this week she's been pecking at me: *What did you do that for? That blonde is ageing on you. Those extensions make you look like bloody Rapunzel.* I stare back at her, too tired to argue. Eventually she sighs.

'I saw a girl in Brighton last weekend with a jet-black Vidal Sassoon bob that would look amazing on you. Right now you look like you're about to enter an American beauty pageant. I mean that in a bad way.'

'Are you done?'

'You're still coming, right? You'll be okay for the party?'

'Yes. I've already said all this. Just go. Go on. I'm going to have a bath and a sleep.'

She looks me over, not bothering to mask her concern. I want to tell her that she is mistaken, that she has it wrong, she and Marco both have it wrong. I am not my mother. I am braver than her. More resilient. The thought makes tears spring to my eyes, and I lift the book to my face so Carmel does not see.

I hear the front door quietly close an hour later as I'm lying in the bath watching the sun move from the far wall across the floor. I'm not expecting Carmel, or Tia – they are going straight from the wine merchants to the hotel near the venue to get ready. Perhaps they have forgotten something? I sit up slowly in the cool water.

'Carmel?' I wait. 'Tia? Hello?'

There is no answer. My skin ripples with gooseflesh as I strain to hear. There is a soft creak as someone starts to climb the stairs. I can just make out the rustle of clothes, the soft tread on the floorboards. I can't remember whether I locked the bathroom door and from here it's impossible to tell. My mind instantly recalls the cyclists from upstairs telling us about the burglaries this summer.

I call out again, my voice shaking. There is no response, but this time a floorboard creaks just outside in the hallway. From where I'm sitting I can see the frosted glass of the bathroom door, and there is someone moving out there. Tall, broad. All the saliva in my mouth dries up. My skin prickles with cold. Now I'm thinking about those phone calls I've been receiving, the silent ones. Long exhalations of breath in the darkness. Joey Fraser asking me where my muzzle is and someone else, Lesley Patterson maybe, who'd played Lucy in the show, saying, '*They call female dogs bitches, isn't that right, Joey?*'

But she is dead now, isn't she? Carbon monoxide poisoning. Suicide. But Joey Fraser isn't. He's got a film coming out. He's come back to England.

I look around me frantically for something I can use as a weapon. I'm naked and vulnerable, still with the bruising on the inside of my elbow where the nurse had taken my blood. She'd asked me what I wanted to do a silly thing like kill myself for, and I hadn't answered. Outside the door the shadow moves, growing taller. I watch the handle slowly turn, my heart hammering in my throat. Carefully, so carefully, I pull the shower curtain closed around the bath so that I am hidden from view. I hear someone come into the room, and the curtain ripples gently in the draught.

Now they are crossing the floor with a slow careful tread which makes me want to scream. The nearest thing to hand is a shampoo bottle which I have wrapped my fingers around, weighing it carefully. I can swing it, I figure, maybe enough to hit them on the temple, stun them perhaps. Despite the cold I am sweating. Whoever it is has stopped in front of the bath. I can see the shape of them through the filmy curtain, and as I watch, horrified, I see them raise a hand and stroke their fingers down the plastic, making a shrill squeaking sound. I want to shout but before I can, before I can spring forward with the urgency I feel coiled in my muscles, I hear a voice say, 'Stella?'

'Marco?' It's Marco. I am flooded with relief. He draws the curtain back.

'Are you hiding?' He sees the bottle in my hand and a look of concern creases his face. 'Stella? Were you going to attack me?'

'I didn't know it was you. Why didn't you say something?'

'I thought you were asleep.'

'Didn't you hear me calling you? God, you had me out of my mind.'

'Out of your mind is right. You look awful.'

'Great, thanks a lot. Pass me that towel.'

He helps me out of the bath because my legs are shaking. When he folds me into a warm towel, I lean against him, smoothing out my ragged breathing. He lifts my face to look at me, cradling my chin with his hand.

'I mean it, darling, you don't look well. Have you slept?'

'I've done nothing but sleep for the last twenty-four hours. How did you get into the house?'

'I had a key cut. After what happened I thought – I thought it would be prudent.'

'You spoke to my aunt.'

'Yes. Are you mad at me?'

'I am, a bit.' I start drying myself. He watches me wrap a towel about my head, turban style. The weight of my new extensions presses down on me. 'You've worried her. You didn't need to do that.'

'I'm sorry. I was trying to help. Come on, get dressed. I've got something for you.'

It's food. The grease-spotted bag is sitting on the table and inside, silver foil cartons, a rich smell of spices, hot fluffy naan bread. I hadn't realised how hungry I am.

'I'm trying to be healthy,' I tell him, not meaning a word of it.

'I won't tell if you don't.' He's brought us cold bottles of beer and now he cracks one open, handing it to me and kissing me full on the mouth. When we sit down, he takes my hand. When we speak, our voices overlap.

'I think—'

'Stella, I—'

'You first,' I say.

'Okay.' He draws a deep breath, rubs his palm along the length of his thigh. It occurs to me then that he's nervous. I immediately brace myself.

'I *did* call Jackie. You're right. But not quite for the reason you think. Or not just for that, anyway. Uh—'

He's reaching into his inside pocket, sweat prickling his brow. For a moment, one crazy moment, I think he is going to pull out a gun on me. But then I see the little box in his hand.

'In the absence of your father I need to ask someone for permission so I thought it should be her.'

He opens the box. Inside, a ring. Glittering emeralds in a plain silver band. I put my hand over my mouth.

'Stella, I – God, I knew I'd make a mess of this. Stella, will you marry me?'

I am silent. The time expands like foam, a balloon slowly inflated. It is thick and almost tangible. In it everything seems frozen, a perfect clarity.

His voice is prickling with nerves. 'Do you want me to go down on one knee? I'll do it, if you want.'

'No, Marco, no. This is – it's beautiful. It's just right.'

'Is that a yes?'

'Yes, of course it's a yes!'

His smile widens, teeth gleam. He takes the ring from the box and slides it carefully onto my ring finger, telling me – almost babbling – that the ring had belonged to his grandmother and how she'd bought it in Penang ('*That's in Malaysia, Stella*') and how he'd kept it a secret these past few weeks – and all I can think is, *How could you have thought he was pulling a gun on you?*

After sex, because of course there is always that – lust like a hot scalding liquid – after that we lie in my bed looking up at the ceiling. I have my head against his chest and he is tangling his hands in my hair. He loves it long, he tells me. Much better. Prettier. After filming the very last episode as Katie Marigold I'd cut it all off; that beautiful, waist-length, honey-coloured hair. I was sick of it. I've never grown it past my shoulders again. I lift my hand to look at my ring and hear myself say, 'When I came out of hospital there was a piece about me in the papers.'

'I know.'

'I just – I mean, I've been thinking about it, and—'

'You think I sold them the overdose story on you?'

I shrug miserably. 'Did you?'

'Of course not,' he says softly. 'If you want my opinion, whoever did that was pretty desperate. I mean, no disrespect to you, Stella, you know I loved that show, but – it's hardly news, is it? You haven't been on television for a long time. Financially speaking, it would hardly be worth it.'

He leans onto his elbow to look at me, half smiling in that way he has. 'You happy?'

'Yes.'

'Good. I love you, Stella. You know that, don't you?'

'Yes.'

'And when we're married it will just be us, just me and you.' He lifts my hand and presses it to his lips. 'Will you keep your last name?'

'I don't know. Maybe not. I'm the last of the Wisemans, after all.'

'Have I told you about Bruce at the golf club?'

'I don't think so.'

'When he married Wendy they couldn't agree on a surname and both their names were too long to hyphenate so they changed it to a whole new one by deed poll. He's Bruce Griffin now.'

'Is that what you want to do?'

'It's an option, if we can't decide.'

'What to?'

He smiles again. 'Marigold.'

He looks at me and just for a moment I think he is serious. 'Can you imagine,' I say, and then we both grin.

'Anyway. Tonight. It's party night. The big party that you've paid for with your ever-dwindling reserves of cash. What will you wear?'

I laugh. 'It's not that bad. I have savings.'

'You keep saying that. When was the last time you looked at your balance?'

I stiffen. I don't remember. I think about those rings in my dad's freezer, fossilised. Marco looks at me gently. I know what he's going to say. Exactly what Carmel had said. *Time to wake up, Stella, time to face the real world.* But I can't. I'm not ready. I can't.

'Tell you what,' I say, 'you choose what I wear tonight. I've got loads of clothes.'

He brightens.

I laugh again. 'Oh, and I haven't, by the way, paid for the party.'

'No? How can Carmel afford it then?'

I don't know what to tell him. Carmel hadn't needed the money in the end. She had told me not to worry, not to worry about anything. She'd get it from somewhere else. And so she had. It was only a few hundred pounds. Maybe she'd borrowed it from Martha. Maybe she'd finally sold some of her vintage clothes on eBay like she was always threatening to do. Idly I wonder how much you could sell a story for, even a pathetic little story about a former child star no one has thought of in decades. Got to be worth a hundred at least, maybe two.

I look up at Marco. 'Jackie said you'd mentioned seeing a doctor.'

'Yes.'

'Do you really think I need to?'

Without hesitation. 'Yes.'

'Can you arrange it?'

'Yes. I've seen him before. He prescribed me those pills.'

'Why?'

'I work very hard – too hard. It's what comes of inheriting your father's legacy. My old man had a heart attack at forty-two and another three before the one which killed him in his fifties. When they opened him up they said he had the heart of a seventy-year-old. That's what stress does to you, Stella. Doctor Wilson thought I was going to kill myself if I carried on. He gave me the pills to help me relax. Switch off. To sleep.'

Switch off. That gets my attention.

'Can you get me an appointment with him?'

'Sure.'

Marco climbs from the bed and opens my wardrobe. I lie back, full of food, suddenly sluggish. The beer has gone right to my head. Marco pulls out a fringed black dress, tight, mid-length, and pulls a face.

'No,' he says firmly, putting it back, pulling out another, strapless, shimmering metallic grey. 'No.'

'Why "no"?'

'You need something simple. You're so beautiful. Why distract from that? Where's the one I bought you?'

I push myself backwards into the pillows. My eyes are so heavy. I know the dress he means: it's navy, long-sleeved. Plain. I just want to sleep. I can hear the rattle of coat hangers, Marco asking me why I need so many clothes, why I don't have any proper dresses. I open my mouth to ask what he means by a 'proper' dress and then I am sinking, so tired. Just a little nap. So tired.

I'm woken by the thin morning light, and Marco gently shaking my arm. 'Stella,' he is saying, 'Stella, you need to wake up.' I groan, screwing my eyes up. My head is pounding, although it doesn't feel like a hangover. Not yet. It's at the base of my skull, a tight, vicelike pain.

'What time is it?'

'It's nearly eleven.'

'In the morning?'

I sit up in horror. I'm in bed, a blanket pulled over me. I'm not wearing any clothes and the disorientation I feel is like vertigo, like swooning. Marco is holding my phone out to me. I can't read the expression on his face. Pity? Resentment?

'I tried to wake you but—' He shrugs, his face inscrutable, and I am stricken with worry. That I have done it again. I've got mad at him. Hurt him. I massage my jaw with my fingers. I think I have been grinding my teeth in my sleep. Or biting.

'Oh my God,' I say, scrolling through the dozens of missed calls. Martha, James, Tia. Carmel, of course. Loads from Carmel. Some from a withheld number, although that was later, much later. The last one recorded was at 04:27. 'I missed the party.'

'I spoke to her at about midnight when it became clear I couldn't get you up. She told me to leave you. Said you'd be better off sleeping.'

'Was she upset?'

He nods. He has made coffee and now he passes it to me. I scan his arms for bite marks or scratches while I'm listening to my voicemails. Carmel's voice is tight, frustrated. *I'm sorry you're going to miss all the fun, you silly cow. Call me.*

Then the last message, just after three. A voice I don't recognise, wet-sounding, bronchial. There is no background noise of the party, no music or shouting. Just that rasping burr, thick intakes of breath.

'You're next.' Silence. Then, 'Lucy. Bonnie. Katie. You all look so beautiful when you're dead.'

I sit looking at my phone for a moment and then run to the sink, sure I am going to throw up, but there is only the slow roll of my stomach and black violets blooming in front of my eyes. Marco is rubbing my back, talking to me gently, urging a glass of water into my shaking hand as I replay the message for him.

'I'm calling the police. It's a threat.'

'They won't do anything,' I tell him, but he calls anyway, insists on it. He has high colour on his neck and cheeks, clenching and unclenching his fists, frustrated. As he speaks and paces the room I go and have a shower, my eyes ringing, my blood high. By the time I come out I'm calmer, less jittery, but he is still flushed with anger.

'They're useless. You're right. They don't give a shit.'

'What did they say?'

'Keep a record. It's not considered harassment because this is the first time you've actually had a threat. All the silent calls, all the middle of the night calls, they don't count, apparently. You know what else she said?'

I do, but he needs to get it out of his system. I've been through all this before when I was a kid.

'She said the good news is that if they were planning on hurting you they'd probably just go ahead and do it. These threatening calls are just that. Threats.'

'I don't even remember falling asleep last night.'

'No?'

I shake my head. My head full of needles. Now I feel hungover. That rough, abrasive feeling behind the eyes. The lurch of my stomach. I can't face Carmel, or Tia or Martha. *You all look so beautiful when you're dead.*

'I hate this. What if this man knows where I live?'

Then Marco says something which jerks me upright, taller. Scared.

'What makes you so sure it's a man?'

The pill is small and round and grey. It is unbranded, like the bottle, and almost entirely unremarkable. I am used to swallowing them now. At first they left a metallic taste in my throat, like pennies. Now I barely taste a thing. Sometimes I drink them with juice or coffee. I used to take them with wine, but all that's changed now. It's all changed.

And so. I'm standing in my bathroom, water puddling at my feet. I look down at myself, noticing that I'm dressed but no shoes. The light coming through the window is the dirty grey of smog or a ruptured exhaust. It's early, and I am at home. The heating hasn't come on yet, and I can see my breath. Winter frost on the windows. I am shivering with cold. And I must take this pill.

There is someone at the door. I can see the shape of the figure through the patterned glass. I swallow the pill dry. My hair is wet, and he is knocking against the glass, saying, 'Are you done yet?', and he is saying, 'Stella, we need to get going', but I can tell by the set of his shoulders that what he means is I will swallow you, I will swallow you whole, and I am afraid.

Chapter 10

By the time we leave the motorway we have been driving for nearly four hours. I know all the roads we've been on because Marco has sworn at each one, individually. '*The bloody M4*', '*The bastard A30*'. The car is hot and uncomfortable and smells stale; coffee and nicotine and Marco's aftershave. When I look at him askance I can see the little muscle ticking beneath the shelf of his jaw, his muddy brown eyes staring ahead. His leg is jittering and when I put my hand on his thigh the muscle stiffens. Still, he will not look at me.

There is a bag by my feet, canary-yellow leather. I found it in a charity shop in Kent three years ago, and I used to think it was the most beautiful thing I owned. It doesn't fit right though. I can't work out what it's doing here. Then another wave hits me, a pleasing numbness, and I pull a phone from the folds of the bag, old and slightly battered. I turn it around in my hands.

'Whose is this?' I ask, and Marco tells me, 'It's yours.'

'Is it?' I'm frowning, confused. 'It doesn't look like mine.'

'It's your new phone, Stella. I gave it to you, remember?'

'Okay.'

Marco is speaking slowly, patiently, but I can tell he is tired. He rubs his temples with the tips of his fingers. I open the phone, scroll through it. Messages are blank. Photos are blank. In the address book just three numbers. I look up at him.

'Where are all my numbers? Where's my phone?'

'In your other bag, the one you lost. Honey, we've talked about this.'

'Don't be mad at me.'

'I'm not— I'm not mad at you, Stella, I'm just – you know? This is hard work.'

The sign reads 'KERNOW a'gas dynergh'. I crane my head to look at it through the smeared glass.

'What does that mean, that sign?'

'"Welcome to Cornwall".'

'They have a different language here?'

'Don't worry, I bought you a phrasebook. You'll soon pick it up.'

It is almost impossible to tell when Marco is joking, and when he does it feels as fragile as a robin's egg. I do not laugh, in case it breaks. There is a strange urgency in my flesh, a prickling. I feel very far from home.

Outside it begins to rain and the clouds turn to ash, a vast leaden grey. Through the window the landscape shimmers, vast rapeseed fields undulating like the mounds of a woman's hips and thighs. The slippery unease increases as we drive past signposts with goblin-esque names: Perranzabuloe, Marazanvose, Goonbell. Rain turning to drizzle as we pass through a dull town, grey blocks of houses against the backdrop of china clay pits. I press my head to the window, catch sight of myself in the wing mirror. Pale and pinched with a crown of wild blonde hair, slightly darker at the roots. My eyes are polished marbles, pupils thick and black and round as coins. There is a graze on my chin, and I don't know how it got there. Marco is asking me if I'm all right. My jaw aches and my arms feel heavy. Blows to the head. I have done something bad. *Put a muzzle on, Katie Marigold. You look so beautiful when you're dead.* I close my eyes, and when I open them we are driving down an avenue of trees thick with shadow, and then I close them again and when I open them Marco is saying, 'Here we are, Stella, we're here', and all I see is a sign choked by the spiny hedgerows growing thickly, skewering glossy black fruits and berries. It reads 'Chy an Mor'. I turn to look as we drive past it. The drizzle has turned into a hard, driving rain. He is peering out of the windscreen, slowing the car to a crawl. The hedges press up against us. I can hear the leaves whispering against the windows.

I turn to Marco. 'What is "Chy an Mor"?'

'It's the name of the cottage. My parents bought it from a man in the seventies and never changed it. Here it is. Look, can you see?'

He points through the window. I catch sight of a little white cottage, a grey slate roof, wind-blunted trees.

'See that upstairs window? That's your bedroom. I asked Kennecker to tidy the garden for you and sort out a few things inside.'

'Who?'

'Kennecker, the caretaker. He was working here when I was a kid so he must be in his seventies now. He said he'd show you how the boiler works and the heating. I can't stay long.'

But. But I do not want to be alone.

Marco sees my face and his lips tighten. 'I know. I know. But I have to work. I have to finish some things. You know what it's been like. Just a few days, and then once I'm done I'll come straight back down, I promise. Please don't look at me like that, Stella. Please tell me you'll be okay. I'm worried about you as it is.'

'I'll be okay.'

He smiles, but he is not reassured, and my heart is fluttering like a trapped bird. I do not want to be here. I do not want to be alone. I cannot trust myself anymore.

◆ ◆ ◆

Marco opens the back door of the cottage, drawing in a breeze of ozone and sea salt and the sibilant sounds of the waves. I stand in the doorway, blasted by the wind, hair floating about my face. The cliff sweeps dramatically down, threaded with canary-yellow gorse. The grey waters of the Atlantic roll sinuously, close enough that I can see the white caps of the breakers steaming towards the shore. The sky is charcoal strokes drawn by an amateur hand.

'You'll get cold,' he tells me.

'I don't care.'

He puts his hands about my waist; they are warm and fleshy, pressing through my thin cotton T-shirt, pulling me towards him firmly, until we are pressed together. The curve of my spine is flat against the leanness of him. His breath is warm against my ear. He is saying my name, telling me it will be all right, that he will look after me. As he moves around he breathes against the back of my neck, feathering the hair there, and I flinch, pulling away. Marco sighs, rakes his fingers over his scalp. In this light I can see how tired he looks, how disheartened, and I know that I am losing him, and the fear fills my mouth like seawater. As I open my mouth to speak his phone begins to ring. He looks at the screen, shrugs.

'Look, I have to take this. Why don't you get your stuff from the car?'

I stand for a moment in front of a silvery, fly-spotted mirror in the hallway. I have to keep reminding myself that this is for my own good. The doctor said so, and Marco had agreed. A break from everything. Getting away from it all. Outside the rain is easing, and the day fills with an eerie tobacco-coloured light. I flick the keys at the car, hear the clunk as it unlocks. I feel an uncomfortable sensation of being watched – no more than a prickle – and I look back to the house. For a moment I see a silhouette in the upstairs window, grey and insubstantial like a veil of smoke, but when I step forward it has gone.

Clouds. Clouds moving across the sky on the glass.

In the car boot a spare tyre, antifreeze, Marco's golf clubs. I stare at the empty space where my bag should be. Close it, reopen it, close it. My blood thickens. I move slowly around the car, peering into the footwell, cupping my hands against the darkened glass of the windows to look into the back seat. I look up at the sky, chrome-coloured, sucking my breath from my lungs in silver ribbons. I open the boot once more, and it is still empty. I stare and stare and heat builds in me like a fever.

'What is it?'

Marco is standing in the doorway, his phone in his hand. He tells me it is cold, to keep the door closed. He reminds me I am not well and on this score he is absolutely right. I am not well.

'Did you bring my luggage into the house?'

He stares at me blankly, shakes his head.

'It's gone, Marco. My suitcase with all my clothes in it, my toiletries, everything, gone.'

'Have you checked the back seat?'

'Yes, the front too.' I drum my fingernails on the roof of the car with a sound like tiny bullets. I can feel a hectic colour in my cheeks.

'Do you think someone has taken it?' I ask.

'What do you think?'

'I'll tell you what I think, I think coming here was a mistake and that this is a – I don't know – some sort of sign. Fate telling me to go back to London.'

Marco smiles slightly, but his eyes remain cool and dark, watching me. 'A sign, Stella? This isn't the Middle Ages. Your first-born isn't going to die because the cock crowed thrice this morning. You've obviously just left it at your flat—'

'I put it in the car. I put it in the car this morning, along with my jacket. I know I did because I remember not wanting to put it down as the ground was wet. So I put it straight in the boot.'

Marco tilts his head a fraction, as if listening to a faraway sound. 'Think, Stella. Think back. Do you really remember doing it? It was early, and you were still half asleep. Maybe you intended to put it in the car but got distracted and you've created a false memory. Remember what Doctor Wilson said.'

I stand, blood buzzing in my ears, chin bent to my chest. I try to remember but it is hard. I can remember unhooking my keys from where they hung by the coat rack. I can remember Marco asking if I was sure I had packed everything I would need. The dawn air had smelled smoky and exotic and the neighbour's cat Tonto had wandered over as I'd stood beside the car. Had I put my bag down to stroke him and not picked it back up again? Is it still sitting on the thin strip of littered concrete which serves as a parking space near our Lewisham flat? But in the next moment I'm sure I stroked Tonto on my way back from the car, because I had had both hands free. Hadn't I? Hadn't I?

Marco says softly, 'I think you left it behind, didn't you?'

I nod, and my eyes brim with tears. What a day. What a lonely day.

'Let's . . . Okay, let's sort this out.' Marco is scanning through his phone. 'Don't worry. We can fix this. Doctor Wilson said to expect these sorts of things to happen, didn't he? It's all part of your recovery, Stella.'

I hurriedly wipe my eyes with the backs of my hands. 'Who are you calling?'

'Alice.'

'What can she do?'

'She can go to the flat and see if you left it behind. Then she can have it couriered down here.'

'How will she get into my flat?'

'She'll use my key,' he replies. 'You'll just have to manage for tonight.'

He turns away from me as he begins talking to Alice. I find my thoughts wandering to Carmel and instantly force myself to stop. It is too painful.

'Okay. She's on her way there now. She'll call and let me know. Why don't you get some sleep?'

'Sleeping is all I'm doing these days.'

'It's the pills. Doctor Wilson said—'

'I know what he said, Marco. I'm just – so tired of being tired. You know?'

'You're not the only one, Stella. Sometimes I think—'

I stare at him. 'What? You think what?'

He looks exasperated and puffs his cheeks out in a long, loud sigh. 'I'm worn out, Stella, I really am. I'm trying so hard to help you. I've driven you all this way and – well. Leaving your bag behind like that, it's a pretty lame trick.'

'You think I did it on purpose?'

He raises his eyebrows at me but says nothing.

'I thought I'd put it in the boot. I honestly did.'

'I just can't believe anything you say anymore. All I'm doing is trying to help you.'

Back in the kitchen he leans on the work surface, head bent. I wait. I can feel a headache building in my temples, something as dark and ponderous as a storm.

'In the car you asked me about the numbers in your phone.'

I nod.

'You asked me where the numbers for your friends were. Don't you remember?'

He is speaking softly, cushioning his words. Tears prickle again. Sometimes I just feel like screaming.

'Stella?'

'Huh?'

'Do you remember?'

'Yes. I asked you where my numbers had gone.'

'They've gone, Stella. You lost them.'

'I can get them back.'

'I mean your friends, honey. Carmel, Martha, James.'

He reaches his hands forward, I take them. He begins to rub my fingers, gently building warmth.

'You're cold.'

'I'm frightened. I don't want to be left on my own. I want to go home.'

He is not being unkind when he tells me: 'You've nothing to go back for.'

I feel that dull sense of cauterisation which has become so familiar to me in recent weeks. A sensation of distance, of depth, the unbearable itch of amputation.

'Lost your job, your friends – you're in a limbo right now. You certainly can't go back. What would you do? Where would you live?'

More tears rolling down the curve of my cheeks, making my vision blur. Marco says, 'Oh, darling', and he says, 'Oh, Stella.' He rubs my knuckles with his thumb.

'I'm just trying to – don't cry, honey – I'm just trying to make you see the reality of it, of your situation. It's no good me pretending to you that everything is as it was. It isn't, and it won't be for a while.'

His phone begins to twitter in his hand. He looks at it and smiles apologetically.

'I really do need to take this. One second, okay?'

He moves away from me, across to the back door and onto the little stone path which leads out into the garden, voice low. I close my eyes, only half aware that I am swaying slightly, only half aware that the knocking sound I can hear is at the front door.

'Marco,' I call out, 'Marco, the door.'

I walk into the hallway, back again. Fidgeting. Someone is here at the house. My hands curl and uncurl at my sides.

'Marco?'

More rapping, this time more urgent. I walk down the hallway on legs which are not quite steady. When I reach the front door I allow my fingers to hover over the latch.

'Who is it?'

'Caretaker,' comes the muffled reply. And then, when I hesitate, 'It's starting to get cold out here.'

I open the door, pinning a smile to my face rigid as rigor mortis. The man standing in the doorway is middle-aged, bullish, thick beard threaded with grey. He is smiling, revealing a row of small, even teeth.

'Oh,' I say, 'you're not Mr Kennecker.'

'True.' He pushes his cap back on his head. 'What gave it away?'

'You're too young. Marco told me he'd been looking after the house since he was small so that would make you at least seventy.'

'Correct. And I am to assume that you are not Mr Marco Nilsen?'

'Very observant. What gave it away?'

'If I'm honest, ma'am, it was your tits.'

I bark laughter once, shocked. He is still smiling, arms folded across his broad chest. *Carmel would have liked you*, I think briefly,

90

and with that comes a pain somewhere in my chest so I shut the thought down.

'Do I hear a trace of an accent? Are you American?'

'Nope. Canadian.' He rolls back the sleeve of his parka to reveal a maple leaf tattoo. It is old and faded and the colours have bled.

'Terrible, isn't it? I got it done in my teens when I was in Vietnam so that people wouldn't keep assuming I was an American. People are much friendlier to you when they find out you're from Vancouver, not Texas.'

'It's a pretty permanent form of identification.'

'Yup, I guess. But you don't think of permanence at nineteen, do you?'

I shrug. He tilts his head slightly, narrows his eyes.

'I'm Frankie.' Extending a hand. 'Like the Sister Sledge song but more irritating. Can I come inside? I'm getting soaked.'

◆ ◆ ◆

The caretaker, Mr Kennecker, has been in hospital.

'Gallstones,' Frankie explains. 'Painful but not fatal. He's fine, he's recovering, but he won't be back at work. I'll pass on your best wishes, shall I?'

'Yes, please do,' Marco says briskly. He moves around the table to shake Frankie's hand. 'We were expecting you half an hour ago, so I hope you'll understand that I'm not going to stay here long. I need to get back to London.'

Since coming off the phone his face has darkened. He looks like a caricature of himself, swiftly drawn. Dark and brooding, wide mouth set in a firm line.

He pulls me towards him, saying quietly, 'That was Alice. She found your bag. It was in the hallway by the stairs. She said she'll get it down here as soon as possible.'

'I don't understand how that happened.'

He squeezes my shoulder, looking into my eyes. 'Stop it.'

'Stop what?'

'Going over everything. You've done the right thing.'

'I wasn't—'

'And stop thinking about Carmel. You're better off without her. She was a leech.'

'I wasn't thinking about Carmel.'

I am, of course. I look at the bracelet on my wrist, the one with the inscription next to my skin. I wear it all the time. And so I think of her.

Frankie has a box beneath one meaty arm, and now he puts it on the scarred surface of the old oak table. He pulls his cap off to reveal dark curls peppered with silver. He has another tattoo, I notice, on the back of his hand. Blue ink, a geometric shape, fuzzy with age.

'Shall I put the kettle on?' Frankie asks.

I clear my throat. 'I'm afraid I haven't been shopping yet, so we have nothing in.'

'Aha!' He sounds pleased with himself and opens the box. 'It's a sort of welcome pack. It was Mrs Kennecker's idea, so I can't take the credit. Just to help you on your first night.'

From inside he produces teabags, milk and a small bag of sugar. Holding up a finger – 'Wait, wait, I'm not done' – he continues to extract a bag of apples, cornflakes, sausages, potatoes and a box of chocolates. With a final flourish he produces a bottle of red wine.

'Uh – Frankie. That's very kind, but Stella won't be drinking the wine this evening, I'm afraid,' Marco says.

'Well, then she can splash it on her cornflakes, can't she?' Frankie stares at the label. 'Should certainly liven up your morning.'

'Do you want to tell him, Stella?'

It stings. My guts turn slippery with anxiety. A blush is building on my chest, my neck. Instead I look down, hands ghost-white stars spread on my knees. I shake my head.

'No?' Marco turns to Frankie. 'Stella isn't drinking because Stella is an addict. We can't have any alcohol in the house. She's here to get better. London was ruining her, and she's left it all behind.'

Marco says all this impassively, tanned forearms crossed in front of him. The glint of his thick gold watch hangs in a loop about his wrist. Distantly, I hear Frankie say that it's cool, no problem, he'll take the wine home, and would I like him to show me the boiler, it's just upstairs. I follow him on hollow feet.

London, home, suddenly seems as remote as a moon orbiting a distant planet. I have shed it like a skin, a ghostly imprint, fading. I miss my friends, although it feels like a long time since I have spoken to Carmel or Martha or James. Marco told me it was all behind me now; the commuting, the unendurable deadlines and unbreakable glass ceilings, the flirting, the pubs, the traffic. But, still. I miss it.

My bedroom is at the back of the cottage, with a long window overlooking the sea to the west. The room is bisected by a dark beam, and beneath my feet are honey-coloured oak floorboards worn smooth with passage. I lie on the bed, my arms over my head. My bones are tired, lead-heavy, like my flesh. I cocoon my memories, the ones which are stark and indelible, the ones the pills haven't eroded away. I keep them safe because they are all I have.

My last birthday. My thirty-fifth, just last month. Black Friday, I had called it.

Chapter 11

It had been eight thirty in the evening when we reached the restaurant, a little bit drunk and a little bit high. Carmel had arrived home earlier than expected, wearing a royal-purple dress and looking at least seven feet tall in her heels. Her eerie grace was astonishing, her skin a gleaming blue-black like polished marble.

'You're early,' I told her. 'And you look amazing. You're not meant to look better than me. It's my birthday. Sort it out.'

'Happy birthday!' Carmel sang, reaching for an ashtray. She tucked the bottle under her arm and headed for the kitchen. 'Consider my punctuality my gift to you.'

'Can I exchange it for something else?'

Then Carmel's voice, floating in from the kitchen. 'Guess who I've just seen?'

'I've no id—'

'Oh, come on. You're no fun! Guess! I'll give you a clue.'

Carmel made a complicated mime swinging her arm between her legs.

I snorted laughter. 'The Elephant Man!'

'Yesssss! God, I love this hot weather.'

The Elephant Man had become our pet name for one of the two cyclists who lived above us on account of his generously stuffed Lycra and his much-imagined sexual prowess. The other was known affectionately as The Anaconda. We were children, Carmel and I, snorting giggles into our cupped hands.

'Did he say hello to you?'

'No. God, no. Never spoken to me since that time he caught me looking at him with those binoculars.'

I laughed, filled with warmth and good feeling. Carmel poured champagne into glasses, handing one to me.

'Where's Marco?' She flicked through a magazine. 'What did he get you?'

'He's meeting us at the restaurant. I haven't had my present yet.'

Silence.

'Did Marco choose this restaurant, Stella?'

'Yes.'

Our eyes met and she shrugged. 'Yeah, I thought so.'

'Listen, I know it's expensive, which is why I asked you all not to buy me anything. This is your gift to me, coming out for this meal. I don't want anything else. You are coming, aren't you, Carmel? Please say you are.'

'Sure. Sure. Got an advance on my wages.'

'I said I'd pay for you.'

'And I said I wouldn't let you. It's your birthday, you dick.'

Carmel turned the page of the magazine delicately, wetting her finger to do so. She looked up at me, head slightly tilted.

'This is what you wanted tonight, isn't it?'

'Yes.'

'A meal out at your boyfriend's favourite restaurant?'

'That's right.'

Valkoinen Huone served reindeer and crayfish and salted liquorice liquor at extortionate prices, and without Marco paying for me, I would never have been able to afford to eat there. Out of all the people I had invited, only a handful had been able to accept, and of those, two had already dropped out earlier in the week. I had asked Marco to consider changing the venue to somewhere less expensive. We had been in bed, our legs tangled together, my hand against his firm chest, feeling his heartbeat beneath the soft pads of my fingers. He had shaken his head with what seemed like genuine regret.

'Afraid not, baby. You understand, don't you, how hard it was to get this booking, how popular this restaurant is?'

He leaned over to kiss me. 'Your real friends will find a way to be there,' he had said.

I swallowed the champagne quickly and immediately refilled my glass.

'I've got you something,' Carmel said.

'I told you not to!'

'I know you did.'

A little black bag tied up with ribbon. It was matte and smooth and very plain. Inside, tissue paper, and inside that a bracelet of thick silver.

'Oh, Carmel. Oh, this is so pretty!'

'You sound surprised.'

I was surprised. Our usual gifts to each other were always tat.

'You remember the present you bought me that Christmas at my parents'?' Carmel said, her eyes glittering. 'What was it called again?'

I laughed.

'The Butt Buster. I did warn you not to open it in front of everyone.'

'That was a good Christmas.'

'Yes, your brother still talks about it. Do you think it scarred him for life?'

'I hope so,' she said, still grinning.

I lifted the bracelet and turned it this way and that in the light. 'Oh, this is beautiful, thank you. I shall wear it always.'

Inside, an inscription: '*I love you, you dick x*'

Carmel crossed the room and hugged me, enveloping me in the comforting musky scent of her perfume.

'Happy birthday. You'll always be a dick, but I do love you to pieces.'

On the tables of the dimly lit restaurant were wild flowers and rosemary in hand-thrown clay vases. Marco greeted us with a mild frown of puzzlement.

'Been drinking, Stella?'

'It's her birthday.' Carmel smiled pleasantly, before taking a seat. 'Let go of the reins a little, Marco.'

I looked around, smiling. My friends, I thought. Those who had been able to make it. Those who had been able to afford it, I corrected myself.

It was good to see Martha and James again; it felt as if it had been a long time. Perhaps it had. I was losing days sometimes. They had recently moved to a bigger house just outside London and as I sat next to them I felt a guilty stab at skipping their housewarming, their invitations to dinner, for drinks. Things have just been busy, I had told Martha over the phone, but we'll see you soon though, I promise. Her hair was tucked up in blonde curls so light and soft and feathery that I wanted to nest in them.

'Happy birthday, Stella,' James was saying, leaning across to kiss me. 'Great restaurant. We've had to take out a second mortgage to come here, obviously. We're just drinking the college funds for our kids.'

'He means thank you for inviting us,' Martha said. 'It's lovely to see you.'

'No, thank you. I'm thrilled you're here. The waiting list is nearly eighteen months long. Marco only managed to get the table because he plays golf with the owner.'

'Oh yeah?' James said in exactly the same way Carmel had; the same measured, careful tone. He sipped his wine. 'We figured it had been Marco's choice. Didn't he want us to come or something?'

I saw Martha dig him carefully in the ribs with her elbow and quickly looked away. Marco, sitting opposite me across the table, caught my eye and smiled. I returned it, pouring myself a drink, but I felt sour and cold. A thought then, dark and toxic like a droplet of ink in water. *Didn't he want us to come or something?*

After dinner we had gone on to a late bar and then to a basement in Brixton where we drank and danced until I lost a shoe and my make-up had become a sooty blur. Towards the end of the night Marco put one hand on my hip and the other, the one holding a bottle of beer, around my neck.

'When do I get you to myself?' he said, into the crease between my collar and my ear, and ten minutes later we were in a cab, two hours from sunrise and twenty minutes from home. I had yawned, leaning my head against the window, watching the lights, the neon blurs, the eyeless city.

'Rise and shine, sleepyhead. You're home.'

I'd stuttered awake. I could see the orange streetlights and the building on Griffin Road where Carmel and I lived. It was dark. The taxi driver was leaning over me in the back seat, shaking me gently by the arm. My head rattled against the window. Marco was gone.

'Come on then. Do you want a hand getting indoors?'

'Where's Marco?'

'That your boyfriend, is it? Got out at Battersea.' When the taxi driver smiled his skin crinkled as though clutched by an unseen hand. 'He paid the fare. Come on, out you get.'

'He left me behind?'

'He did, yes.'

'Why?'

The taxi driver shrugged, embarrassed. I thanked him and wandered into the building, fumbling my mobile from my bag. Marco answered as I stood in the hallway of our building. He sounded irritable and tired.

'What?'

'You left me! You left me in the taxi by myself!'

For a long moment there was just the sound of his breathing. Then a noisy exhale. 'You don't remember.'

My head was starting to ache and my mouth had that sour hungover tang. Something moved restlessly in the pit of my stomach, some creeping dread. I slid to the floor with my back to the wall.

'You don't remember the things you said? The things you did?'

'Wh-what?'

'We've been here before, haven't we? You have a few drinks and you're fine and then—'

'Then what? Then what, Marco?'

Down the hall a door opened to one of the flats, and a head poked out. I ignored it. Quieter now, I said, 'Then *what*, Marco?'

'It's like you have a trigger. You turn on me. I don't know, maybe it's me, maybe I'm the problem. I'm not sure it's a good idea for us to be around each other anymore.'

'No, Marco, no, don't say that.'

'I've got bruises on my shoulder. I can see the marks your teeth left on my arm.'

'But – I don't remem—'

'No, of course not. Of course you don't. You'd had a lot to drink and you blindsided me. It came out of nowhere: just a fury I've never seen. I'm still shaking, Stella.'

I felt the cold floor beneath my stockinged feet and the quick pulse of my heart. It was as though someone had wrapped a flex around my throat and was tightening, tightening.

'I don't remember,' I managed. I stared at the reflection in the gilded mirror opposite. My face was waxy beneath dirty hair. Make-up clotted about my eyes like tar. The contents of my bag had spilled across the floor; a beautiful silk scarf streaked with grime, loose change, a half-empty carton of cigarettes. I pulled these towards me and lit one with fingers not quite steady.

'The taxi driver didn't mention it.'

'Of course he didn't. He was probably as embarrassed as I was.'

'I will change, Marco. I will be better, I promise.'

'Yeah,' he sighed. 'Yeah, so you keep telling me.'

'Excuse me.' A voice came from down the hallway. I looked up, red-eyed. There was a woman there – I'd seen her before, her and her little yappy dogs, the types which tremble in your arms. She was wearing a dressing gown pinched at the throat with her fingers.

'Any chance you could move this conversation upstairs? It's five o'clock in the morning.'

'Hold on,' I said to Marco, and then I stood unsteadily and told her fine, told her I'm going.

She gave me a hard look. 'And you can't smoke in here. It's against the building regulations.'

Slowly I gave her the finger. 'I'm not in the mood,' I told her. 'Leave me alone.'

She smiled nastily, showing me yellowing teeth. 'Give over, love. You're not a teenager anymore. Papers always said you had a bad attitude and looks like they were right an' all.'

'What?'

'I know who you are. I remember that show. Used to like it too, once upon a time. But reading about all the stuff that happened left a bad taste in my mouth. You were a right little prima donna, weren't you?'

I stared at her, suddenly furious. In my ear I could hear Marco saying my name, asking me what was going on, but it was as distant as the moon.

'You don't know anything about me.'

'I know what I see. I know that you're a drunk. I've seen you staggering in through the front door five nights out of seven. I've lost count of the amount of times you've lost your keys. I know you live with another woman. What more do I need to know?'

Her dogs had started barking so I needed to raise my voice. I could just see them in the doorway behind her. She had a stairgate there, like you'd use for babies. All the little dogs were clustered about it, throwing themselves at the bars, yipping. I could smell her flat from where I stood, that musty canine stench.

She snorted. 'I see you, Katie Marigold. I see what you've become. The shine rubbed off you a long time ago.'

Another door opened down the hall, then someone asked what all the fudging racket is. That's the word they used, *fudging*. I started walking upstairs, suddenly leaden and drunk. I could barely get my key in the door and all the while I was thinking *I am losing my mind*.

That evening Marco turned up at the flat and held my cold hands between his own. He showed me a livid bruise on his shoulder, scratches on the flesh of his neck. There was a welt on his wrist where I could see the tiny imprints of teeth. I had apologised effusively, afraid. The fear that he was going to leave me made my skin crawl.

'I promise to change. I will do anything, Marco.'

Chapter 12

The next morning I wake dry-mouthed, full of a nervous leporine energy. I shower and dress, taking my pill at the bathroom sink, scooping a handful of metallic-tasting water into my mouth. Through the window the cliffs, sheer rock faces like advancing leviathans. Gulls pinwheel against a grey sky, heavy with unshed rain. I pull my jeans over my hips, brush my teeth and wait for the pill to start to work as though descending dark fathoms. The fuzzy edges, the thick, cottony way it fills my ears, I welcome these things. I want them to creep in before the doubts do, before the anxiety and the low hum of despair.

A walk, then. Fresh air. God, but the day seems long.

The road which leads from the cottage to town is pitted and narrow with a stripe of long grass growing up the centre. It is bordered on either side by fields, and in the distance, the sea. I raid the cupboard beneath the stairs and discover an oversized oilskin the colour of egg yolk which reaches my knees. Buoyed by a cup of strong coffee, I leave the house, idly wondering what Carmel is doing, where she is now. Then I remember and feel a sour, childish petulance rising. Marco was right about her. She is a leech.

◆ ◆ ◆

The town of Tyrlaze curls in the lap of the valley like an affectionate cat. A scattering of cottages in flint and stone, the thin steeple of a church. The little graveyard is neatly kept, the stones leaning at odd angles, cantered towards the sky. The sea glimmers like silvery scales just beyond and the air smells of salt, of wood fires and rain. A handwritten sign is propped outside a cottage – 'Fresh EGGs LaiDe This MORNing' and beneath that, in smaller print, 'Our ChiCkKens Rule The RoOst'. On the ground is a stack of empty cartons next to a tray of eggs lightly speckled with rain. A mud-splattered Land Rover is parked outside the house, surrounded by bickering hens. Bird droppings decorate the garden, the car and the windows like a Pollock painting. I am just leaving when I see an old woman in the doorway, watching me. She has appeared as silently as a fog, marking me with round glassy eyes. Her hands are caked with blood to the wrists. There are spatters of it on her apron, dried to a dusty maroon. I open my mouth to speak but already the pills are making my thoughts thick and treacly. Before I can say anything she has slowly closed the front door, all the while never taking her eyes from me.

Along the sea wall the bright shops in the inclement weather feel like a forced smile at a funeral. Most of the seafront shops are closing for the season and those that are still open are empty. Windbreakers crammed against dusty windows. A little rack of postcards washed out in the wintry sunshine. In the shop window are yellowing posters, long faded. A pantomime. A church fair. A town carnival. I look at the date on it. 14th July 2004. I think for a moment. Where was I in July 2004? What was I doing? And then, of course, with a jolt I remember. Thailand. Carmel and I had booked flights one evening after a session on cheap wine. We had been thrilled by our impulsiveness. It had been a freewheeling adventure: blistering heat and soft white sands, the drink, the weed, the mushrooms, the sex. In Bangkok, I had got my hummingbird tattoo. There is a photo of me somewhere – it used to be pinned to the corkboard in the flat – a cigarette clamped between my teeth, beer in one hand, gripping Carmel's fingers tightly with the other as the muscular, gleaming back of the tattooist bends over me. In the photo I am tanned and grinning and look younger and happier than I can ever remember being. Thinking of it now makes my stomach curdle. That laughing, reckless figure seems so distant. A lump of alien rock, drifting in space. Had it been me? It must have been, once.

That night the mist comes in from the sea, thick and heavy as a cloak. It gives the rising moon an eerie blue light that picks the bones of the landscape silver. I wake, becoming immediately cold, skin prickling. I sit up, covers pooled about my waist, straining to listen for the sound which has woken me. At first I think it is a hard rain but slowly I realise it is coming from inside the house. The sound is soft and sibilant, like heavy material being dragged across the floor. I creep to the doorway, peering into the darkened hall. Water. I can hear it more clearly now. My hand gropes for the light switch in the dark hallway.

The bathroom door is ajar. Inside, the taps and the shower are running, filling the room with steam and a thunderous roar. For a moment I simply stand there, skinny arms folded across my chest, cupping my elbows in my palms. I blink rapidly. I do not need to look in the mirror to see that a crease has appeared between my eyebrows; a vertical frown line like a stitch in my skin. It is the look of my father as he hunched over betting slips, lottery tickets, scratch cards. The look he got moments before the loss set in. He passed it on to me the same way he did his thin hair and dimples.

I turn the taps off and open the window to let the steam out. The tiled floor is glossy, the walls damp. The water has been running for some time. I try to remember if I'd left the taps on and I can't. It's like a switch has been thrown, a circuit which can't be completed. A mirrored cabinet hangs over the sink, and I swing it open and take out the bottle of pills. I hold the brown glass bottle up to the light and shake it. Inside, the little grey pills rattle like shaman bones, runes. I take two more from the bottle, grinding them between my teeth. The taste is chemical and astringent. I wipe the condensation away from the mirror and study myself. As I do so I catch a sudden movement behind me. Something moving towards the open door. I gasp and just for a moment fancy that I see the ivory oval of a face hanging in the mist, framed by curtains of dark hair. But when I turn there is nothing there. Just shapes in the fogged-up bathroom, grey and indistinct. Nothing except the lip of the bath and the laundry basket in the corner. Nothing except the black-and-white tiles and the towel rail with a solitary pink towel folded over it.

I'm losing my mind, I think. *I'm losing my fucking mind here.*

I make my way downstairs, hand clutching the banister so hard that my knuckles whiten. The kitchen is very dark, the wind a thin, fluting howl in the old soot-blackened chimney breast. A cold clutch of fear threatens to topple me. The sink. The taps are running down here too.

This time I turn them off so sharply that my wrist bristles with pain. My heart is a drum, my fear a rapid percussion, slowly building. I walk about the house distractedly, not really sure what I am looking for, what I expect to find. In each room I turn on the lights and run my hands over the window locks. After that I check the front and back doors. I peer beneath the bed and in the airing cupboard. I look in the old stone pantry full of cobwebs. I find nothing, of course, except the fossilised corpses of woodlice and balls of lint.

I make tea and sit in bed and the pills lift me, turning the night into something uncomplicated and dreamy. I fall asleep with the lights on, just as the sky is brightening, clouds turning the pearly colour of oyster shells. I fall asleep and there are no dreams. But even in my sleep I am listening, and I feel my fear growing like mushrooms in the dark. I need to heal. I need to feel as though I am scar tissue, being repaired from the inside.

There are just three names in the address book of my phone – Marco, Doctor Wilson and Alice. I wonder if Aunt Jackie is worried about me. Marco has contacted her, he tells me, to reassure her that I am getting better.

'I think she saw it coming, love,' he'd said to me solemnly. 'You've been unwell a long time.'

'I need her number,' I'd told him, and he'd said sure and he'd written it down on a piece of paper, folding it smaller and smaller and pressing it into my palm. 'Here you are.'

And of course I'd lost it. I must try to remember to ask him for it again. I must try to remember.

Marco calls me while I am washing dishes in the cold morning.

'Hello?' he says. 'Stella? How are you?'

'I'm all right. Tired. When will you get here?'

'Honey, you know what? I'm going to have to give it another couple of days. Chances are I may have to go to Zürich for a while. I need to work on the Tybourne account.'

'What?'

'It's my business, honey. It's not as easy as checking people into a hotel. I can't just abandon it.'

'There was more to my job than that.' I'm automatically defensive. 'And you can't just abandon me!'

'Is that what you think I've done?'

I don't know how to answer that so I ask instead, 'Have you heard from Carmel?'

'I think you need to face facts, Stella, she's not going to want to speak to you again. Not after what happened.'

My stomach sinks. I know this, of course, but I am hopeful. Optimistic. My mother had called me 'starry-eyed'. She would say it in a sour way, her lips twisted. The seagulls are shrieking and it's making my head hurt.

'Can you call Jackie for me? Give her my number?'

'Sure, I'll do it this afternoon. Can you email her?'

'No, I – I can't get into my emails. I'm not sure of my password. It's been changed. I must have done it; I just don't remember.'

I haven't been able to access anything since I arrived at Chy an Mor. I can remember a rainy afternoon as a teenager watching old films with my dad. *The 39 Steps*, *The Great Escape*, *Some Like It Hot*. He'd been slumped in his armchair, the one which always smelled of tobacco and hair wax, and his eyes were unfocused and far away. In one of them, something black-and-white and slow-moving, a war general in the trenches turns to his officer and says, '*All lines of communication are down. We are out here on our own now*', and over their heads the thunder of artillery.

'I love you, Stella, you know that, don't you?'

I tell him yes. I tell him fine. I tell him not to worry. He reminds me to keep taking the pills, to look after myself. 'Stay out of trouble,' he says as he hangs up. Next, I call Frankie, dialling from the note he left me on the fridge. He doesn't pick up. The message I leave is brief with only the slightest tremble in my voice. I tell him about the taps and ask him to come and have a look at them. At the root of my words are all the things I don't say: Please can you come over; please can you help; I am afraid.

All lines of communication are down. We are out here on our own now.

Chapter 13

I tell myself I have to pull it together. I'm meant to be getting married next year and I can't even remember the last time I showered. Two days ago? More? When my naked legs rub together I can feel the burrs of the hairs growing there like a dark pelt. My hair extensions are falling out in cobwebby strands. When I take off my top in front of the mirror I find clumps of wiry hair like spiders' legs beneath my arms. It is soft and springy to the touch. I've gone to seed, as my mother would say, as though talking about a rundown house, derelict, in need of demolition. I take two pills and head downstairs.

I try to imagine planning a wedding without Martha and Carmel. What was it Marco had told me? *You lost them.* What did that mean? Would they even come to the wedding if I invited them? The thought of their absence makes me cold. I wish I could remember what happened. I'm distracted and burn the porridge I'm cooking to the bottom of the pan. The kitchen fills with smoke and I open the back door to let the worst of it out. Outside the rain has passed and the sun is high in an enamel-blue sky. Thistles are growing along the old stone path, furred with moss and treacherous in the rain. The garden has been left to grow wild with bramble and nettles beneath the stunted palms which stand sentry by the house. I sit on the little stone seat speckled with lichen, my foggy mind turning over and over.

The first time I'd met Doctor Wilson, he had taken my outstretched hand and instead of shaking it had turned it over to look at my palm.

'Your lifeline is very strong,' he'd said, as his fingers had caressed the soft pillow of flesh at the base of my thumb, 'and this, this is called your Mount of Venus. It symbolises romance and sensuality. Are you very romantic, Stella?'

'I suppose.'

'Yes' – he'd nodded – 'yes, I see that you are.'

Later, he had given me a prayer scroll hidden inside a silver charm.

'It's a Tibetan Gau,' he had told me, 'it's Buddhist.' Except he pronounced it the American way, '*Boo*-dist'. Then he had leaned closer so that I could faintly smell aniseed on his breath: 'Alcohol is a demon, Stella.'

I'd looked around the room, unsure if he was joking. It had a lazy, tropical feel to it – almost colonial – with Indian tiles and soaring ceilings and overgrown, luscious plants. A large rug covered most of the polished wooden floor, depicting jungle vines intertwining with one another. The wall space between bookshelves was hung with fabrics in maroon and gold. I could hear the fans whirring overhead.

He'd leaned closer, lowering his voice. 'But like all demons, it can be exorcised.'

I'd thought him mad, of course. Told Marco I thought he ought to be struck off.

'I honestly can't believe he's legit. What is he, some sort of shaman?'

But he had given me the pills, a whole bottle of them, just for me, all for me. I put them straight into my bag. Mine. I tried to ignore what he had told me about my drinking; those words which had sounded so much like a concealed warning. 'You drink to forget, and soon all your memories will be lost.'

◆ ◆ ◆

In the garden the sun is growing hotter, the clouds of that morning burning away. As I walk slowly back inside the cottage I can hear a tapping noise, like skeletal fingers on glass. The old pipes rattle noisily beneath the sink. I freeze when I hear the knock at the front door. I've only had one visitor since I arrived at Chy an Mor a week or so ago. The courier, bringing me my forgotten luggage. I answer the door and find Frankie, holding his phone.

'I was just calling you.'

He is wearing an old T-shirt, the picture long faded, the words 'Moose Creek '89' barely legible. He is bigger than I remember, and broader in the stomach. Bulky, like a badly wrapped package.

He grins at me. 'Are you all right? You look pale.'

'I'm fine.'

'Beautiful day, isn't it?'

'Yes, it is. Why are you here?'

'You left me a message, remember? Something about the taps.'

Had I? I suppose I must have done. Otherwise how would he know?

'Yeah, sure,' I say. 'Come on in.'

Frankie doesn't though. He continues to stand on the porch. He tilts his head backwards, looking up at the vast expanse of sky, now deepening to a periwinkle blue.

'The air up here is amazing. It's so clean it's almost clinical. Did you know the Victorians would send their sick children to convalescent homes on the coast? They claimed the bracing sea air had health benefits.'

I wait, smiling patiently, one hand on the door.

'They were right as well. It does. Negative ions in the air or something. It improves your sleep, gives clarity to your brain, helps with depression—'

'Well, this bracing sea air is bloody freezing. Hurry up and come inside.'

Frankie accepts the offer of a cup of tea and stands at the windows admiring the view while I tell him how the taps have been running of their own accord. I mention the rattling pipes, the brownish, foul-smelling water I have found pooled in strange places; in the cupboard, beneath the coffee table, on the windowsill. I do not tell him about the strange chill in the bathroom or the way the shadows can sometimes look like they are creeping along the walls because I don't want him to think badly of me, that I am mad. He nods solemnly, occasionally interjecting with a question before falling silent, stroking his beard.

'Okay, just one thing. You contradicted yourself before. You said "the taps in the house had been switched on", then you said they were "running by themselves". So which is it? Have they been switched on or were they running by themselves?'

For a moment I simply stare at him, uncomprehending.

'What I mean is, and I'm not trying to scare you, but if what you're saying is that they are coming on by themselves, well, then we can call out a plumber and sort this. If what you're saying is that someone is switching them on and that person is not you, then we have a bigger problem.' He sips his tea, looking at me levelly. 'Do you think someone has been breaking into this house?'

I shake my head.

'Okay. Okay. Thing is, Stella, I'm not a plumber. I'm happy to look for you, but I think you'd be better off with a mate of mine who can fix this properly. Do you want me to give him your name, see what he says?'

'No, not my name. Give him Marco's name. Marco Nilsen.'

'Ah, the boyfriend,' Frankie says, and while that brilliant smile is still in place his voice has taken on a sing-song lilt.

'That's him.'

'You been together a long time, you and Marco?'

'Just over a year.'

'That sounds serious.'

'It is. We're engaged.'

'Congratulations.'

I look down at the ring on my finger. The Tudors believed that a vein ran from the fourth finger of the left hand directly to the heart. The thought of it makes me uneasy.

'He's a good man, and he works hard. I owe him a lot.'

'I don't doubt it,' Frankie says. 'Well, I'll tell you what I'll do. I'll take you into town for breakfast and then we can drop in to that friend of mine. I'm sure he'll know about the gremlins in your pipes. Deal?'

'I've already had my breakfast . . .' I say.

'So have another breakfast.'

'And town is so far away.'

'It's five minutes in the van.' He looks at me with mischief and good humour. 'Come on, for goodness' sake. It's only breakfast, not a witch burning. It'll do you good to get outside for a bit. Change of scenery and all that.'

'All right,' I surprise myself by saying, 'but just give me a second to get ready. I warn you, I am deranged through lack of sleep.'

'Well,' Frankie tells me over his shoulder, 'sounds like you need some bracing sea air.'

Upstairs I pull a brush through my hair and rub blusher into my cheeks with the tips of my fingers. It stands out in vivid circles against my pale skin like a sickness. I change my jumper for a T-shirt and cardigan and go to the bathroom. I feel surprisingly happy. I take the pills from the cupboard, tipping two into my hand. I put them on the windowsill while I brush my teeth.

Walking down the landing I notice for the first time the loft hatch at the end of the hallway. It is set into the ceiling, a little to the left of the door to the spare room. There is a bulky-looking silver padlock on it, looped through the catch. I stand beneath it with my head tilted back, wondering if there are rats up there. Squirrels perhaps. It would explain the scratching sounds I've been hearing, pattering like footsteps. It makes me think of a child running the length of the hallway in a nightgown, hands trailing along the thick cottage walls. I make up my mind to ask Frankie to go up there and see. When I spit my toothpaste into the sink there is a little blood, a pinkish hue. I pull down my lip and study my gums. They are pale, fleshy. There's a knock at the door and I turn, surprised.

'Are you coming, Stella?'

Frankie has a large white van, slightly dirty and smelling of dog and engine oil. The front seat is covered with a violently colourful blanket. ('It's from Mexico,' Frankie explains when he sees my doubtful face, 'and I suppose some would call it a bit garish.') The back is full of tools and coils of wire and ladders which rattle around as it jolts along the country road. I lean my head against the glass. Frankie asks if I am comfortable and points out the distant shape of the tin mine and the naked trees like stitches embroidered against the landscape.

'See that beacon over there?' he asks. 'There's a legend that a giant called Bolster could stand with a foot on that beacon and his other foot on Carn Brea six miles away. They said he ate sheep and cattle and sometimes children. He died, of course, in the legend. Died because of love. Bled out into a bottomless hole.'

'Yikes.'

'Yup, legends are gory as hell most of the time. The good ones, that is.'

He pulls up in the deserted seafront car park, opposite a café. The wind charges the waves to shore, sending spray and foam crashing over the rocks. There is a scatter of dog walkers on the sand, which is as dark and glossy as treacle. Lifeguard flags flutter in the high wind, black-and-white like a chessboard.

'What do the flags mean?'

'Surfing, but no swimming. There are nasty rip tides along this coast, could pull you out a good way. Know what to do if you get caught in a rip tide, Stella?'

I tell him no as I climb from the van.

'Swim at an angle towards the shore. Don't try to swim against it. If all else fails float on your back and go with it. We've had a lot of tourists get into trouble because you can't see the rip. It's under the surface, sneaking up on you. Know what I mean?'

I stare at him pulling on his hoodie in the wintry sunshine. I can't help feeling that he is teasing me. When he emerges he grins, his eyes glittering.

'You want to go in the water, you come to me first. I've got a wetsuit that'll fit you. The cold will kill you quicker than anything else.'

Sand, blown in from the beach, scratches underfoot as we cross the road.

'What's the deal with all your tattoos?' I ask. 'Do they have some sort of significance?'

'Uh,' Frankie says, his face hidden beneath his hood, 'I actually got them in prison. An inmate called Tito from Guadalajara did them for me as a mark of how much time I served.' He winks at me as he opens the café door. 'But don't worry. Those old people I killed were going to die soon anyway.'

I hang back, just for a second.

He grins. 'Stella, come on. I'm joking. As if I'd kill old people.' He leans closer, almost whispering. 'Just those two hitchhikers but that was it, I swear.'

We pass through the café doorway, and I smile weakly to show I can take a joke. Overhead the bell jangles. Frankie raises his hand to a man reading a paper who nods back. As we reach the counter side by side Frankie says, 'You know I'm kidding, right? You know that. I've never hurt anyone. Never killed anyone. I haven't even had a parking fine.'

'Frankie!' The woman behind the counter leans across and hugs him, making a noise like a slow puncture, a high-pitched *wheeeeee*.

I stare at her red hair, the colour of a freshly painted pillar box, twisted up in an elaborate roll. She has a ring through her nose and a smattering of freckles across her cheeks, one of which has a deep scar running across it. It puckers when she smiles. A crease in the skin like she has been hacked at.

She smiles at me. 'Hi!'

Frankie introduces us. 'Stella, Heidi, Heidi, Stella. Heidi runs the café here,' he tells me, taking a menu from the counter and handing it to me.

'It's my baby,' she says, smiling.

'How long have you had it?'

She looks at Frankie, frowning in concentration. 'A few years, maybe? It seems longer.'

'Every second I spend with you seems like an eternity, my dear,' Frankie says without looking up, but smiling just a little.

'Ha. Ha,' she deadpans, rolling her eyes at me as if to say *how do you put up with this?*

I can't take my eyes off her. She looks like a comic-book hero-ine, richly pigmented. I feel a sudden stab of envy. I will never look that exotic, that abundantly confident. Once, maybe, when I was younger and brighter. Not now. Heidi bends forward, the bright plume of her hair like an exclamation mark. Frankie is saying some-thing which makes her laugh and I feel a painful jealousy at their intimacy, a needle slowly inserted into skin.

We order breakfast and two coffees and take a table by the window looking out to sea.

'How's the not drinking going?' he asks.

'Harder than I thought.' I look into my lap. I've picked up a napkin and begun to twist it between my fingers. I force myself to stop. I don't want to look mad. *Don't look mad*, I tell myself, *pretend to be normal*. Sometimes I feel sick with the panic.

'It's the boredom, mostly. The days go on forever. Hours and hours and hours. The worst for me is the evening, right after din-ner. I really miss that glass of wine, you know? It helped me relax.' I laugh bitterly. 'Ha, listen to me – "It helps me relax" – what a cliché.'

Frankie shrugs and sips his coffee, wiping his moustache with his fingers. On the beach a toddler is running heedlessly along the sand in the ramshackle way of toddlers everywhere, feet tangled and spilling, head raised to the roof of the sky, laughing. We watch for a while, silently.

'Do you have support? Meetings? Alcoholics Anonymous or something? It's hard to do something like this by yourself. As far as I understand it – and I do understand it, Stella, my uncle died of cirrhosis and was still necking the bottle at the end – boredom is one of the biggest triggers for any relapse when it comes to addic-tion. You can't underestimate it. It sounds trashy, but you need to keep busy.'

I shake my head. I can't remember how we've got into this conversation, and I open my mouth to tell him to stop, to tell him I don't need his input, and then I have one of those weird memory jags which happen sometimes, a tiny implosion in the brain. I remember Carmel's new job, and the cake I'd made. Something so small and yet – yet there is something else, below the surface of that memory, something circling, circling, a shark beneath the water.

'I'm sorry, what did you say?'

Frankie puts down his cup, looking at me earnestly. 'I said, what about finding a therapist down here? Or if you don't feel as though you can face it you can go online. Pretty sure the Internet is hooked up at the house. You need something. Everyone needs something.'

'No. It's fine, really. I can do this.' I think of the ghostly shape I'd seen in the mirror. 'The doctor has given me some pills to take. He said the best thing is to recharge for a little while. Take it easy.'

Frankie blinks. 'The best thing for what? For alcoholism?'

'Yes.'

'He said the best thing for alcoholism is a holiday?'

I stare flatly at him, looking exactly like my mother when she was angry.

'Do I sound incredulous? That's because I am. I'm surprised you were just given some pills and told to take a break.'

'He said "recharge",' I correct him, but inside, deep inside and whispering like the wind in a cave, something stirs. I'd thought the same, of course. *Is that it?* I'd thought as Doctor Wilson had handed me the little brown bottle and given me his obdurate advice: no more booze, take a break. *Is that it?*

'You know what? I think the Victorians had it right. Fresh air, sunshine, the sea. Bracing walks and freezing water temperatures. That's what you need.'

'Wasn't the life expectancy of the Victorians something like thirty years old?'

'No one likes a smartass, Stella.'

I thank Frankie for breakfast and insist on getting the bill. We tussle good-naturedly over it for a few moments before he shrugs, palms tilted upwards.

'Sure, okay then. But I'll get you out for a walk on the beach one day soon, yes? It's the best time of year, when all the crowds have gone. Please have a think about what I said, about keeping busy.'

We are outside now, facing away from the wind. The sun is warm on the places where my skin is exposed: my hands, the back of my neck, my cheeks. I want to lift my face to it.

'Do you think it was me?'

'Do I think what was you?'

'The taps. It's just you've mentioned keeping busy twice now and I just – it sounds like you think I'm a fantasist.'

Frankie says nothing. He puts his hands in his pockets. 'Stella, taps don't just run by themselves. Not the way you described, at least. Not all of them at once, at varying flows. It's impossible. I mean, look, if you want we'll go and get that plumber I mentioned, I'm happy to do that and get Marco to pay for it, really. But I think you'll be embarrassed when he doesn't find anything wrong. I think it'll make you feel worse instead of better.'

'I know what I saw, what I heard.'

Frankie remains silent.

'Look, I don't know what else Marco has told you about me, but I can promise you I'm perfectly okay. You don't need to keep checking up on me, pep-talking me.'

'Now you do sound crazy. Marco hasn't said a word about you, other than in the kitchen on the day we met. I'm looking out for you because it must be hard up there. If you want me to stop, I'll be glad to.'

I can see he is telling the truth and immediately feel like shit. My thoughts are foggy, like a bad head cold. I can't think straight. Instead, I hold out my hand and he shakes it.

'Sorry, Frankie. I didn't mean to judge you. But really, I'm fine, everything is fine.'

Chapter 14

I see it as soon as I open the garden gate. Something has been left on the doorstep. As I approach I feel suspicion; my nerves are trembling wires crawling the length of my spine. Looking about me, there is just the long grass, the house and sprawling, wind-sculpted trees. The object is small and plain and as I get closer I see it is just an egg box. Just that, sitting there. I lift it and flip the lid. Eggs, of course. Eggs of differing pastel hues; one the purple-grey of a faded bruise, another a tawny brown, lightly freckled. A tiny feather still clings to it so I peel it carefully away and the wind lifts it from my fingers. Beneath the box and anchored by its weight, there is a note. I unfold it with slightly trembling hands. I have noticed I am shaking a lot these days. Delirium tremens, I suppose. Isn't sobriety interesting, isn't it fun?

'Pay AttenTIon' is printed in blocky black writing. Just those words, with no signature. I do not recognise the writing. I go inside feeling shaken and a little intruded upon.

I prop the door open and hang up my coat. Inside, that strange smell again, a briny, waspish odour. I stand still in the dim hallway for a moment, just breathing, just taking it in. My head feels cloudy and opaque as I walk into the kitchen.

All the cupboards and drawers have been opened, the contents emptied and lined up on the floor in neat rows. The inventory takes up most of the stone floor. I put my hand out to steady myself, looking around me with mounting dismay.

Everything has been lined up in order of size – espresso cups at the front, eggcups then teacups and glasses until the chunky Cornishware mugs at the back. Then there are the dinner plates, tea plates and saucers, saucepans, frying pans, woks and steamers, cleaning products and tea towels carefully folded, and a long line of tinned goods. There is an almost perfect circle of candles to my left, some used and little more than thick stumps of tallow, others still wrapped. It reminds me of an installation I'd attended as an art student, hungry and always broke. The exhibition had been called 'Galenskap' and featured everyday objects neatly displayed in intricate patterns across the gallery floor. *Galenskap*: a Swedish word meaning 'madness'.

I stare for almost a full minute, my skin tight with goose-flesh. A movement catches my eye and I jerk, gasping. It is a moth, trapped against the windowpane. It is bracken-coloured and as big as a cotton reel.

I have been forgetting so much. So much.

I find myself kneeling in front of the cupboards, piling every-thing back inside. I am trying to remember this morning, the moments before I left the house. I had gone upstairs to the bath-room, hadn't I? While Frankie had waited. Had Frankie done this? Had I done this? Is that even possible, to do this and not know it? Perhaps whoever had brought the eggs around – the eggs and that eerie little note underneath, the one which sounded so much like a threat – had let themselves inside to do this, to scare me. But then why leave the eggs on the doorstep if they had keys? Round and round it goes, none of it making sense. I sit back on my haunches, my hands pressed together at my mouth as though I am praying. I think back to the moment in the bathroom, the moment I had taken the bottle of pills from the cupboard. I had poured two into my hand and put them on the windowsill. Had I taken them? I don't remember. I dust my hands off on my thighs and head upstairs to the bathroom. The sun is bright and golden and the clarity of the sea air coming in through the bathroom window is wonderful and the pills are not where I'd left them.

Where you *thought* you left them, I tell myself. They are not on the windowsill. I check the floor and lift the towel hanging there but they have disappeared. *You must have taken them*, I think. But I don't know. I don't *know*. I open up the cabinet and reach for the bottle. The bottle is not there. Now my heart starts to race, *tick, tick, tick*. Where is it? I rake the contents out of the small cupboard into the sink; packets of aspirin and waxy lip balm and throat lozenges grown sticky and furred with mould. I search the room, look behind the bath and in the little cupboard next to the radiator. I look in the cabinet, in the pockets of the dressing gown hanging on the back of the door and behind the toilet where I find another of those puddles of dirty stagnant water. But I cannot find the little brown bottle with no label. With growing unease, I search the bedroom, stripping the bed, pulling the covers from the pillows. I look under the rug and in the wardrobe and behind the curtains. I even go downstairs and look in the fridge. I cannot find it, and now I begin to really panic, almost relieved I have something concrete to hang my anxiety on. I pace the small rooms and back to the bathroom, checking and double-checking in frustration. I think I have found it when I lift my handbag and hear a rattle but it is just my keys loose at the bottom. I sit down at the kitchen table and rest my head on the surface, ignoring the growing sense of dislocation as adrenalin is dumped into my system. I think again of how much simpler my life was just over a year ago, living with Carmel, having fun. And again, that brain zap, my head turning inwards to that day in our flat – the day of Carmel's new job – and the outside world dims around me like the flame of a gas lamp lowering.

Chapter 15

Carmel had been standing at Blackfriars waiting for her train when she found out. A dull, drizzly English lunchtime. It was me she called first.

'I got the job.'

'You're kidding.'

'I'll take your congratulations as implied. Soon I will be known as Mademoiselle Silky Bollocks and you will have to call me Your Highness.'

I laughed. 'Amazing. I always knew you'd do it. When do you start?'

'A month. They're flying me to Paris again to sign the contracts. God. God, this is really happening!'

'It is.'

'God bless them. God bless France. *Liberté, égalité, fraternité* and all that.'

'Yes. *Très bien.*'

'Uh – *je ne comprends pas.*'

'*Mais-oui.*'

'This needs work. Are you home? I'm heading back now.'

'*Oui.* Let's go out and celebrate.'

'Not the pub. Something proper. Dinner?'

I had looked over at the doorway where Marco was standing, his arms folded across his bare chest. Dark hairs coiled like wire wool on his skin. He had called me that morning, persuaded me to let him come over, told me he had cancelled all his meetings. He told me he was desperate to see me, compared it to a thirst. A need. 'I need you,' he had said, and laughing I had replied, 'All right, okay then. Yes.' We had barely been apart in the last two months. That's how it happens for some people, he'd told me, and I'd said how what happens and he'd said, 'Love.' He'd twined his fingers on mine, bearing down with a pressure just short of pain. It had turned the beds of my nails white. 'Love,' he had continued, pressing himself against me. 'I love you.'

'We're all going out for dinner tonight when she gets back, and I'm baking a cake,' I enthused when Carmel had hung up. 'I'm baking a cake in the shape of a bra.'

'You can't cook, Stella,' he said, leaning against the fridge and tucking his hands beneath his naked armpits, 'and can't you put the heating on? It's freezing.'

The poky second-floor flat was permanently cold, and in the winter a knife-sharp draught blew in through the gaps in the windows. I ignored him, pulling open the kitchen cupboards. We rarely had much food in, and today was no exception. I picked up a bag of caster sugar which had formed into a hard, solid rock.

'It's a brilliant job and good money. She's done well.'

'Yes, but it's not your brilliant job, is it? What are you so pleased for?'

'Because she has worked hard for this. I'm allowed to be pleased for her.'

'We all work hard, Stella. I started off working seventeen-hour days. After my dad died I took on his business at nineteen years old. No one baked me a cake.'

He wrapped his arms around me, pulling me close. His hands dug into the soft flesh of my middle.

'Aw, poor guy.' I pouted. 'Would you like me to bake you a cake too? Would man baby like a cakey?'

'What I'd like,' he'd said, turning me easily in his arms so we were face-to-face, 'is for you to get out of this rut you're in.' He ran his hands down my back, drawing me closer, a frown tightening his features. 'You're too thin.'

'I'm fine.'

'You're not. Look at this.' He lifted my T-shirt gently, pointing at the flare of my ribs. 'There's nothing on you.'

'I've always been skinny.'

'No, you haven't.'

I looked at him, confused, and he smiled.

'Katie Marigold's nickname was "*Pudge*", wasn't it?'

'Oh. Yeah, I suppose it was.'

That's what Daddy Marigold had called her, at least. I'd been a plump little kid, 'delightfully chubby', as so many articles had referred to me. It was an asset, a part of my appeal. As I edged closer towards my teens some of that fat dropped away, shed by my nerves and hormones, pushing food around my plate with the back of my fork. Mum had wanted me to go on a high-calorie diet, terrified I would lose my trademark dimples. I stubbornly resisted. By that time Katie Marigold was an albatross around my neck.

'Maybe I should make a cake just for you.' Marco laughed, slapping me playfully on the behind as I turned away. 'Get some flesh back on your bones.'

'I don't want a cake, Marco. I just want to make this one. Now go on, piss off. I need to make a list. I need to get ingredients. Most of all I need to concentrate.'

'Why are we celebrating London's biggest slut whoring knickers again?'

'Marco, please.'

'Okay, okay. Don't know why you don't just buy one. All that time and effort, you know you'll only end up binning it.'

'I can do this.'

'Fine, I'll get out of your way. I'll pick you up at seven. Don't burn the bloody thing.'

But Marco hadn't arrived at seven. I had been waiting, pacing the hallway in heels which clattered noisily. I was sore that he'd stood me up. When it was nearly eight o'clock, I called Carmel.

'Where are you?' Carmel demanded. 'We're all waiting.'

'Bloody Marco hasn't turned up.'

'What do you mean? He's here. He's been here nearly an hour.'

I blinked.

'Do you want me to put him on the phone?'

'No, I – no, I think I must have got confused. I'll come now.'

I had left the building, carrying the cake in a box, my stomach already knotted. I hadn't always been absent-minded, and it worried me in a way I couldn't articulate, like being lost in a forest full of mist and lights and false turns.

By the time I reached the restaurant, my head had started to ache. It was a very specific pain, pin-sharp, and it deadened my thoughts. Marco stood and helped me take my jacket off, took the cake from my hands.

'Where were you?'

'Here,' he responded. 'Like I said I would be.'

'But you didn't. You didn't say that.'

'Stella, I did.'

'But you didn't. Why do you think I was waiting at the flat for you?'

I became aware that people were looking over at us and forced myself to smile, to lower my voice.

'But why would I say that? Look. The restaurant is here.' He picked up a pepper grinder and placed it on the table. Then he picked up his fork and showed it to me. 'This fork is my flat, see? That goes here, near the restaurant. Now, watch this. See this drink? I'm going to put that all the way over here because that is your flat. Now. Why would I come so far out of my way?'

'Because you bloody said so, that's why.'

'Oh, you lovebirds,' Carmel chimed. 'Please. Stella, you're here now and I'm thrilled. Well done me on being so excellent and getting a job.'

'Sorry, Carmel. Well done.'

'Have you seen what Marco brought along?' Carmel asked, smiling just a little. She pointed to a box in the centre of the table. A big box. A cake box. I stared at it. The pain in my head was humming brightly.

'It's very thoughtful. I'm surprised. I always think of you as being such a wanker, Marco.'

Marco raised his glass to her wryly. *It can't be*, I stupidly told myself as I stood to look inside the box. *It can't be. She must be wrong.*

But she wasn't. It was a cake. A huge sponge cake fashioned to look like a pair of breasts in a bra. The blue icing had been piped on in delicate filigree patterns to form the lace of the cups in a pale blue. There was even a diamante clasp in the centre. It had been professionally made, with a scattering of icing flowers about the edges and 'Congratulations' spelt out in cursive icing at the top. It was enormous, and it was beautiful. Tears stung my eyes as I gasped and sat down a little too quickly. Marco grabbed my forearm, face creased with concern.

'Sweetheart, are you all right?'

'I can't believe you did that.'

'Did what? Are you okay? Do you want some water? You look awful.'

'I can't beli— You knew I was making a cake for her.'

Just for a second he looked at me blankly and I thought, *Okay, there will be a punchline. There will be an explanation, and we'll laugh and fall into each other*, but his face remained still, frighteningly still.

'Stella? All right?'

'No, I'm not, I'm not bloody all right. You knew what I was planning. What do you think is in the box next to you, for God's sake?'

He lowered his voice. 'Listen to yourself. I thought we'd agreed this. We all know you can't cook. Isn't it better this way?'

I blinked at him.

'Honey, don't you remember? We talked about it earlier, about how you burn everything you bake, how you can't be trusted in the kitchen.'

He laughed, looking around the table, appealing to the others sitting there.

'Come on, you can't be mad about this. Don't you remember? When I said we should just buy one?'

My mouth was opening and closing. He laughed again mildly.

'I just wanted to do something nice for Carmel,' he continued, 'and I thought you agreed with me.'

'Why? You've never liked her.'

Someone whistled, long and low. The sound of a bomb falling. I didn't look up.

Marco's face darkened, and he said quietly, 'Stella, lower your voice. People are staring.'

I closed my eyes, opened them, Marco was looking at me. There was nothing on his face, no expression. He was a blank page.

'Stella?' Carmel was saying as I stood, picking up my unopened cake box, my eyes full of tears. As I walked away towards the toilets I heard Marco saying that he was sorry, that he didn't know what my problem was. The pain in my head was glittering.

Inside the toilets I tried to catch my breath, to slow the tears which I knew were coming. Sadly, I lifted the lid of the cake box and stared at my own effort, lumpy as hand-thrown clay. I had written 'Silky Bollocks' across it in wobbly red icing and covered the bits where it had stuck to the cake tin with thick layers of too-hard icing. It was too dark, too dry, too shit. I stuffed it into the bin in the toilet, slamming the lid against it, and cried and cried.

Chapter 16

Alice answers when I call Marco's office. I can hear her nails clattering against the keyboard and imagine her with the phone tucked beneath her beautifully straight jawline, pastel-pink lips moving ever so slightly. Alice would never do anything as vulgar as speak loudly.

'Did you get your luggage, Stella?'

'I did, yes. Thanks.'

'You'd left it right by the door. I'm surprised you didn't trip over it on your way out.'

'Can you – please can you get Marco? Tell him it's important.'

'He's in a meeting. I can't interrupt him at the moment.'

'Please, Alice . . . I – I—' I'm horrified to discover there is a lump in my throat and I remind myself to breathe, breathe. 'I think someone has been breaking into the house.'

'Are you safe? Have you called the police?'

'No. Not yet, I mean.'

'Has anything been taken?'

'Maybe. I think so. I don't know. Things have been moved around. Please, Alice, can't you get him for me?'

'He isn't here, Stella, and this meeting is taking up most of his morning. He's not due back till later today.'

'Okay, okay.'

'What kind of things have been moved around?'

'Cups. Bowls. All the cutlery in the drawers. And someone has left a box of eggs on the doorstep this morning with a threatening note.'

'What does the note say?'

'Uh, it said "Pay Attention".'

Alice is quiet for a moment although I can still hear her typing. Finally she says, 'Are you in danger?'

'I don't know. I can't find my pills. I can't think straight. I'm sorry.' My voice cracks, and I start to cry. I apologise again, breathlessly.

'It's all right,' she tells me as I sob quietly to myself for a second or two, shoulders shaking, my hand over my mouth immediately wet with tears.

'I'm better now, sorry,' I say again after a moment has passed. 'That took me by surprise.'

'No problem.'

'It's just – I got scared, didn't I? When I came home. The mess that was everywhere and now I can't find my pills although I'm sure' – I release a shuddering breath, my cheeks are damp – 'I'm sure I had them before I left the house.'

'Where did you go?'

'For breakfast wi— Just for breakfast.'

I don't want to tell her about my breakfast with Frankie, and I don't know why. Partly, I suppose, because she would almost certainly tell Marco but mainly because he is my secret. My friend. He feels like the only one at the moment.

'Where are you now?'

'At the cottage, at Chy an Mor. In the garden.'

'Is it sunny?'

'Uh – yes. Not a cloud in the sky.'

'Can you see the sea?'

'Yes, I can.'

In the background, in the busy office in which Alice is currently sitting, I hear a phone ringing. In her normal, adult life three hundred miles away. I sigh. I'm done crying. The force of my tears frightened me, but now it is weak and watery. I give one last shuddering breath.

'Go on,' she says.

'Whenever I see paintings of the sea it's always a blue-green. I don't know why they do that because the only time I've seen the sea it's been grey, like silver. Mercury-grey.'

'Are there any gulls?'

'Not today. But I hear them sometimes.'

'How's the garden looking? Need work?'

'Lots. The old caretaker has been in hospital, and it doesn't look like it's been touched since the spring. Nettles everywhere.'

I know what she is doing. She is distracting me, calming me down. I am at once grateful and infuriated by it, by the implication that I am a child. Poor old Stella, can't deal with reality. Poor old Stella can't handle her life. I inhale deeply, wipe my eyes with the back of my hand and squeeze the snot from my nose. I feel better. I thank her. She tells me not to worry, that she is used to it. It won't be until later that I will think what a peculiar thing that was to say.

Without my pills I can't sleep. I lie awake and listen to the sounds of the house, the groans and scratches. The way the floorboards creak. My shallow dreams are full of noise, and I wake up to get away from them. I think there is someone in the house with me. At one point, I imagine I see a shadow pass the doorway, as though running. The rustle of fabric, a watery sigh. But there are no footsteps, and no doors open and close. I think I hear the taps switching on only once, as I lie with my ear pressed to the pillow, but I can't be sure and by that time a peach dawn is breaking, and I am drowsy again.

◆ ◆ ◆

The noise is soft and unremarkable, the clink of the letterbox. It wakes me with a jolt, and I push myself up onto my elbows, staring wildly around. The light filtering is a dirty grey smudge, and I can hear the restless patter of rain. When I open the curtains I notice that the ocean and cliffs have been spirited away by nature's great conjuror, a thick sea mist. Below me the waves are booming in the lightless caves. A movement in the garden catches my eye, and I press myself against the cold glass, but there is nothing but creeping fog. The house is cold as old stones. Downstairs I find a white oblong on the mat, an envelope. There is no writing on it, and inside, nothing but a photograph. It slides out into my outstretched palm, face up.

The woman in the picture is me, and it gives me a jolt. It's me and then, when I look closer, I see it is not, not quite. She is looking directly up at the camera – neither smiling nor frowning – she looks uncertain, suspicious. Blonde hair swept back from her face, and all that can be seen of her shoulders is covered in a red-and-white scarf knotted at the throat. Her skin is pale and slightly sickly-looking, the colour of milk which has turned over in the night. The horrifying thing is the bruising. Plum and violet and a sickening nicotine yellow across the bridge of her nose. Her eyes are set in swollen cushions of skin, a rich deep blue. It looks like she's been hit by a truck. It shocks me. My hands start to tremble.

I turn the photograph over. There is writing on the back in blue ink.

'Pay AttenTIon', it tells me, and that is all.

I stand in the cold kitchen, turning the photograph back to front and back again. The edges have softened and curled with age. I stand as the kettle boils and cools, as the mist presses close to the cottage like an overcoat. In the background the news plays out on the television screen just visible through the living room doorway. A fire in a department store. A stabbing in Manchester. A new policy to cut funding to nurseries. This piece contains some graphic footage. I walk to the drawer and pull out the piece of paper which had been beneath the box of eggs. I smooth it flat with the side of my hand. 'Pay AttenTIon', it read, and the handwriting on both was the same. 'Pay AttenTIon'.

I do not know the poor, injured woman in the photo, nor do I recognise the writing. I make toast with marmalade and find an old radio under the sink and tune it in. Some music. I put the photograph together with the note on the table, weighed down with my mother's jar with the coins inside. Her earthly remains. I must have picked it up when I left London, although I don't remember. It had been in my suitcase, lying on top of the clothes I'd packed. Anxious, I call Frankie. The reception is bad and I can hear the wind blowing across the line. It is a lonely sound and I'm glad when he picks up. Frankie sounds pleased to hear from me and when I tell him about the notes he tells me he'd be happy to stop by.

'Weirdest thing,' he says. 'But I'll have a look, and of course if I can help you I will.'

I call Marco again and leave him a voice message. 'Marco, I'm scared. Please call me, please come back. I need you.'

I hang up and pace the floor. I need something, something to get me through the withdrawal of these pills. I wish I had some Valium or a sleeping pill. Anything. Hell, I think brightly, I'd snort some ketamine if I knew where to get some. Anything to stop this. I think about calling Doctor Wilson, but then a memory floods back to me, sharp as lemon juice.

◆ ◆ ◆

It was my second appointment with Doctor Wilson. I was calmer that day, less agitated. Perhaps it's because Marco was with me. Perhaps it was because I would be getting more pills.

'Guess how much it's worth,' Marco said, as we'd pulled up outside the vast Edwardian building. 'Go on, guess.'

'I don't—'

'Five million. A five-million-pound house. You could fit ten of your flats in there, easy.'

This time a young woman opened the door; a pale housemaid with a strong Eastern European accent and white-blonde hair. She led us through the hallway to Doctor Wilson's study.

'Mr Wilson, it is your guests.'

The housemaid turned, smiling, revealing lines of tiny, regular teeth like a cat. 'He says to go on inside.'

Doctor Wilson had risen from his desk smiling, eyes impossibly blue and glassy, like polished jewels.

He nodded to Marco and asked us both to sit.

'Excuse the mess' – he indicated the paperwork on his desk – 'I'm only just back from holiday.'

'Anywhere nice?'

'Yes, weekend in St Tropez. Anita was pining. All too brief, unfortunately. Tea or coffee?'

'Coffee. Stella?'

I nodded. Doctor Wilson held his hand up, three fingers raised, to the maid who was hovering by the door.

'Lovely girl,' he confided as she closed the door behind her, 'you wouldn't know she came from a war-torn country. She laughs a lot.' He folded his hands on the desk. 'Let's get on with it.'

'Thank you for seeing us again at such short notice,' I heard Marco say, 'I know how busy you are.'

Doctor Wilson was nodding, his fingers steepled beneath his chin, eyes on me. He'd picked up a small statue no bigger than a fist from his desk and turned it towards me.

'Do you know who this is?'

I shook my head.

'It's Shiva. The destroyer. His purpose is to destroy in order to rebuild. What do you think you have in you – inside you, Stella – which needs to be destroyed?'

He looked from me to Marco and back again.

'Hindus believe that death is not an end, only a beginning. It makes way for a rebirth. So let's talk about how we can create your death, Stella, how we can do this.'

I must have looked startled because he laughed and said, 'Metaphorically speaking, of course.'

The maid came into the room, padding softly, carrying a tray. She poured the coffee at the end of the long mahogany desk, sneaking looks at the three of us occasionally from beneath lashes so fair they were almost white. Doctor Wilson was addressing Marco.

'You, sir, I'm afraid, will have to leave. You can take your coffee into the conservatory. Estelle will show you where it is.'

I turned my head and watched him go, realising I was holding on to the arms of the chair so tightly my knuckles were white. Nothing frightens me more than scrutiny.

'So, Stella, let's talk. Open up. Tell me about yourself.'

'I don't want to talk about me.'

'Well, we need to start somewhere. How about you tell me what you do for a living? Do you enjoy your job?'

'Oh, oh no. It's not what I planned to do.'

'What did you plan to do?'

I hesitated, looking down at my lap. 'I studied art history. Hoped one day to curate a gallery, maybe in New York.'

'No more acting?'

'God, no.'

'I remember the show. "*Let's take a walk to Honeypot Lane, let's meet the fam-a-lee*".' He stopped singing and looked at me, eyebrows raised.

I laughed nervously. 'Well, that was a long t—'

'You in your little dress and that dog. You remember there was one episode, when – uh – when the dog had to wear the little bonnet you made it, for the parade?'

'Yes.'

'And you told him off, right? You said "Make sure you walk behind me" and what do you know? He did! Right up on two legs. Man, that was one clever dog.'

'Nine. There were nine of them. They kept dying.'

'I'm sorry to hear that.'

'People used to think we were cursed. The show, I mean. We went through so many golden Labradors I'm surprised the RSPCA didn't press charges. One of them was poisoned.'

I looked down at my hands. That wasn't quite right, was it? I'm thinking. One dog or two? Or more? I could remember seeing a bulky shape hidden beneath a tarp in the corridor, and my mother ushering me past. '*Don't look, Stella, love*,' she was saying. '*Keep walking.*'

'You know my favourite? That brother of yours, the oldest one.'

'Eddie.'

'Eddie! That's him. Eddie Marigold.'

'All the Marigold children had "e" sounds at the end of their names: Bonnie, Lucy, Katie, Eddie, Mikey – even the dog, Frisky. It was lame.'

I'd spiked his gentle good humour a little. He lifted the statue of Shiva again, studying it.

'What kind of person would you say you are, Stella? Happy? Calm? Morose?'

'God, I'm – I don't know – neurotic? A little bit prone to fantasy.'

'I deal with a lot of addicts, Stella. Drugs, booze, porn, gambling.'

I wasn't sure if it was my imagination that heard the stress he put on the last word. But he couldn't know about my dad, could he? The betting slips and scratch cards and the clamorous beating of hooves. I blinked rapidly.

'One thing they all have in common is a refusal to see themselves as they are – as they truly are. And when that happens it makes my job more difficult, do you see? I wonder what will help you to understand the depth of your problems.'

'Problems?'

'Well, yes. You've been drinking too much, taking risks. I heard about the violence, the paranoia you've been displaying. It's much more pleasant for you not to look at yourself though, I understand that. Do you know what arrested development is?'

'Something to do with drug addiction, isn't it?'

'It's theorised but yes, it's thought so. The impact of trauma can have the same effect too. A stunting of the emotional growth and psychological development at the age when the addiction or the event occurs. Now, your childhood was far from normal, and the death of your mother at such a sensitive age – well – that is bound to have had an effect on you.'

'This is ridiculous. I'm not drinking because my mother is dead. I'm sick. I've been ill. I can't sleep. I'm only here to get the pills, that's all I want, it's the only thing that works.'

My teeth were grinding in my head. The ceiling fan paddled lazily overhead. Incense was burning on the desk, a language of smoke and perfume.

'The last time I saw you, Stella, your hands were shaking so much you could barely sign the consent forms. I thought I was going to have to sedate you.'

'My father died. I'm in shock.'

Doctor Wilson crossed his legs so that his right foot rested on his thigh. He was rangy, long-limbed. It made him look like a diligent spider in a web.

'Your father died nearly two months ago. I appreciate that grief is subjective but—'

'But what?'

'Do you think you're managing?'

'I feel like this is all irrelevant. These are leading questions.'

'Think of it like a trail left through the woods. You've heard of Hansel and Gretel, yes? A little trail of breadcrumbs to help them find their way home?'

I stared at him without speaking. I was thinking about Hansel and Gretel, nearly eaten by a witch who had pretended to be good and kind and sweet but, of course, she had not been. We knew that, the reader. We knew she was a cannibal.

Later that day I discover pools of water beneath the table, strange and sour-smelling, like an animal has crept inside. I receive a silent phone call a little after noon, and another just before two. In them I can hear the wind whistling on the line, and a panting, hurried breathing. Like panic. I fall asleep on the sofa with my book tented on my chest, one hand curled beneath my head.

And I do not know if I am dreaming. In the past when I have been sleepwalking I have woken in strange and unfamiliar places, shivering with cold. Now though, now, my eyes are open, and I can see my hand at the end of my arm. I can feel the chill in the air, the way the cold tiles feel beneath my feet. I am in the bathroom, and the light is grainy as though it is late afternoon. I am holding the bottle of pills. *There they are*, I think, *thank God*. I watch as my hand unscrews the cap from the brown glass bottle; I can even see the silver bracelet I am wearing, the one Carmel bought me for my birthday. I watch as my hand tips the bottle, and even as I realise what is about to happen I can't stop myself. It is as if I am standing separated from my body by a wall of thick, soundproof glass. No, I cry out, no, no, no. But there is no sound and my hand is still moving as the pills begin to tumble out of the bottle and into the toilet. I can see every detail; the cracks in the old porcelain, the shallow bowl of water rippling as the first pills break the surface and here I am tipping them all away, the sleeping, somnambulant me while the other me is shrieking, 'Don't, don't', and there are tears, real tears, salty and hot, I can feel them. 'I need those, I need those to get better,' I say, but they have all gone, the bottle upended in my hand. I stare down into the toilet at the pills already turning to a grey sludge. Then I begin to shuffle off, I can see my feet moving over the cold tiles, my chipped nail varnish, the hem of my T-shirt just loose of my jeans' waistband. When I look up it is into the mirror of the bathroom cabinet. I am smiling and it is horrible, skin stretching like sentient wax. And behind me, behind me in the bathroom, is the other me again, face bruised and swollen. I can see a thin trickle of blood coming from her smashed nose, black eyes like raisins pushed into dough, thick and swollen. She is smiling too, and she is wearing that dress, my dress, my dress and I wake up and I remember.

'Holy shit,' I say out loud to the empty room. 'What was that?'

In my dream the dress had been the blue-green of the sea, with iridescent scales on the skirt, which was full and frothy with petticoats. It was a dress for a mermaid, and the reason I know that is because I had worn it once as Katie Marigold in a show entitled 'Katie Marigold All At Sea'.

I take the stairs two at a time and dash to the bathroom even though I know what I will find. That chalky residue in the toilet, the empty bottle on the floor. I have spirited away my only hope of sanity, and I don't know what will happen to me now.

Chapter 17

When my phone rings I almost don't answer. I do not recognise the number and so I don't speak when I pick it up. I am expecting silence, more of that rattling breath. So I get a shock when a voice says my name.

'Stella? Stella Wiseman?'

'Who is this?'

'You don't know?'

It's a strange accent and I can't place it; masculine with a soft edge, almost camp.

'No. No idea.'

'We knew each other a long time ago.'

'Oh yeah?'

'Shall I give you a clue?'

'Can't you ju—'

The voice changes. High-pitched, manic-sounding. It is eerie. '"I want chocolate milkshake! One for me and one for my dog!"'

My heart, my heart is beating so fast. I know who this is. I grab hold of the sink and wait for the stars in my vision to clear.

'Heh. You still there?'

'Yes. It's you, isn't it? Joey Fraser.'

'Correct. Ten bonus points if you can tell me which episode that line came from.'

I don't even need to think about it. Funny how the brain works. 'Episode six, series four. "Give Me Your Answer Do, Katie Marigold!". You're sitting at the counter of the milkshake bar with Frisky.'

'That's right. What a show it was. Whoever heard of a milkshake bar in a rural village in 1980s England? Whoever heard of a family with five kids who didn't bitch at each other all the livelong day? Plenty of that behind the scenes though, am I right?'

'Joey, how did you get my number?'

'Same way I got your address. By asking the right questions.'

I stiffen, turn slowly. I imagine him standing in the kitchen behind me, smiling, the phone pressed to his long face. But there is only the table and chairs and the bookcase and the back door. Even from here I can see it. The door is open, just a bit, moving slightly in the wind. The old-fashioned iron thumb latch is clinking against the jamb. While I was sleeping someone has opened the door to go out. Or come in.

The skin of my scalp tightens. A litter of leaves has blown into the kitchen, reds and browns and rich, vivid orange. The door rocks back and forth gently, the latch chattering. Wet footprints run from the door to the stairs.

'Stella?'

'I'm here.'

'We should really meet up. You know I was offered nearly twenty grand to get some of the old cast back together? Turns out we're still pretty big in Japan. That's a good sum of money.'

'Uh-huh.'

'But after you and me, who's left? I made some calls, and you know what I found out?'

'What?'

'Don't you keep track? Lizzie Noble died last week. Drove her car right into a tree.'

'God.' Lizzie Noble had played one of the little twins in the *Marigold!* series. I could picture her clearly, straight dark hair down to her waist. Like a little Gothic doll.

'Yup,' Joey was saying. 'Unpleasant. Very unpleasant. Still . . .'

'Still what?'

'You know. It puts us back in the papers for a bit. It was trending on Twitter on Monday afternoon. "Hashtag *Marigold!*"'

'You haven't changed.'

'I'm glad to hear it.'

'Where are you, Joey? Where are you right now?'

Silence. I almost think he has gone and then, 'I heard you're losing your mind. About time, I'd say. Surprised it didn't happen sooner. How's your mother?'

'Dead.'

'Oh yeah? Well, that's a real shame.'

'What is it you want?'

'You and me, one interview, some photos. A film crew maybe. They want to make a documentary but they can't do it without you, of course. The star of the show. We can do that, can't we? We can sit in the same room for an hour without—'

'I haven't forgotten what you did. I could still put you in prison. There's no statute of limitations in this country, you know.'

'Oh man, not this again. Not again. We were kids, Stella. Confused, crazy kids.'

'I haven't forgotten that time in the trailer, I—'

But I was talking to an empty line. Joey Fraser had hung up.

The back door is still ajar, moving slightly in the wind. As I walk around the sofa I see a line of straggling footprints, gleaming little pools of water. Something has come inside. I am so afraid. I am afraid of the way my heart is hammering in my chest, and I am afraid of the way my throat has dried, my nipples stiffening against my T-shirt. I can smell that scent again, like a dark high tide. It is a dank and rotting odour. It is the depths of the sea where the water fades from green to midnight blue, where the fish swim out of darkness in fast-moving shadows with stricken, bulbous eyes.

I look over at the back door again. It opens, just a little, and I see someone is standing there. Standing outside in the garden, dark eye pressed against the crack. I scream, drop my phone. It skitters along the tiles and under the table. My heart vaults into my throat, my ears.

The figure moves, running away from the house and into the mist which is creeping up the garden. I am propelled without thinking, opening the back door and striding outside. The ground is cold and wet beneath my bare feet and I can hear my own hoarse breath.

'Who are you?' I'm shouting, walking across the tall grass. 'Who are you? What are you doing here?'

There is no reply, but I can hear the rustle of the dress she is wearing. The mermaid dress. I've been dreaming about it. As I reach the end of the garden I stumble over the snarls of fallen wire fencing and barely notice the slice it takes from my ankle. My fingers become immediately bloody as I untangle myself breathlessly. I rise, brushing myself off, cursing under my breath. Although it is not visible through the fog I know that beyond the wire is the clifftop, the gorse and the heather and the bracken which drops away sharply to the Atlantic below. There is only a slight wind but the glittering mist is dampening my clothes and I shiver. I am about to turn around when I see, just ahead of me, movement through the fog. A shadow dimming and looming, arms preternaturally long against the grey. Someone is out there, moving away from me.

'Hey!' I call out. 'Hey!'

I start to run, and I am on the clifftop proper now. Adrenalin is making my nerves vibrate as the figure turns and just for a moment I think I see a face, dark eyes wide with alarm. Then there is only the sea mist again, thick as velvet, and I can't be sure if I saw anything at all. I push ahead with my arms outstretched.

'Hey!' I say again, and even though I know that soon the land will drop away beneath me I continue to run, fingers outstretched like the fronds of a sea anemone, blindly searching. The sea is louder now and I can taste salt. Beneath the damp furze and long grass, a pothole opens up in the rocky ground, spilling me to the floor. The light has taken on the ochre tinge of an old sun-bleached photograph. Blood rushes in my ears. I am disorientated as I lurch forward, scrambling against the alarming tilt of the ground, and I don't know which way is home. I turn and turn again, feeling the soft press of heather beneath my bare feet which are sore and bleeding. I call out, but this time I don't say 'Hey!' I say 'Help! Help me!' over and over, and now I'm struggling to find the narrow twisting path or find my way back to level ground, and the curve of the land is frighteningly steep and I am afraid. If I fall into the sea will it hurt? Will I know that I am falling or will the shock be taken away from me like the scream from my lips? How long until someone knows I am missing? I think of the coldness of the water, the silvery churning depths, and I shout 'Help me!' and a white hand sneaks out from the mist and touches me on the forearm. The feel of it is cold and chill as the grave, and I scream, sure the ground is dropping away beneath my feet but then I am being pulled upwards and up, staggering slightly, and I hear a voice saying, 'Okay, it's okay', and I am falling roughly onto the damp ground. A throbbing stitch opens up behind my ribs, and I clutch at it, gasping. Frankie is bent over, his hands planted on his thighs, his face bleached pale. He is panting.

'My God, Stella.'

'Did you see them, Frankie? What happened?'

'I didn't see anyone.' Frankie is massaging his chest. 'Wow. I'm having a heart attack, I swear. What were you trying to do? Run off the edge of the cliff?'

'There was someone else. Someone was in my house.' I sit up. 'What if they fell over the edge? What if they're drowning? Frankie, what do we do?'

The coastguard is silver-haired and sleepy-eyed. His face is deeply seamed with age, as wind-blasted as tough leather. He kneels in front of me, talking in a low voice. I have been wrapped in a silver thermal blanket, like a marathon runner or an astronaut. The coastguard is telling me off, gently. He tells me it is a bad day for walking out on the cliffs, that the fog conceals the lethal drops, that sometimes the poor visibility can make you believe you are seeing things which aren't there. He says this last bit pointedly and looks at Frankie as he does so. Frankie is standing behind me, his hand on my shoulder. I look at my knees. They are muddy, my jeans ripped. I remember the figure in the silvery gloom, how it had been shimmering as though under murky water. I think of the footprints, the pills in the toilet, that smell of dank and dripping caves. I am so tired, and I am becoming so afraid of my mind.

Frankie tells the coastguard that he had heard me calling out to someone in the garden and gone around the side of the house where he'd seen me slipping away into the mist. That's the phrase he uses – 'slipping away' – and it makes me shudder, makes me think of things becoming untethered and adrift, makes me think of dying in the still of the night. He had followed the sound of my voice and when he had finally caught up with me, it had been just three feet from where the cliff dropped away to the jagged spines of the rocks and cold grey water below. No, he tells the coastguard, he hadn't seen anyone else, certainly no one of the description I had given. But that's not to say – he adds with discreet loyalty – that no such person exists.

'We haven't recovered a body,' the coastguard tells us, rising to his feet, 'which isn't to say we'll stop looking. We can have another boat out there before it gets dark and if the weather is clearer tomorrow we'll set out with the helicopter too. If your friend did fall—'

'Not my friend,' I say. 'I don't know who it was. They were in my house. Watching me. Wearing my clothes. Old clothes, from the show.'

The coastguard gives Frankie another look, frowning.

'Well, that's a matter for the police, Stella. I advise you to be honest with them.'

I feel wrung out, invisible hands drawing me tightly together, closing me. Frankie squeezes my shoulder.

'Come on inside,' he says quietly.

Frankie asks me if I want to speak to the police and when I reply no, he shrugs. 'You don't think you should tell them? About the footprints and the notes?'

'No.'

'Do you want me to call Marco?'

'No.'

'What about your friends? Someone to come and sit with you?'

I give a hard laugh. 'Who exactly did you have in mind?'

He frowns, but his only response is to ask me if I want tea. This time I say yes.

As the kettle boils, he opens up the back door and goes outside. There is a lean-to which has been built onto the side of Chy an Mor, with a corrugated-iron roof and a door held together by flaking green paint. It is padlocked, but Frankie tells me he has the key. When he comes in, he is carrying split logs in his arms and begins loading them into the grate.

'I cut this wood a few weeks ago when Kennecker told me you were coming down. I can't believe it's stayed dry in there through all that rain, but there you are. I'll leave you the key so you can get in and out.'

'It's already so cold.'

'It's October.' He looks at me levelly, and I am careful to measure my expression of surprise. How did that happen? Wasn't it only summer last week? Me and Carmel sunning ourselves on our crappy little balcony? Where has the time gone? *You know where*, a sober voice intones somewhere in my skull. *You're losing your whole life, girl.*

'What were you doing up here, Frankie?'

'I told you, I saw you from the side of the house.'

'But why were you at the house?'

He sits back on his heels, looking flustered. 'To give you the key to the woodshed. Weather forecast for the rest of the week is dire, so I thought you'd want to get a fire going on cold nights. I forgot all about it till I found it on my keyring.'

I take the key from him and stare as he strikes a match, holding it close to the kindling.

'I don't suppose you found the key to the padlock, did you?'

'What padlock?'

'The one upstairs. For the hatch.'

The kettle is boiling and Frankie stands up, shaking his head. 'I've only got what Jim Kennecker gave me. His instructions were "Keep her warm, keep her safe".'

'"Safe"?'

150

'Uh-huh. He's old-fashioned. I'll get the tea.'

'Yeah, sure. Thank you, Frankie.'

'What for?'

'For catching me.'

'I thought you were going to die,' he says plainly, hands in his pockets. 'I don't mind admitting that I was absolutely terrified.'

I sit on the sofa with my knees tucked up beneath my chin. I wrap my arms around my shins and watch the fire. It is building, building in the grate, and the wood is beginning to char and blacken at the edges. Frankie goes into the kitchen, ducking his head beneath the low doorway. I miss the pills. They were keeping some of my thoughts at bay: the worst ones, the ones which hurt and scrape like blunt instruments.

'Did you really see someone?'

'I did.'

'She was wearing your clothes?'

'Yes – sort of. A costume I used to wear, a long time ago.'

There is a pause and I can hear Frankie moving about in the kitchen. The cupboard doors open and close. He appears in the doorway, hands in his pockets.

'Stella, you've barely any food. Your milk went off two days ago.'

'I'm sorry. I keep meaning to go to town.'

'I'm not . . . Look, I'm not trying to patronise you – but what have you been living on? Dust and air?'

I press my hands lightly to my stomach where I can feel the bony protrusion of my ribs. I have been eating – I see the evidence of it: dirty plates, empty packets, apple cores growing fuzzy in the bin – but it has no rhythm, and I can't remember when I last felt hungry.

'Tell you what,' he continues, 'I'll go and get you some stuff, shall I?'

'Can I come with you? I don't want to be on my own.'

'Of course. You've had a shock and a shitload of adrenalin. I'd probably feel the same.'

Frankie whistles as he goes back into the kitchen, and I momentarily entertain myself with the thought that I am going with him because I want the company. I tell myself that it is because I do not want to be alone and that is partly true. I can tell myself that because it is easier than entertaining the paranoid daydream that Frankie will call Marco once he has left the house. Informing him, telling on me. *She can't cope, and she's not eating, and she nearly died today.* I shiver.

'I have to make a quick stop,' Frankie tells me as we walk to the van. 'Shouldn't take more than five minutes. I've got someone I'd like you to meet.'

Although the fog has lifted now the sun is still a hazy disc in the sky and the air is bright and cold. We drive into town, parking in a little mews facing a row of workshops and lock-ups. The clock on the dashboard shows me it is nearly four o'clock in the afternoon. And here is a new sensation, so unfamiliar to me that at first I do not recognise it. I feel hungry.

Frankie tells me he will just be a minute and disappears through one of the dark doorways opposite. I climb from the van and walk over the cobbles in a circle, head tilted to the clear blue sky. I only see him as I turn back, the man standing and watching me just a few feet away. He looks like a low-rent Johnny Cash, greatly weathered. His face is deeply lined, long brackets about his mouth. A geriatric teddy-boy, hair slicked back into an oily pompadour. Beneath the sleeve of his T-shirt a carton of cigarettes is just visible. His mouth is hanging open slightly, eyes wide. I know that look. It's fear. I raise my hand, and he takes a step back, crossing himself as he does so. Forehead, chest, shoulder, shoulder. He can't take his eyes off me, and I'm starting to feel uncomfortable, wishing Frankie would hurry back.

'Hi,' I say. 'I'm just waiting for someone.'

'You're her.'

I get it. I nod, slowly. Katie Marigold. He's about the right age to have seen it as an adult after all.

'Yes, I am. Older now, but no wiser, ha-ha.'

He squints across the courtyard, shielding his eyes from the sun. 'You,' he says, and spits between forked fingers. 'You're more real than I am.'

Movement behind him; it's Frankie coming out through the doorway. He stops when he sees the man I am talking to, and I have a moment to read the expression which crosses his face. He's rattled. Why?

'Stella, cool. You've met Jim Kennecker.'

Kennecker. I think on it for a second. Then, of course. The caretaker. I hold my hand out to him but he stares down at it, dumb. Frankie puts a large hand on the man's scrawny shoulder.

'You should probably get inside, Jim. Phone's ringing.'

'I was sorry to hear about your spell in hospital,' I tell him. He looks at me, scratching his lip with a thumbnail and I know, *I know*, that what will be coming out of his mouth next is a lie.

'Oh – yuh. My heart. I have a bad heart.'

'Right.'

I look to Frankie who, I realise, is holding something. It is a lead, and at the end of that lead is a dog, a collie with amber eyes.

'Uh, Stella, this is who I wanted you to meet. This is Blue.'

'Hello, boy,' I say. 'Hello, Blue.'

'Are you okay with dogs? Not allergic?'

'No, it's fine. Hello.' I'm scratching him behind his ears, patting his flanks. Blue is standing up now, tail wagging. As I stand he nuzzles against me.

153

'I'm sorry about Jim,' Frankie says in a low voice as we climb into the van. 'He puts some work my way occasionally, rents me the space over the workshop. Sometimes he can get confused.'

'Yeah,' I say, but I can see that neither of us believes that, and I'm relieved when we leave the workshops behind. His heart, he'd said. But it hadn't been, had it? Not according to Frankie. What was it he'd told Marco and me that first day? My brain is soft as a cushion.

By the time we get back to Chy an Mor it is full dark, and I am ravenous. The moon is a bone-white rind hanging between the trees. In the kitchen Frankie is removing cartons from a plastic bag, stacking them next to him on the table.

I study him as he sifts through the cupboards, removing plates and cutlery from the drawers, occasionally talking to Blue. His skin is dark, tanned from summers of work outdoors. His eyes crinkle into amused half-moons when he smiles. Frankie brings plates to the table, catching me yawning.

'Are you staying for dinner?' I ask.

'Do you want me to?'

'Yes.'

He studies me indifferently. I know I'm not his problem and I tell him so.

He laughs. 'You're no one's problem. What a strange thing to say.'

'I just don't want to be by myself.'

'That's why I brought Blue over, to keep you company. He can do the night shifts, look after the place for you.'

'Here, you mean?'

'Where else?'

He lowers himself into the chair opposite and his eyes don't leave me. I reach across the table and put my hand on top of his.

'Right now I just want some human company. Do you understand?'

He nods. I am embarrassed by my neediness and wish I could have a drink. I miss it, glasses of white wine, slightly frosted. Long stems of gin and tonic poured over ice. The crisp, slightly cloying taste of cider. Whisky, peaty and earthy and amber-coloured. All those ghosts of cigarettes and beer and spirits and nights which bled into mornings. I miss drinking. I miss my friends.

Later, when we are clearing away the plates, Frankie retrieves my phone from beneath the table, handing it over to me.

'You know, they have satellites that can pinpoint your exact location just from your mobile signal,' he says. 'Every time you switch that thing on, you're never alone.'

I stare down at it in my hand. It's so bulky and unfamiliar still, this phone. What had happened to mine again? Lost, Marco had said. Like my friends.

'What about me?' I ask him. 'Can I find someone else through their phone? See where they are?'

'Depends. I guess you could. Who did you have in mind?'

Joey Fraser, I think immediately, remembering the phone call of earlier, the way his voice had snaked into my ear. *I heard you're losing your mind. About time, I'd say. Surprised it didn't happen sooner.*

'Stella? You okay?'

'Huh?'

'You're away with the fairies.'

'I'm sorry. I heard some bad news today. An old friend died. Actually, not a friend, not really. We worked together. Long time ago.'

'I'm sorry to hear it.'

'Drove her car right into a tree. The *Marigold!* Curse, they're calling it. One by one we're all dropping like flies.'

'You don't believe that though, do you? Curses, I mean.' Frankie leans his knuckles on the table, voice soft. 'Because I can put your mind at rest there. They're not real.'

'Oh! I almost forgot!' I say, and hand Frankie the photograph and the note I'd found beneath the box of eggs. Frankie holds them inches from his face, shaking his head in puzzlement.

'This is weird. You said they just turned up? Out of the blue?'

'That's right. Do you know anything about it?'

'Nope. Don't recognise the writing. Don't know who this is either. Do you?'

I shake my head, disappointed.

'It's horrible. Looks like someone beat her up pretty bad. You need to go to the police, Stella. This is more than trying to scare you. This is an out and out threat.'

'They won't do anything. I've had this before, with a stalker. He used to send me stuff to my home when I was a kid. Seven or eight years old. I was – sort of famous for a while, on the television. He was a fan. He signed his letters "Uncle". The envelopes would be full of really weird stuff. The police said they couldn't do anything until he actually did something to physically harm me. The threats weren't enough. We moved out not long after, and it seemed to stop.'

'Jesus.'

'Lost a bit of faith in the process after that, to be honest.'

I consider telling Frankie about the phone calls, the ones in which the silence bristles with menace and static, but instead I pick up the photo and slide it with the note between the pages of the *Reader's Digest Book of Perennials*. Frankie watches me carefully, his hands in his pockets. Something is nagging at me, I can feel it persistently, like a toothache. It wasn't there before, when I first arrived.

'You'll keep Blue here with you tonight then, yes?'

I nod.

'He's a loud barker, an excellent mouser and a rampant breaker of wind. So be warned. I've bought him some food. It's in the fridge.'

Blue is looking over at us, head tilted.

Frankie winks at him. 'You'll look after this lady tonight, boss? Make sure she sleeps safe?'

Blue whines down in his throat and wags his tail. Frankie and I laugh.

'Good boy.' He turns to me. 'Found him hiding under my truck about six years ago. He spent nine days under there, shivering. I had to pass him food and water.'

'How did you get him out?'

'Persistence. I'm a dogged bastard.' Frankie flashes me that easy, roguish grin again.

'Poor Blue. Poor baby.'

'Oh, keep talking, darlin', he's going to love you. If you need more wood, you'll find a stack of it in the shed. Don't lose the key, it's the only one. And – uh – careful as you go in. There's piles of boxes in there, really old stuff.'

We move into the hallway and I switch on the light. Frankie whistles long and low.

'Wow. How long has that been there?'

A huge patch of damp covers the wall from floor to ceiling. It is black and wet and ugly-looking. Frankie presses his hand against it, but the thought of touching it revolts me, turning my stomach. Blue flattens himself low to the ground, walking down the hallway in a crouching gait. I stare at it.

'I don't know. I've never seen it before.'

'It almost looks' – Frankie is hesitant, turning his head this way and that – 'like a person. Wouldn't you say? Like the outline of a figure.'

I bristle with a sudden chill. He's right, of course, that is exactly what it looks like. A looming silhouette beaded with condensation as though something were pressing through from the other side of the wall.

Frankie fixes me with a firm gaze as he gets ready to leave. 'You have my number. You can call me if you need to. If I don't answer just keep trying – I sleep like the dead.'

'Won't your wife mind?'

He looks down at the plain band on his wedding finger, almost as if he is surprised to see it.

'If she does she's going to need to use a Ouija board to tell me about it.'

It takes a moment for me to make the connection.

'Oh, Christ, oh, Frankie. I'm so sorry. I feel like – oh – I'm so sorry.'

'Well, you didn't know, and it was a long time ago now. Take that look off your face, Stella, you've done nothing wrong. She had a brain aneurysm as sudden and lethal as being hit by a fourteen-wheeler. There was no warning, no history and no second chance. I've made my peace with it, so you mustn't worry. Okay?'

'Okay.'

'Again, with feeling.'

'Okay.'

Chapter 18

It has been just three days since I stopped taking my pills – the 'drifters' – and I'm wide awake. It feels like a circuit has blown in the soft tissue of my brain. My thoughts knot and tangle and the clarity, when it comes, is so stark I immediately shrink from it. The room is cold. Blue, lying at the foot of my bed, lifts his head and barks once, sharply. He looks at the ceiling and stands, whining uneasily, ears flat against his skull. The air feels electrically charged, an imperceptible buzz. I check the time, it is nearly a quarter to three in the morning, and I am starting to shiver. Blue begins to pace, and I cross the room to open the door for him, pulling my blanket around my shoulders. In the hallway the smell is rising like heat. Something like lakes and deep water slightly corrupted. Vegetative and overripe. With the light on I can see another huge damp patch on the stairwell. It covers nearly a third of the wall, right down to the skirting boards. I can see the places where it has dripped down onto the carpet. It looks to me like a figure in profile, one hand raised. I think of immurement, of being walled in. I can even see cracks in the plaster spreading out like tendrils of hair.

Blue is whining downstairs, back and forth in front of the back door. I open it for him and he disappears into the dark garden. I switch on the lamp and see another damp patch on the wall, blooming like a toxic fungus. Another in the sitting room, slightly hidden by the sofa, so wet it is almost black. I call for Blue but my voice has shrunk. It is a whisper. 'Blue.' There is a patch of water on the floor beside the back door. I'm sure it wasn't there when I let the dog outside. I smell it but it is not urine, it is briny and rich. Seawater.

'Blue!'

This time I hang in the doorway, peering into the darkness. There is no movement in the garden, no barking. The rain has stopped but the branches are still dripping, I can hear it.

'Blue?'

I go outside. The moon is barely visible behind the clouds and there are no stars, just a perfect darkness. I cannot see the dog anywhere and I think of the cliffs and their lethal drop-offs and I am suddenly afraid. I call him again and turn back to the house thinking I should go after him, thinking I should get some wellies and a torch.

It's not the movement I see first, although something has drawn my eyes to the upper window, my bedroom window.

There is a hand pressed against the glass, long, pale fingers which leave no residue, ghost-white. I stare and stare and then something shoots past me, moving at speed, and I see it's Blue cowering in the doorway, and when I look up again there is nothing there at all.

The next afternoon I take Blue to the beach. We take the main road, walking carefully along the overgrown grass verge. The bluster of the wind lifts my hair, fussing it about my ears. Blue walks ahead a little way, always throwing cautious glances behind him as if to reassure himself I am still there. By the time we reach the outskirts of town I am so hot I have tied my jumper round my waist. I have noticed that the waistband of my jeans is roomy and my engagement ring has worked loose, sliding to the first knuckle of my finger. I must remember to eat.

'Blue!'

He is sniffing around the wall of the house selling the eggs, the one with the old Range Rover marooned on the grass.

'Blue!'

Too late. His head lifts and he sees a chicken in the yard, scratching in the dirt. He barks once and takes off, bounding over the low wall and into the front garden. The chicken makes a noise like an engine sputtering and lurches for the doorway. Blue utters another volley of barks, and I call him from the road. 'Come back! Come back, Blue!' Just for a moment I think he will, but then he pushes his nose against the gap in the door and slides through it, following the chicken into the house. I am just in time to see his tail disappear into a thick wedge of darkness. I stand there for a moment, breathless. Any second I expect to see him creep back out, looking up at me with a guilty expression, but after a minute has passed I realise I am going to have to go and get him. I can remember the way the woman in the doorway had looked at me, the way she had lifted her red hands. A warning, or a bloodied supplication. Lady Macbeth. Head down, I cross the yard quickly.

The doorbell is hidden beneath a screen of ivy. The button is missing, leaving just a small black hole like the pupil of an eye. I knock and wait. The red paint of the door looks new but the frame around it is rotting, the soft wood splintering away. This close I can see that the house is in a state of quite advanced disrepair. The windows are streaked with bird shit and dirt, and most of the panes are cracked. Gaps in the roof like a mouthful of rotten teeth. Brown, scorched grass, moss stippling the walls. A chicken appears from a little outhouse and pecks at the ground by my feet. One of its claws is shrunken and deformed, curled against its belly.

161

I push open the front door. Looking in, I can see a length of faded red carpet, worn wooden floorboards. There is an archway to the left of the stairs leading, I assume, towards the back of the house, to the kitchen or the dining room. There's a closed door immediately to my left, and next to it a telephone mounted to the wall, the old-fashioned type with a rotary dial. There are no pictures or ornaments or decoration of any kind. It smells warm and musty, like a sunlit barn. I call out.

'Hello? Blue?'

I am walking slowly down the hallway, listening. I can see holes in the wall where the plaster has fallen out in great chunks. It crunches beneath my feet. There is a sudden clatter just up ahead behind the closed door, something falling to the floor. I walk towards it beneath an archway where plaster cherubs gaze at me with sightless eyes. I push the door open and go into the kitchen.

It is full of chickens. A large black bantam is roosting in the sink. Others clutter the shelves and scratch on the surface of the table. A pot rack is suspended over the table and the metal pans rattle together tunelessly as more birds settle on the bars. A drift of snowy white feathers like snowflakes. Everything is covered in bird shit, white and hard and cracked like old porcelain. Blue is darting about the room, mouth agape while the hens shriek and shuffle. I make to grab one to lift it away from him, and it pecks at the ridges of my hand, where the skin is thin and easily torn. I cry out, dropping the bird, cradling my injured hand to my chest.

A voice from behind makes me jump, and I have to stifle a scream.

'I eat them, you know, the birds. I kill them and cook them. What do you think of that?'

It's the woman who had shown me her bloodied hands – an ancient little figure with a tiny, nipped-in waist and clouds of silvery hair like wire wool. Her skin looks like parchment. She is wearing a dirty apron and scuffed house slippers. One of her yellowing eyes is running thick tears.

'I break their necks.'

She steps closer to me, and smiles. Her teeth are tobacco-coloured, soft-looking, pulpy.

'I'm sorry about my dog—'

'I know who you are,' she whispers, coming close enough that I can smell cloves on her breath. 'You're a dead woman.'

I've managed to grab Blue by the scruff of the neck and am hauling him towards the door but when I look up I see there is someone blocking my way. Another woman, slightly younger, her face carefully made-up. She has her hair in a chignon but there are crescents of black beneath her fingernails and her lipstick is smudged, just the tiniest bit. I haul Blue to my side, hearing myself apologising again. She darts her eyes over me without smiling.

'You'll have to mind my mother-in-law,' she says flatly. It's hard to place her age. As she steps into the light I can see that she is older than I had previously thought, in her sixties at least. 'She has good days and bad days. This is one of her bad days. We have more and more of those as she gets to the end. Come on, Beverley. You're scaring Stella.'

I blink at the sound of my name.

'Ellie?' the little woman says to me, lifting one knuckled hand to my cheek. I back away. I don't like to be touched. It makes me clench my teeth.

'Not Ellie, no.' The woman looks at me over her mother-in-law's head.

'How did you know my name?'

'Oh, we all know who you are, Stella Wiseman. Since you moved into the cottage up there the town has talked of nothing else. A star, however faded, is still a star.'

'Oh, well, I wouldn't say—'

'You know they say that the light you see is from stars which are already dead? That explains why it's so cold.'

I am standing with Blue between my legs, holding him in place with my knees. She puts her hands on her mother-in-law's shoulders and smiles.

'I'm Penelope Dalton. This is Bev, but don't bother introducing yourself, you'll only have to do it again the next time you see her. How are you finding it up at Chy an Mor? It's been a while since I've been up there.'

'Yes, it—'

'Of course you're probably still settling in, aren't you? It must be very boring for you here, with all of us old folk and nothing to do. I expect you're desperate to get back to the city. You're bleeding.'

I look down at my hand, where hair-thin scratches are already growing into welts dotted with blood, criss-crossing my pale skin.

'Ellie,' Beverley says to me again, lifting a finger, which shivers slightly. She points at my chest.

'No—' I begin, and Penelope cuts me off.

'That's the Nilsen house, isn't it? The one you're in. You're with Marco, I suppose. Will he be joining you soon?'

'He – uh . . . He has some work to finish abroad. Look, I really need to go.'

'Of course. Come on, Mother, let her pass.'

'You mustn't worry about her,' Beverley says to me quietly as I squeeze past. 'She's always been a bitch.'

Penelope barks a strangled laugh and squeezes Beverley's shoulders. 'Good God, are we going to be forced to do this in front of our guest? You'll frighten her off! Come on,' she says to me, 'I'll walk you to the door.'

As we go down the hallway I hear Beverley say something else, but I don't quite catch it as the kitchen door closes on her. The last glimpse I have of her, she is standing beneath a hanging rack bristling with chickens, her sallow face hangdog and worried-looking. She is mouthing something at me, but the door closes before I can see what she is saying.

'Dementia is very cruel,' Penelope tells me. 'Sometimes I wonder who suffers more. I do hope you aren't struggling too much up there on your own. They say all these old places are full of ghosts.'

I am instantly cold.

She studies me carefully as she opens the front door. 'It's funny,' she says, wrapping her cardigan around her bony shoulders, 'I never thought of Marco as having a "type" but now I've seen you, well – maybe he does after all.'

While I stand there staring, wondering what she means, Blue squirming beside me, she closes the door.

I've arranged to meet Frankie for tea in the café. As I'm crossing the car park my phone rings in my pocket. I call Blue to heel and answer, turning my back to a wind which dusts fine grains of sand against my bare legs. The stinging sensation is almost pleasant.

'Stella? It's me, Marco. Can you hear me all right?'

'You're a bit fuzzy.'

'I'm just at the airport. Heading back to London. I should be down with you by the weekend. I'm sorry it's taken so long.'

'I'm so pleased you called, I—'

'Listen, I don't have long. Are you okay? How's the house?'

I hesitate. I don't want to worry him. *Everything's fine, darling. I've started seeing shapes in the walls.*

'Not bad.'

'Yeah? You still taking the pills?'

'Sure!' I say so brightly I have to grit my teeth. *I'm sabotaging myself, flushed them all away. Buh-bye, sanity.* 'Up and down, you know? Peaks and troughs.'

'You sound tense. Are you sure you're all right? I shouldn't have just left you.'

'It's fine, I promise. It's good for me. This space. Like a retreat.'

'Okay, baby girl. I have to go. It's boiling here. I'd love to bring you one day, although we'd give the bullfighting a swerve. I'll call you when I land, okay?'

'Okay.'

He hangs up and I am left staring at my phone. *Bullfighting?* I think. Before, Marco had said he was in Zürich. Hadn't he? That tangle of confusion knots tighter, making my skin itch. I scramble in my bag for a pen and a scrap of paper and write on the back of it 'Zürich/Spain??'. My handwriting looks a little better, not spidery and shaky as it has been these last few weeks. I fold the paper and slip it inside my pocket and go and meet Frankie.

He listens as I tell him the story of the hand at the window and the strange woman I'd met in the ruined house.

'Do you want to keep Blue for another night?'

'Yes, I think I'd like that, I really would.'

'Have you heard from the police? The coastguard? Anything on the news?'

I shake my head.

'You still worried that someone's been in your house?'

'I'm more worried that – what if it's in my head, Frankie?' I feel absurdly close to tears. For the millionth time I wish I had my pills. 'That's what worries me. I'm hoping they'll find a body just so I can be reassured that this person existed. Is that an awful thing to say? That I hope they find them dead?'

'Yes and no,' he replies. 'Listen, Stella. Are you quite sane, do you think?'

I check his face to see if he is laughing at me, the way Marco does sometimes.

'How would I know?'

'You wouldn't. But if it helps, you seem quite sane to me. A little fragile' – he pronounces it *fradge*-ill, smiling as he says it – 'but not mad. Not yet, at least. But you – you're all on your own up there. Are you taking the pills this "doctor" gave you?'

'Why do you say it like that?'

'Say what?'

'"Doctor". Like I've made him up.'

He looks down, smiling, although when he lifts his head again the smile has disappeared and I'm wondering if I ever saw it at all. 'I don't doubt you, Stella. Please don't think that.'

'I'm not – thank you, I mean. I just feel a bit out of my depth at the moment.'

'Sharks under you, yeah?'

I must have looked puzzled because Frankie laughs. 'It's a family thing, I guess. My grandmother used to say I was always getting out of my depth and the sharks were circling. It was her way of saying I was always getting into trouble.'

He studies my stricken, sleepless face and puts his hand very carefully on top of mine. 'Tell you what, why don't I come over one evening, keep you company for a bit. We could play backgammon.'

'I don't know how to play backgammon.'

'Well, then I'll teach you. I'm the best backgammon player in four counties. We'll have hot chocolate. You just need to get the fire going. How does that sound?'

'Can you come over tonight?' I don't want to sound desperate but I am, I am desperate. *Don't leave me alone in that house of ghosts.* I look down to see that I am gripping his arm.

'I'm busy tonight. I'm helping Jim with something. Are you going to be all right?'

What can I say? I tell him yes, of course, yes, I'm fine, and it is not until he has gone that I realise a small but vital thing. Frankie has taken off his wedding ring.

Heidi catches me as I walk out of the door. She is sitting in a sheltered spot with a crossword on her lap. She smiles and calls out 'Hey, Stella!' Heidi is wearing cut-off denim shorts and tights the colour of cherries. Her hair is in a perfect Dutch braid. Again I feel jealousy, sour and as thin as gruel in my mouth. Heidi is too much, way too much. Too confident, too pretty, dainty like a little doll. Frankie clearly adores her.

'How are you? Frankie says the cottage is beautiful.'

'Yes. It is, yes.'

'You're lucky to be up there – the sunsets must be awesome.'

'Yes.'

'You taking Blue to the beach?'

'Yes,' I say again. I feel dumb.

'Listen, I've been meaning to talk to you—'

'I really have to go.' I have had enough for this morning. I just want to be alone. She smiles, open and friendly.

'Sure, sure. How about tomorrow? About eleven?'

'Tomorrow sounds great.' I have already decided it won't be because I won't be there.

'Okay.'

'Okay.'

A fringe of seaweed stretches the length of the beach, stranded by the high tide. At the far end are the giant boulders, grey and ominous like earthbound comets. I take off my wellies and socks, digging my toes into the wet sand. Blue charges into the surf, paws sending up a fine spray. My mind turns back to the conversation with Frankie, the way he'd asked me about Doctor Wilson. Because of course I'd felt the same, hadn't I? The day of my second appointment. I'd wondered about him, but then I'd simply smothered it with the pills, which he had referred to as 'drifters'.

Chapter 19

When I get back to Chy an Mor, I feed Blue and switch on the computer. The desk is in front of a small window overlooking the garden. Beside me is a notepad and on top of that – and here I blink because I really don't believe my eyes – is the photograph and the note. I stare at it for a moment and then slowly push my chair back. I go to the bookcase and take down the *Reader's Digest Book of Perennials*, opening it at the place where I was sure I had left them. Only they aren't there. They have been put on my desk where I will see them. Pay Attention. I feel edgy, with a raw nervous energy. I turn and look around the empty room, ask it if I am going mad.

There is only one person who saw where I'd hidden them. He'd been here when I'd slid them between the pages. I swallow, dry-mouthed. That day on the cliff when he had just happened to be there. He said he'd been coming to give me the key for the wood-shed but that could have waited till Marco was here, couldn't it? Frankie, the only person with a spare key to the cottage. I sit down hard in my chair. I'm shaken by my meeting with Mr Kennecker, the original caretaker. Frankie had told us he was in hospital – 'gall-stones', he'd said. But Kennecker had said his heart, hadn't he? And had either Marco or I checked out this little fiction? We'd taken Frankie at his word.

I'm thinking back to my fan, Uncle, the one who used to write me all the letters, those ragged envelopes containing such strange gifts. Once it had been a bloodied tooth, an incisor. It had rolled out into the palm of my hand. I'd shrieked and dropped it on the floor, where it lay like a pearl on the seabed. And those dogs. I remember now. There is light coming through the cracks of my memories.

'Poison in the meat,' I overheard my mother say to my father. 'Someone slipped it in. It's the third one this year. Police don't give a damn, but as I've said to them, if some psycho can kill an animal what's to stop him going after Stella next?'

They'd arrested someone in the end, hadn't they? An older man, with thick grey hair and bifocals, one of the cleaners. I can remember him being escorted from the building. How old had I been then? Ten, eleven? My mother saying, 'You're safe now, Stella', her hand on my shoulder. They'd found rat poison in his locker. It's what he'd been giving the dogs. When they'd searched his house they'd found newspaper clippings of the show and signed pictures of me stacked up next to his big television set. I don't remember what happened to him. My mother kept it all from me.

I look down at the photograph next to my elbow, the one with the woman in it who looks so much like me. It's a threat. I can feel it. I look closer at her and something jolts sharply in my memory.

I've seen that woman before.

I pick up my phone and call Marco's office.

'You know I really can't do that.' Alice's tone is clipped, like I am being told off. Perhaps I am.

'Please, Alice. I really don't know who else to ask. It needs to be a surprise, you see, something special.'

I close my eyes, open them. Inch my bare feet into a warm patch of sunlight on the floor. She doesn't believe me and that's fine. What is more important is that she doesn't tell Marco that I'm asking her this favour.

'What's it for again?'

'A surprise. I want to make him something. I'm collecting old photos together and I'm doing a collage.'

'Right.'

It is the screensaver I'm thinking of, the one on Marco's computer. The day I'd lost my purse and had to wait in his office while Alice called a taxi, there had been that series of photos sliding across the screen.

'It's a particular picture – um – Marco and a woman, arms around each other, in front of a fountain. Looks like it could be Italy. Can you see it?'

'Nope, but if not I can find it in the file. I know the one you mean.'

'Can you email it to me without him knowing?'

Alice hesitates, and I say quickly, without thinking, 'Please, Alice. I really want to do this for him.'

'Give me your email address. I'll have to think about it.'

I've had to set up a new account so I give her the address, reading it carefully.

'Thank you, thank you so much.'

'I can't promise anything, Stella. It certainly feels too much like snooping.'

'Can I ask you one more thing?' I ask, smoothing the crumpled piece of paper I've taken from my bag in front of me. 'Marco called me earlier from the airport and I wanted to track his flight. He's flying from Zürich, right?'

'Uh—' For the first time Alice does not sound composed. 'I'm not currently at my desk but I think it's Madrid. Gets into Gatwick at seven thirty tonight. Do you want the flight number?'

'No. Just send me the photo, please.' *Madrid?* 'I must have misheard him.'

I can picture Alice standing in Marco's office, with its view over Fitzrovia towards the BT Tower. The smells of coffee and printer ink, new carpets, paint. His beautiful chair behind the desk, an antique carved in oak with a leather seat the colour of dried blood. Hadn't I straddled him in that chair one late afternoon in August, after everyone had left the building? I had, and had sunk my teeth into the wood as I'd orgasmed. As far as I know, the teeth marks are still there. 'You've always been a biter,' he'd said to me afterwards, and I'd laughed, but something in those words now makes me feel strange. *You've always been a biter.* Have I? I think of asking Alice to check, to run her hands over the hard material to see if the little indentations are there, where my incisors met the wood.

'Are you still there, Stella?'

I pause. I've been staring at a framed picture hanging to the left of the window. It is a watercolour of the sea, gilt-framed. But the painting isn't what I am looking at. I can see the room reflected in the glass; the dark shapes of the sofa, the coffee table, Blue lying on the floor. Beyond that, silhouetted in the doorway, I can see the shape of a figure, a woman.

'Yes,' I whisper. 'Yes, I'm still here.' I swallow, a dry click. 'Alice. There's someone in my house.'

I am watching the milky glass. I can make out no detail in the figure, just a suggestion of thinness and cold. The shoulders are slumped, skinny arms hanging loosely.

'What – Stella, what do you mean?'

'I can see someone behind me, in the glass. I'm so frightened.'

I am whispering now. Blue approaches me, shivering, a whine trembling in his throat. He pushes his skull against my leg, needling. I can hear the steady drip, drip, drip of water onto the floorboards. I know if I were to turn my head I would see water pooling there.

'Is the door locked? Can you call for help?' And then, after only the slightest pause, 'Are you sober?'

'I have to go, Alice. Send me the photo. It's very important.'

I end the call abruptly. Blue is scrabbling to get into my lap. He is afraid, and so am I. There is a thick gurgling as of milkshake being drained from an empty glass through a straw. The sound of a throat struggling to work in uncompromising flesh. Drawing breath, or trying to, into wet lungs.

'You don't frighten me, you know,' I whisper. I squeeze my eyes closed and when I open them and turn slowly, so slowly I can almost hear my tendons creak, there is no one there. There is no one there. The doorway is empty, bar the long afternoon shadows. On the floor, a little pool of water. And all about me is the smell of the sea, the sea.

Chapter 20

It's dark, and I am awake with a sharp jolt like a single handclap. I lie, my eyes wide, staring at the ceiling. The dreamcatcher spins on the end of its thread. Blue is pacing the room. I can hear his claws clicking against the wood, but that is not what has woken me. I sit up. I'm listening. I can hear voices.

I walk to the bedroom door and pull it carefully, quietly open. There are people talking downstairs. I can't make out what they are saying but there is the murmur of conversation, lifting and falling. My skin prickles with cold. I don't like this. Blue huddles beside me in the doorway, a whine trembling in his throat. I walk the dark hallway to the top of the stairs. Down there, in the darkness, a light is flickering. More voices, and then laughter, the canned kind. It's the television. I put my hand on Blue's flat skull and tell him it's all right. But even as I walk down the stairs I am listening and a hard ball of ice is forming in my stomach. I know those voices. One of them is mine.

'What are we plantin' here?'

'Lettuces, tomato, carrots . . .'

'Parrots? I want to grow parrots!'

(Audience laughter)

'Not parrots, Pudge. Carrots. You know, the ones that you eat?'

'I don't want to eat parrots! The feathers will get stuck in my teef!'

(More laughter)

'He means carrots, Katie Marigold. You know, the orange things?'

'Oranges? I want to grow oranges!'

(Audience laughter, the sound of a doorbell)

I am standing at the foot of the stairs in the darkness. From here I can see into the sitting room, the light flickering from the TV set. It is playing my old show. I step into the room, eyes quickly darting around. There is no one here.

'Come on, we'd better be quick. We need to start digging. Bonnie, grab that fork.'

'I thought we was diggin', not eatin'.'

'It's a garden tool. You know, like a spade or a rake?'

'A snake? I don't wanna see no snake!'

I sit slowly opposite the TV. My face is lit with jittering shadow. There I am, tiny, doll-like. My face dimpled, my hair tied up in irregular bunches. I remember this episode. It was called 'Look What's Growing, Katie Marigold', one of the later ones. By the end they were all called things like that. 'Here Comes Katie Marigold!' and 'Katie Marigold Rides Again!' And now, here it is, me, running to keep up with the older kids, me with all the funny lines, the eye rolls, the catchphrases. Me, with all the applause. I hug my knees tight to my chest. I can't stop watching and my eyes are full of tears. Here is my childhood; in make-up, on set, in production meetings. Just off screen is my mother, arms folded, mouth a thin line, head tilted to one side. She was always there, I realise, every single episode, a copy of the script curled up beneath one arm. I don't remember any of the other parents being there, but maybe it's because they were a couple of years older than me. Maybe.

'Uh-oh, what's this?'

'Katie Marigold, what have you found?'

'What is it?'

'I fink we'd better ask Daddy!'

176

(Laughter, applause.)

I stand up and turn it off. It's a video, I realise. I bend down to the machine. I hadn't even seen it when I'd arrived but now I do see it I realise how long it has been since I saw a VHS player. It is top-loading, and I press the eject button with the pad of my thumb. The tape rises and I pull it out. On the label in felt-tip is written 'Marigold! Series 4-6'. It is childish, blocky writing. I put it on the table and lie on the couch, waiting for sleep. It is a long time coming.

The next morning I walk into town. I am going to meet Heidi, I have decided. That videotape in the night was enough for me to want to get out of the house and have company. I'd held it in my hands that morning, turning it over and over between my fingers. *Where had it come from?* One thing was certain, I was sleepwalking again. I must be. Because how else would it have got into the house?

She is waiting outside the café, her coat pulled up against the wind. She holds a flask in one hand and waves when she sees me. She is like a sprite, fizzing with energy.

'Hi, thanks for coming,' she says, and then kneels to nuzzle Blue, slapping him gently on the flanks. When she straightens she gives me a smile.

'I thought we'd go to the beach. I've brought a flask and some croissants. The forecast said rain but not till this afternoon, so I think we'll be all right.' She hooks her arm in mine and I flinch at the familiarity. If she notices she doesn't let on, keeping up a steady stream of chatter until the dunes are behind us, rising at our backs like the tundra of a vast and distant planet. On the beach the wind is strong and thick with salt, the sand treacle-coloured and shimmering.

I let Blue off the lead and we scramble up rocks studded with mussels and barnacles. Pools are cradled in hollows, and much of the moonlike surface is slick with treacherous gutweed.

'How are you?'

'Good,' I reply. 'Fine, fine. Fine.'

'I'm hungover,' Heidi groans. 'White Russians and some awful cider. I feel like death. Times like this I can understand why you don't drink. I must look like shit.' She nods to Chy an Mor at the top of the cliff. 'Is that your place up there?'

Shielding my eyes, I follow Heidi's gaze and see the squat little cottage with the warped roof, long chimney like a finger raised to the sky. I've never seen it from this angle. It looks so remote.

'Yes, that's it, that's the cottage.'

'Is it haunted?'

I turn to her, not knowing what to say. She hands me a croissant. 'That's what people say. Is it true?'

'I don't believe in ghosts.'

'Aw, that's a shame. I was hoping you might have some good stories for me.'

The sand is dimpled with the scars of the retreating tide. Blue charges into the shallow river where the seaweed floats in the current like witch's hair. He rolls his wet body in the sand and then veers off, tail high in the air.

'What a life that dog has.'

'Yes. And look at this. It's lovely, isn't it? I will never get tired of this view.'

I nod towards the surfers right out past the breakers where the mist hangs over the sea like a nimbus. 'They're brave.'

'They're nuts, more like. It must be freezing.'

'I'd love to try it.'

'You should ask Frankie to teach you. You could talk about wipeouts and hang ten or whatever till the cows come home.'

'Frankie?'

'I know, right? You look at the size of him, and you'd think he'd have no centre of gravity at all but he's actually very agile, like a cat.'

I think of the time he caught me on the clifftop, the sure manacle of his hand about my wrist.

'See?' Heidi points at a dark shape in the water. 'See him there? Sitting on his surfboard. Posing, some people would call it. Do you want some tea? I hope you like it sweet.'

I do. She pours us both cups from her flask and I cradle it, ruffling the surface with my breath.

'You must miss your boyfriend.'

I don't reply. Heidi reaches over and touches my cup to her own. I look at her, surprised.

'I hear you. Fond of your own space, right? "*Besser allein als in schlechter Gesellschaft*",' Heidi says and smiles. 'I have German grandparents. It means "Better to be alone than in bad company".'

I feel a brief jolt of memory, sharp as jagged glass. Martha, of course. Sweet, kind, generous Martha, who had been afraid of swearing during labour. I feel a flare of loneliness then, and perform a quick mental calculation as to when the baby would be due.

'What do you mean by "bad company"?'

She ignores me, looking out to the horizon. 'Listen. I wanted to speak to you. I hope I have this completely wrong and that you'll tell me to shut up and stop being so paranoid, but someone has been looking for you.'

'Who?'

'He wouldn't give his name. At least not to me. He's been in the café a few times, just asking around. At first I thought he was just interested in the area – we get a lot of that, you see – geologists,

179

botanists, historians – so I was happy to answer his questions but after a while I just' – she shrugs – 'I just thought something wasn't right.'

She points at the scar on her face, the one like a curving sideways smile. 'Although, as you can see, I'm a pretty lousy judge of character.'

I don't know what to say to that, so I say nothing.

'My husband did this to me. I'd like to tell you it was the last straw, the very last, but you know what? It wasn't. It was just one in a very long, very boring list of injuries he liked to inflict on me.'

She holds out her hand, and I can see that two of the fingers on her right are misshapen, as though from arthritis. 'Ask me why he broke my fingers.'

'Why did he break your fingers?'

'The volume on the TV was too loud, and I didn't get to the remote fast enough. That's the punchline. Pretty funny, huh? Pretty funny.'

I don't think it's funny, and I tell her so. She smiles, watching the brace of the waves hurtle towards the shore.

'It's a chemical process, love. I found that out a while ago. The hormones which are released have an effect on the brain similar to mental illness. Did you know that?'

I tell her I did not.

'It's that little chemical that makes you stay with a man even when he's breaking your fingers or cutting up your face. Just a little hormone with a lousy name, making you blind. When Tony hit me, he was relaxed, in good humour. That's what made it so frightening. He told me the trick was to relax, to breathe through the pain.'

'That's awful. I'm so sorry.'

'Well. Long time ago. But the scars are still there, you know? The person who got me out of it was Frankie's wife. Amazing woman, she was. It was she who told me to change my name and do something crazy with my hair to draw attention away from my scar. She helped me with a place to stay and food to eat. She was incredible. You better believe I cried my eyes out when she died. I always told myself that if I ever saw a woman in the same kind of trouble as I'd been in, that I'd try to help in some way.'

I see a figure emerging from the waves, surfboard tucked beneath his arm. He waves, and we wave back.

'Ah. You think *I'm* that woman,' I say quietly. 'I'm not. I'm happy. I'm getting married soon.' But I'm thinking about that photo, of course, that woman's face so similar to mine yet bruised and deformed, horrifying.

'This man, the one who's been asking questions. I got the same feeling about him. He came into the café but he didn't seem like he was all there, you know? Of course I've told him nothing. But I just wanted to let you know, in case – in case it's a situation like mine, like an ex, someone you don't want to find you.'

'What does he look like?'

Heidi thinks for a moment. 'Middle-aged but trying not to show it. He looks like he's had some work done – cosmetic, I mean – he has that tautness, do you know what I mean?'

I tell her yes, I know.

'His teeth are very white. More work, I think. He's charming, very pleasant. Slight American accent, but only a trace. Nice car, nice shoes, expensive. Either he's rich or it's a mid-life crisis. He smells good too, sort of like clean water.'

'I thought you only met him a few times?'

'I did. I'm capable of taking in a lot of information about people very quickly. I'm always on alert, do you see?'

'Yeah. What did you tell him?'

She laughs drily. 'Not a thing. He'll be asking around though, so he probably already has the answers to his questions. So be warned.'

Frankie has drawn level with us both, his feet planted in the sand, wetsuit glistening like sealskin. He wipes wet hair away from his face. 'What're you two talking about?'

'Your missus.'

'A wonderful woman. Why are you talking about Erica?'

'Just telling Stella a story.'

'Ah,' he says, nodding, and picks up a long branch of seaweed from the sand. 'Old bones.'

'Leave them buried, right?' Heidi replies, head tilted to one side. Her hair blazes crimson.

'That's right. Leave them buried.'

I know who Heidi is talking about. Joey Fraser. That prick. I pull out my phone when I get back to the cottage, scroll through the numbers on the call log.

'Stella.'

'What's going on, Joey? You're lucky I haven't called the police.'

'You're going to need to humour me with specifics.'

'You've been coming to my house, trying to frighten me. Even for you this is low.'

'Stella, please, calm down. I thought you'd grown out of this.'

'I know what you're doing and it's not funny. I can't believe you got hold of a videotape – haven't you heard of computers? Of the Internet?'

'Stella, I— You should hear yourself, you really should. Take a breath.'

'You're haunting me. Leave me alone.'

'You owe me!' I have to hold the phone away from my ear. He is so angry his voice distorts. 'You made my life hell! You made all our lives hell! You deserve to live in fear and panic the rest of your life. Why should you have it easy?'

'Wh— What?'

'Oh, come on. Come on, Stella. Don't play dumb. Your. Mother. Talk about a pushy parent. She hoovered up every good line on that show and had them rewritten just for you. She made sure we all knew we were the supporting cast, the backing dancers. She even had the name of the show changed.'

'Ha!' I'm laughing but it's shrill. It feels like a fist made of ice is sinking into my stomach. 'What are you talking about?'

'You really don't remember, huh? The first series of the show was called *Two and Six*. It was your mother putting pressure on the producers – and we all know how much she liked to do that, right? Getting them to change it, to give you the best lines. Only when putting pressure on them stopped working she started threatening to pull you out altogether. Of course that made them nervous and so they changed the title. Don't you realise that you were the only one in the whole show to be called by your full name? Katie Marigold. Katie Marigold. Only you and no one else. She used to say you were the heart of the show so often that people started believing it.'

'You're making this up.'

'Look it up if you don't believe me. You were a monster. If you didn't get your own way you lashed out, usually at us, the bigger kids. I have a deep, deep scar, sister. Don't you remember?'

I tell him I don't but I do, I think. I can remember standing in a caravan and screaming and screaming, my lungs white-hot, burning. Someone had done something to me, something awful. Joey had been there, glaring at me, not helping. Why hadn't he helped me? I feel furious again.

'I remember how much you bullied me. The things you used to say. How lonely you made me feel. It's not my fault I had the biggest part, I—'

'There you go again! You *didn't* have the biggest part, at least not in the beginning. You had the same as everyone else, one or two lines apiece. And the episodes weren't all about you then either. One of them was about me, can you imagine? Only your mother thought you were Shirley fucking Temple and started causing trouble and before you knew it the whole cast were reduced to bit players.'

'I was a kid. I was just a kid!'

'Look at the first two series. The actress who played Bonnie was replaced twice. No one could stand you, so they quit. The original Mikey quit because you scratched him till you drew blood. A year later our mother was replaced, and still no one stopped you. There used to be a joke on set that even the dogs were dying just to get away from you.'

I am shaking. I was in a caravan, screaming. I had the Katie Marigold dress on, and my hands were sticky and I was screaming. Why hadn't he comforted me? Why hadn't he got an adult? What had he done?

'If you come near me, if you come near the house again, I will call the police. I haven't forgotten what you did.'

'I'm not here to threaten you, Stella. You're turning into your mother, do you know that? You're out of your fucking mind.'

I clench and unclench my fists. I am filled with anger, slippery as a nest of eels. I can't grasp it. I am not used to this rage. The pills kept it at bay. It's overpowering, and I realise I am grinding my teeth together so hard that my jaw aches.

Back at the cottage I lift the videotape from the table and stalk over to the tall bookcases in the corner, filled with the curling pages of Jilly Coopers and Jackie Collinses. But there are no more videotapes on the shelves or in the cupboards of the dresser. I turn it over in my hands, wonderingly. *You're sleepwalking again, princess*, Marco had said to me, and he'd put that soft grey pill in my mouth and I'd ground it to powder before I'd even swallowed it.

I open the back door and let Blue out into the garden. He immediately sits beneath the shade of the apple tree which grows stubbornly against the bracing wind, heavily knuckled branches already bearing fruit. October already. The clouds are low and grey, rolling in from the sea. As I turn I notice that the woodshed door is ajar. I stop, stand very still. The padlock has been opened. It hangs from the handle, the key still in the lock. *Well, there you go then*, I think, moving slowly over the damp grass, *only you could have done that because only you have the key.*

Inside it is dark, soft light coming through the gaps in the tiles. The whole place is strung with cobwebs and dust, long vines of ivy snaking through the cracks in the brickwork. There is the cord of wood that Frankie had chopped before I'd arrived, covered in a tarp. Beyond that are stacks of boxes, soft and water-stained. I open the nearest one and a slew of old 45 singles slither out onto the floor. As I move forward my foot nudges something and I bend down to look closer. It's a stack of videotapes, four in total. They are carefully labelled. I carry them into the sitting room, pulling the one labelled 'Marigold! Series 1-2' from its sleeve.

The theme music is as I remember, that same piano rising and falling, that jolly English voice chiming, 'It's time to meet the Marigolds!', but when the title card comes up it reads *Two and Six* and there we are, Frisky number one and the five of us children waving at the camera. There's my on-screen sister Bonnie, a girl I can't remember, goofy-looking, wild hair tied up in a scarf. A different girl then. The mother is an actress I don't recognise and so is Mikey. Joey was right. I press my hands together and realise I am shaking. What's happening to me?

My phone is ringing and ringing and ringing. The morning sun is too bright. I reach my hand out from beneath the covers and pull the phone back under.

'Stella, I am sorry, I am so, so sorry.'

'Marco? Where are you? Are you here?'

'Oh, baby. Oh, Stella.'

'Marco, what is it? You're frightening me. Where are you?'

His voice sounds panicked, almost breathless. He is pacing, I can tell. I sit up.

'I need you not to worry, honey. I need you to promise you won't worry.'

'Marco, for fu—' I check myself. *Swearing doesn't suit you.*

'I don't know how it happened, I swear.'

I wait. My heart has picked up a neat little rhythm in my chest, running hard.

'About a week after you – you went into hospital I lost my phone. Only for a day or so. Do you remember?'

I tell him no, I don't.

'I just thought I'd left it at the office. I wasn't too worried. In the end I found it down the side of the sofa at your flat. It was barely hidden at all. I was surprised I'd missed it the first time because I thought I'd looked there. I thought I'd looked everywhere.'

'Go on.'

'I just – I want you to know – okay, so. Okay. Do you remember those photos we took?'

I close my eyes. I remember. Of course I do. But I thought he'd wiped them.

'I'm so sorry, Stella. I don't know how this has happened. I meant to delete them, I swear I did. But listen, it's just going to be one of those things, you know? People will talk about it for a few days and then—'

'I can't believe I let you talk me into taking them.'

'You hardly needed much persuading.'

I stare out of the window to the cliffs and the sea. Glassy sinuous waves rolling to shore. 'Are they going into the papers?'

'They're already there. Printed today. Alice called to warn me. I mean – they've pixelated them. You can't see everything.'

'Well, then that's okay then, isn't it? You didn't take any pictures of my face.'

A pause, so slight. An intake of breath.

'Marco, you promised—'

'Listen, after your second drink you were willing to do anything. You said you didn't mind. I mean, I thought you were enjoying it.'

I try to think back. The memory of that night is dense and blurred. How strong were those drinks he was making?

'Fuck,' I say, forgetting myself, forgetting to mind my language. 'Fuck.'

'I thought I ought to tell you before you saw them yourself. Got a nasty surprise.'

'Carmel,' I say flatly.

It was Carmel. It must have been. I can even remember telling her about them. She'd *tsked* and pretended to be shocked but I know Carmel. She's unshakable. I, however, am not, and now I feel a seismic shift inside me, the collapse of everything I thought I knew and trusted. Marco sounds doubtful.

'I don't know, honey. Does she need the money that badly?'

'Paris is expensive.'

'And after your overdose made—'

'It wasn't an overdose; I keep telling you. Why now though? Why wait all this time?'

'I suppose your profile has been raised just enough after your overd— your hospital visit – to make these pictures more profitable. More lurid.'

'What's the headline?'

'Oh, don't. Don't do this to yourself.'

'I want to know.'

I hear a rustling over the line. 'Uh – "*The Honey of Honeypot Lane*". Underneath that it says, "*Katie Mari-Bold Is All Grown Up*".'

'I'm so embarrassed.'

'Don't be. You look beautiful. Scratch that, for a woman your age you look amazing.'

I don't know what to say to that so I say nothing.

Before he hangs up he asks, 'Are you mad at me?'

'I don't know, Marco. I don't know. I need to think.'

I toss the phone onto the floor and bury my head into my pillow and scream and scream.

I don't leave the house that day. I want to cocoon myself indoors. I pull all the blankets from the cupboards and pile them onto the sofa where I sit eating yogurt and watching old reruns of *Friends*. Marco calls and calls. Joey Fraser leaves me three voice messages, and I do not listen to a single one of them.

Frankie turns up, calling through the letterbox. 'I know you're in there,' he shouts. 'I'm not going anywhere.' I think of him waiting outside his truck for a mangy stray dog that would die without his help. 'I'm a persistent bastard,' he'd said. He arrived at ten fifteen and when I look out of the kitchen window a little after one o'clock he is still out there, reading a book, sitting in the garden. Next to him is a small package of sandwiches wrapped in greaseproof paper. I sigh. I can't go on like this. I know that. He looks up when I open the front door.

'Hello.'

'Hi!' He lifts his hand but does not stand up. Instead he goes back to his book.

'What are you reading?'

He lifts the cover to show me. Stephen King. An old one, by the looks of it. Well read.

'Is it good?'

'Yup. Do you like him?'

'I prefer the films.'

I sit next to him on the bench. The old stone is cold.

'You shouldn't hide away. You've nothing to be ashamed of.'

'It hurts.'

Frankie nods.

'It's the betrayal. She was meant to be my best friend. She was meant to be one of the good guys, you know?'

'I know.'

'I mean – what would they pay? A couple of hundred quid? I'm nearly forty. I haven't been on television since 1993. I'm hardly newsworthy. I would have just given her the money. Double the money. I'd have found it somehow. She just needed to ask me.'

Frankie scratches his beard absently.

I look at him askance. 'Have you seen the pictures?'

'I have, yes. Jim Kennecker shoved them under my nose. You made his day.'

'I can't face anyone in this town ever again.'

'You can and you will. Hold your damn head up. You've done nothing wrong. Here.' He is holding something out to me. A bar of chocolate.

'What's this?'

'Happy Halloween.'

I feel myself lean in closer to Frankie and rest my head on his shoulder. He puts his arm around me and squeezes once, briefly.

'Thank you,' I tell him. 'Thank you, Frankie.'

Chapter 21

I sleep most of the afternoon and wake that evening into pitch-darkness, my eyes rolling open like a ventriloquist's dummy. I'm still on the sofa and my bones are cramped. I stretch, wondering what the time is. Blue, who has been sleeping on my legs, has disappeared. The wind presses against the house, causing the rafters to creak and moan like a galleon. I sit upright instantly. I can hear something. Movement. I stand up, listening. There is a scratching sound, like nails against the window. Outside, the bone light of the moon, silver-blue. I hear movement, the soft rustle of clothes, shuffling footsteps. I move forward, trying to peer out of the window but there is just the dark garden and the trees. I stand, waiting. The room is cold and a draught blows about my ankles.

'Blue?' I whisper quietly.

I creep into the kitchen, afraid to turn on the light, afraid to be alone in the dark. The back door stands open, just a little way. There are no footprints this time, just that ghostly cold. I am unable to remember if I'd locked it before I'd fallen onto the sofa but there is a good chance I hadn't, a very good chance. Even though I have not taken the pills for a week I'm still forgetful, my head full of ghosts. I cross the kitchen silently and pick up a knife from the table. It is a sharp one, a boning knife with a twelve-inch blade. I press it to my side and turn to face the stairs, pooled in darkness.

Upstairs then. My heart pulses thickly. It is in my neck, my wrists, the backs of my knees where the skin is tissue-thin. I'm exposed like stripped wire. I sniff. I can smell cologne, something expensive. Something which might be described as smelling like clean water. I tighten my grip on the knife. Overhead, a thud like something being dropped and rolling over the floorboards, a door creaking. I begin to climb the stairs.

There are two things I'm sure of by the time I reach the top. One, it's a man. Two, he's in the bedroom.

Joey Fraser, you bastard.

I am breathing quietly, alert to every sound, every movement. I hear the bedsprings creak and imagine him crawling over it, searching for me, hands spread like ghost-white stars. I pull the knife up and hold it two-handed, rounding the doorway. There is a figure there, in front of the window, his back to me. I do not think he has heard me. I can see he is wearing dark clothes, hood up so his face is obscured. His hands are cupped against the glass as though he is looking for something in the garden. Looking for me, maybe.

I run at him. I am holding the knife out in front of me and just at the last minute he turns, flinging one arm up in front of his face, shouting out, swearing. I bring the knife across in a sweeping arc, and it sinks into his sleeve just below the crook of his arm. As he turns I see his face, contorted with terror.

'Marco?'

A woman is behind me in the doorway, screaming. Her voice rings like a bell, it hurts my ears. Marco is staring at me in disbelief.

'My God, Stella. You've stabbed me.'

We are in the kitchen. I have a bowl of tepid water and a rag and am pressing the wet cloth against the wound in his skin, the one I have made, seven inches long. It is not deep but there is more blood than I expect and when I wring out the rag the water turns a dusky pink. Marco is giving me a plain, hard stare, and I can feel myself shrinking. I apologise again.

Aunt Jackie is making tea at the counter. She is pale with shock. She'd been in the bathroom as I'd crept up the stairs and hadn't seen me until I'd driven the knife into Marco's forearm in the darkness. She wouldn't come near me until Marco had taken the knife from my hand, even when I kept saying, 'I didn't mean it, I didn't mean it.' Even when I clumsily tried to hug her she'd moved backwards a little, out of my reach.

'I just don't get it. What were you thinking?' She puts a cup in front of me.

'I didn't know it was Marco. How could I have done?'

'Who else did you think it would be at this time of night in his own home?'

'I'm sorry. I said I'm sorry. Why didn't you tell me you were coming down?'

He winces and pulls his arm away. 'I tried. You haven't been answering your phone. Please stop doing that.'

I twist the rag in my fingers, worried.

'I let the dog out, Stella,' Jackie says, sipping her tea. 'I can't bear them. Even the smell of them gives me hives.'

'Where did you get that dog from? I jumped out of my skin when I saw it.'

'It's Frankie's dog. I'm looking after it.'

I press the wet cloth to his skin again.

'Can't he look after his own dog? Stella, seriously. Stop.'

'It's just a favour I'm doing him,' I say quietly. I'm shaking myself, a little. Adrenalin, I suppose.

Jackie reaches over the table to Marco and touches his arm. 'Should you get stitches? Do we need to take you to the hospital?'

'I just need a drink. I think we both do. Get my bag for me, will you, Stella?'

I return with his holdall, the black one with the leather straps. He pulls a bottle of wine from the top and looks at me apologetically.

'You don't mind us drinking, do you?'

'No, of course not.' I do, of course. It's a bottle of Cru Beaujolais. It was what he used to bring over to mine on our nights in. We would drink it in bed and watch terrible made-for-TV films. I pour him and Jackie large glasses. Just the smell of it makes my throat ache with longing. She takes it from me with a strange, wary look. I ask if they're hungry and take out some bread and cheese and butter wrapped in parchment paper, as yellow as a spring daffodil. I'm trying to make things nice, make things normal. Jackie asks if I've got any pasta, snapping her gum between her teeth. I tell her I don't.

'Notice you don't have any fresh fruit either.' She points at the empty fruit bowl. 'Amazed you haven't got scurvy.' She circles my wrist with her thumb and forefinger, tutting. 'You've lost weight, not eating properly. Are you sleeping?'

I nod. I squeeze her hand and tell her it's good to see her. She nods back and I notice tears in her eyes.

'I'm so worried about you, Stella. Marco too.'

'Oh, Jackie, no, I'm fine. Please don't worry. I'm coming out the other side now, you'll see.'

She pulls a face which tells me she finds that hard to believe. It's a face which reminds me she just saw me stab my boyfriend in the arm. I think again of that bloodied knife in the sink, and my stomach rolls. I don't remember where it came from. I don't remember seeing it here before.

'I know you've been through a lot, love—' Aunt Jackie begins.

'Look, let me look for a plaster or something. I'm so happy to see you both. I've been feeling so much better recently – I've taught myself how to build a fire, I've been taking walks on the beach. You and Doctor Wilson were right, Marco. I needed the break. I needed the silence.'

'I feel like I've been neglecting you. It must be so lonely down here.' He puts his large hand on my head and turns me so I am facing him. 'Things will be different soon, I promise. I just need to tie up a few loose ends.'

'You haven't caught the sun.'

'What?'

'On the phone, you said it was hot. When you were at the airport.'

'I don't follow you.'

'I thought you'd be tanned.'

'I was indoors most of the time, Stell. It was a business trip. Are you sure you're all right?'

I see the look that passes between him and Jackie and twist the rag so hard my fingers turn white.

'Stella – what have you been doing to yourself?' Aunt Jackie says, pointing at the back of my hand, the one the chicken scratched, my skin there stippled with cuts. I withdraw my hand slowly beneath the table.

'I *am* fine,' I tell them both carefully. 'There's nothing wrong with me. Not anymore.'

'You still sleepwalking?'

Marco has pulled out an old first-aid kit from beneath the sink and is clumsily taping gauze over the wound. I look from him to Jackie, my smile as brittle as frost. I ignore the question.

'You want to know something weird? I found some old *Marigold!* tapes.'

'Oh yeah?'

195

'The strangest thing. There was a pile of them in the woodshed. Can you imagine?'

'The day we first arrived here, do you remember what I told you?' Marco asks me. 'This is my parents' holiday home. We've been coming here for Easter and Whitsun holidays since I was ten years old. I've no doubt they held on to everything. I was thirteen when *Marigold!* came out. They recorded every episode for me. They also recorded every episode of the *Antiques Roadshow* and you'll probably find those tapes in there too. They never threw anything away.'

I think of the old records slipping to the floor and nod. Jackie is looking at me over the rim of her glass.

'Marco thought it would be nice for us all to be together,' she says. 'Maybe we can talk about the wedding?'

'Of course. I'd love that.'

Marco smiles at me. Then he says, 'I know how hurt you must be about those pictures in the paper. For the record, I'm furious.'

'He wants to sue,' Jackie says, not without a small thrill of excitement.

'Sue who? Carmel? She doesn't have anything. Besides, you can't sue her.'

'Why not?'

'Because—' *She's my friend*, I want to say, but somehow the words get lost.

'Oh, I meant to tell you – Doctor Wilson gave me two more bottles of your pills. They're in the bag.'

And my heart lifts. No, it soars. Thank God. More pills, more numbness, more lovely, lovely, oblivion. I give him a genuine smile, rich and warm. I am saved.

'Can I have them now?'

He laughs and finishes his drink.

'Sure.'

I seek them out, careful not to look too keen, too greedy. My chest and heart hurt with the longing for them. It is a physical pain, a needle in the chest. I wonder if this is how my dad felt as he heard the thundering hoof beats, the roar of victory. I no longer care. I lovingly cradle the bottle as I walk to the bathroom and tip two pills into my hand. I am greedy for them. Just as I am about to take them I think of Frankie taking off his wedding ring, the way the exposed skin had been pale against his summer tan. A white circle about his finger, a ghost band. Like wedding rings encased in ice, slipping from fingers. That image, it stays with me past eleven, past half past, my back pressed against the wall and the pills in my hand.

Marco knocks on the door. 'Are you all right in there?' I tell him fine, and still I don't move. I stare at the wall and I think of Carmel at four fifteen on a Sunday morning sitting by my bed in A&E. The way her face had been gaunt and haunted, asking me, 'Do you *want* to die, Stella?' I wonder what she would say to me if she saw me now.

I tip the pills carefully back into the bottle and put the bottle into the drawer. Not tonight. I lie back on the bed with my hands folded over my chest. I think I will never sleep but suddenly I'm gone, and I don't wake up until morning when I notice two things. The sunlight is thick and golden and Marco is not beside me.

I find him downstairs on the couch, beneath one of the blankets kept for storage in the airing cupboard. His arm is folded outside the cover and there is that white bandage wrapped round it, spotted slightly with blood. I shake him awake and he looks at me groggily. Down here it smells of red wine and cigarettes, the butts crushed out into a cereal bowl. I shake him gently awake.

'What are you doing down here?'

'I thought it would be best,' he says shortly, his eyes still closed. 'I got a knife in the arm last night, Stella, in case you'd forgotten.'

I kiss his forehead. 'I'm so sorry, baby.'

'I need you to be well, Stella. I need you to show Jackie that you can manage, so she stops worrying about you. All of this – it's hard for me too, Stella. It really is. You're not the only one suffering.'

'It would help if you were here more.'

'I'm working on it. You want to get in with me?'

He lifts the covers and I consider it, just for a second. Then an idea comes to me, as simple and sudden as an exclamation mark. 'Actually I was going to go into town and get breakfast for us all.'

I kiss him gently on the temple, sweeping his hair away from his face to do so. He murmurs 'You're so good to me', but already his eyes are closing and he is turning over.

As I stand I reach out and grab his phone from the table, quickly carrying it into the kitchen. I'm expecting it to be locked, but as I slide my finger across, it opens easily. I go straight to the phone book without hesitating, staring at the doorway to the front room as I do so, expecting any minute for Marco to walk through asking me what the hell I think I'm doing. I find the number on the second attempt (nothing under caretaker, so I looked under 'Kennecker') and write it on a tiny scrap of paper, which I fold and fold to the size of a postage stamp and tuck into my bra.

Chapter 22

I walk down to Tyrlaze, the sun warm and soft in the morning light. It is too early yet to call Mr Kennecker, but I have resolved to do so later today, and that buoys me a little. I am Taking Action. I am Normal. Overhead, a cornflower-blue sky laced with white clouds. I stop to take a picture of it and only as I am about to walk on do I realise where I am. I'm outside the chicken house, the one which looks as though it is about to collapse any minute. The woman, Penelope, is outside in the yard, watching me. She is wearing pearls and a red lace shawl and wellies thick with mud. She does not smile.

'That of interest, is it? The sky?'

'I think it looks beautiful.'

'It'll rain later. That's a mackerel sky. Ask any fisherman, he'll tell you.'

She reaches into the bucket, throwing grain for the chickens pecking about her feet.

We are silent for a moment. She is scrutinising me.

'Saw you in the paper. Saw all of you, in fact. You didn't look bad, you know. Hell, I'd have done the same at your age if the right man had asked me.' She smiles slightly, drawing back her lips to reveal uneven, yellowing teeth. 'Saw Marco arrived yesterday. Won't be long now.'

Before I can ask her what she means she takes a step towards me, the bucket swinging at her hip. I back away a little, afraid.

'He told you yet? About Ellie?'

I shake my head. 'Who?' I hear myself say. She laughs, dry and nasty, and turns away, walking back into the house.

When I get back to the cottage Jackie is walking in the garden with her hair wet, her phone lifted up towards the sky. She frowns at me as I walk past.

'Can't get a signal. I've only gone and brought Darren's statins with me and left mine at home. His cholesterol will be through the roof by Sunday.'

She looks me up and down kindly and draws me to her in a bony hug I find surprisingly comforting.

'Oh, darling. You've always been such a good girl. Your daddy used to say you were the apple of his pie. Do you remember how he always got it wrong?'

I nod.

'He was so proud of you as Katie Marigold. He used to watch them all the time, although he never admitted it. Pretended it was junk.'

I nod. I remember that too. 'Load of old rubbish,' he'd say, 'I don't know why you put her through it, Marion.' My mother, Marion, with her slantways smile, had only nodded and rubbed her fingers together – money – replying: 'This is her university fund. Someone has to help her out, and we can't rely on you.'

Of course by the time I'd got to university most of it had gone. The dogs and the horses and the slow spin of the fruit machines. My dad, with that line furrowed between his eyebrows.

Jackie follows me into the kitchen. I'd been to the deli and picked up fresh bread, bacon and freshly ground coffee. Jackie is still talking.

'Marco suggested we go out for dinner tonight. We need to properly celebrate your engagement, for one thing. He's done so much for you, been an absolute angel. And you need some food, you're wasting away.'

'I can't, Jackie. Those pictures that got put in the paper. I'm so embarrassed.'

'Nonsense. "Woman takes off clothes" is hardly news, is it? It's your friend who should be embarrassed, the one who sold you out like that. She should hang her head in shame.'

'Thank you, Jackie.'

'It's only a meal in town, love.'

'For everything, I mean. Thank you for everything.'

I have to turn away from her because I am so close to tears, and I don't want her to see me crying. I'm normal, remember? I need to act normal.

Inside, the knife has been washed and cleaned and put away, somewhere where I don't have to look at it anymore. Marco is on his phone, reading the news.

'I need you to look at these damp patches,' I tell him, taking the milk out of the fridge. Marco doesn't look up at me.

'What are you talking about?'

'In the hallway. You can't miss them. They're as big as I am.'

'I haven't noticed.'

'Are you kidding?'

Now he looks up, blinking slowly. Shakes his head. I feel a throb of anxiety.

'Marco, come and see. Put your phone down, come on!'

We walk through, and I look at the wall and back to Marco again. He is watching me levelly.

'It was here. Frankie saw it too.'

'It must have been a shadow, honey.'

He comes closer, placing the flat of his hands on the wall.

'It's cold, but not wet. Feel.'

I do, reluctantly. He's right, of course. Cold but not wet. There is no musty smell of damp, no crumbling plaster. Even the spots about the doorframe which had appeared on my second night seem to have gone. I take him into the bedroom, but the walls are plain, unblemished. The lace curtain moves a little in the breeze.

'I swear, Marco, I swear I'm not making this up.'

'No one thinks you are, honey.' He steps closer to me and touches my lips with his thumb. He speaks to me so quietly I am forced to lean in so I can hear what he says.

'Do you know what happens when you're under a lot of pressure? Something cracks. Inside you. Something cracks and sometimes what comes out is black and frightening and thick as molasses. But we're fixing that, aren't we?'

I think for a moment. Jackie is in the doorway, peering around the room with her blue doll's eyes.

'I think someone's been coming in here when I haven't been around,' I tell them after an uncomfortable silence. He looks up at me.

Jackie pulls a face. 'I had that with a plumber once. Going through my knickers and my personals while I wasn't in the house. We only found out when he'd left. He took all my Marks and Spencers but left the Ann Summers. Darren said it proves he was a pervert.'

'Who?' Marco asks.

'What?'

'Who is coming in here when you're not around?'

'I don't know. I mean, I thought it was Frankie at first—'

'I thought you liked him.'

'I trusted him. I do, I do like him. I don't know.'

Marco laughs a good, solid laugh. I'm feeling stupid now, in the bright morning sunlight. I'm tired and headachy. My whole body throbs, my jaw tight.

'Honey, I can't accuse him without proof.'

'Things have been—'

'Things have been what?'

'Moved around,' I finish lamely, and even as I say it I feel ridiculous.

'Well,' Jackie says brightly, 'maybe we can dust for fingerprints?'

'Or, or it could be Joey Fraser. I know he's in Cornwall. What about the other caretaker—'

'Mr Kennecker? Come on, Stella, he's nearly eighty.'

'You know I met him. His story about the hospital doesn't match with what Frankie told us.'

'You're paranoid,' I hear Marco say. I catch him right at that moment, tapping his finger against his temple and looking over at Jackie. Suddenly I am angry – furious, in fact. The way they're both talking to me: softly, softly, like I am cracked bone china recently glued together. Frankie is the same, and even Heidi, the careful way she'd looked at me.

'Come with me,' I snap, and lead them to the sitting room, striding with a purpose I haven't felt in weeks. I hand Marco the note and the photograph and watch him carefully for signs of recognition – a flare in the eyes or a breath quickly drawn. There is nothing. He looks at the picture blandly, almost without interest, turning it over in his hands before handing it to Jackie.

'I don't know what to say, babes. I don't know who this is, and I don't recognise the writing. It's creepy though.'

Jackie actually performs a double take when she sees the poor woman in the photo, the swelling around her eyes, the dark and painful smudges on her skin.

'It's uncanny,' she says, holding it up next to my face. 'Marco, we have to call the police.'

Marco sighs. 'I'll talk to Frankie this afternoon. Maybe we can get some extra security up here – cameras or something.'

Jackie is nodding so violently it seems as though her head might fall off. 'You know, I read about a family that discovered a man secretly living in their loft! He'd been there seven months before they found him! They caught him on security camera.'

'Don't give her ideas,' Marco says, rolling his eyes.

They're doing it again, talking about me as though I'm a baby. I slam my hand down so hard on the table that the cups rattle. Their heads snap up, eyes widen. Marco steps away from me, creating distance. He's probably remembering the scratches I'd left on him, the imprints of my teeth on his skin. Am I dangerous? *Where's your muzzle, Katie Marigold?* I'm suddenly frightened all over again.

Chapter 23

I escape upstairs and sit on the bed, arms folded, heart racing. Without the medication I feel plugged in, mobile. Every so often I get up and cross the room to the window, peering out of the curtains at the grey skies, the sea. Through the window I see Marco in the garden smoking a cigarette. I take the folded piece of paper from my bra and dial it into my phone quickly, before I lose my nerve. It is a landline. Kennecker's phone rings only twice before it is picked up.

'Hullo?'

'Mr Kennecker, it's Stella. We met the other day an—'

There is a click as he hangs up. I call back again, and there is no answer. I am sweating lightly, and when I see Marco coming back to the house, I get into bed and pull the covers up over my head, heart racing.

Marco comes into the bedroom about ten minutes later, and I pretend to be sleeping. I remain under the covers, keeping my eyes closed, my breathing steady. After a while I hear the front door close, Marco whistling for Blue and Jackie's heels on the path. Finally, there is the sound of Sadie's catlike engine as the car pulls away. Suddenly I am on my feet, running to the door and down the stairs, only knowing that I have to move. I have to be fast, and be home before Marco. I pull on my coat and trainers and tuck a scarf about my neck. Outside the day is chill, gloomy with the threat of rain. I start at a run down the narrow track, feeling weightless, only half knowing what I'm doing, half thinking. I need to be fast but more importantly, I need to be sure.

Once in town it takes me some time to find the little mews and even longer to work up the courage to knock on Jim Kennecker's door. I am sweating. My legs tingle with exertion. There are sprays of mud up my calves and thighs. I knock and then knock again, impatient. My heart is thumping and I'm starting to wonder what the hell I'm doing. Suddenly the door is yanked open so hard it showers dust. I plant my hand on it to prevent him slamming it closed again.

'Mr Kennecker, please don't – don't close the door. My name is Stella Wiseman and I need to know why you lied about being in hospital.'

Jim Kennecker blinks but at least he doesn't look as he did the other day, morbidly afraid. I refuse to drop my eyes and so after a moment he opens the door wider and nods for me to come inside.

The workshop smells of sawdust, cedar and beeswax polish and it is immensely comforting. There is no warmth in his voice as he offers me a cup of tea which I turn down, and a seat which I accept. I tell him I do not have much time.

'You gave me a fright the other day when I saw you.'

'I know that. What I don't know is why.'

'Is Marco up there too? At the cottage?'

'For the weekend. He's working in London in the week, at least for the next few weeks.'

'But you been on your own, haven't you?'

I nod.

'You notice anything up there, Stella? Anything odd or out of place?'

I swallow. I could tell him. I could tell him about the taps and the pools of dark water and the feeling that someone is following me from room to room, right on my heels, cold breath on my neck.

Jim Kennecker leans on his knuckles and looks me in the eye.

'There's a ghost in my house,' I whisper.

He nods. 'I won't go up there no more. I'm done with it. It's a bad place and bad things happened there.'

'Is that why you lied?'

'I don't want to get blood on my hands.'

I open my mouth when I hear the crunch of tyres outside, and I think of Marco pulling up in his gleaming car. He is coming, I think, panicky, with his strong white teeth and long fingers he is coming. I have a sudden olfactory memory of cigar smoke and cooked pork, strong enough to make me double over. I tell Jim Kennecker I have to go.

The door opens. Frankie is standing there in his fur hat looking like a frontiersman, Blue by his side. He looks from me to Jim with genuine surprise.

'Frankie,' Jim says, straightening. 'All right?'

'Not really.' Frankie is looking at me, his brows drawn. He looks puzzled. 'Your fiancé just fired me.'

Chapter 24

The dark is creeping in as the weather gets colder. By four o'clock I can barely see the edges of the cliff or the apple trees at the end of the garden. I take a shower and dry my hair with my fingers, letting the extensions fall apart like cobwebs. My roots are showing through, dark as coffee. There are freckles on my skin, the imprints of summer.

When I come downstairs I find Jackie and Marco in the sitting room watching *Marigold!*; Jackie is soft-eyed, doughy-faced with emotion. Marco has his hands planted on his knees, showing occasional flashes of teeth. I sit on the arm of the sofa and he looks up at me, his eyes soft and glittering. I recognise the episode immediately. It is one of the later ones: 'Katie Marigold, Best in Show!', in which I enter Frisky in a dog competition in order to win the prize money to pay off Daddy Marigold's parking fine. Hilarity ensues.

'Katie Marigold, this show is for pedigree dogs only. What breed is your dog?'

'Sir, I don't know what that means.'

'What kind of dog is he?'

'A bloody hound, sir.'

'Do you mean bloodhound, Katie Marigold?'

'No, sir! My daddy calls him a bloody hound, sir, 'specially when he's mad.'

Audience laughter.

It has me cold. I am remembering again, in that tiny room (a caravan, a trailer), me and Joey Fraser, then thirteen years old. He was holding something away from me, out of my reach, and I was screaming and screaming.

'You're in trouble now, Joey,' I was shouting, and his face was pale as milk. 'You're in big trouble.'

My skin had been burning, hot. Had he hurt me? He must have done. Where was my mother? Why had no one come to help me?

I shiver. Marco squeezes my leg.

'You look beautiful,' he tells me. But he isn't looking at me. He's looking at the screen.

◆　◆　◆

The wind is rising, bringing with it a fine rain which laces everything with glitter. Overhead the moon is ringed with frost as I link my arm through Marco's, and we walk towards the pub. I enjoy the bulk of him, his weight against me. With Jackie a little way ahead of us, he pulls me beneath a streetlight and kisses my cold lips. I lift my head as his hands move around to the back of my neck where the fine tendrils of hair are coiled. I flinch only a little as he brushes against a tender spot there, moving the tips of his fingers with exaggerated slowness over my shoulders until he finally pulls away.

'Come on,' he says quietly, 'I'll hold your hand.'

It is busy in the Star Inn and other than a few curious heads turning towards us as we enter my presence creates little fuss. Perhaps not everyone saw the papers, I tell myself, or maybe they simply don't care.

'Let me get the drinks,' Jackie says, and disappears towards the bar. Marco and I find a table and he pulls my chair out for me. He nods approvingly as I sit down.

'I'm glad you wore that dress,' he says.

I look down at myself. It's one he'd bought me back when we'd first got together: rich navy-blue, long-sleeved, fine-knit. It's modest. Carmel used to call it my Amish dress. (That pain again when I think of her, like a slingshot.) It had been lying on the bed waiting for me when I'd come out of the shower.

'Did you bring it with you from my flat?'

'Not your flat, not anymore. No point paying rent when you're not living there. I've packed up your stuff and taken it to mine. Most of it you won't really need.'

'What do you mean?' I ask as Jackie hands me a drink – apple juice and ice, a little bent straw. 'I don't want you throwing anything away. That's mine. It belongs to me.'

'Food looks nice,' Jackie says brightly, handing us both menus. 'You don't want to hang on to that old stuff, love. This is a fresh start for you.'

'But I thought—'

'We should have a toast,' Marco says, sliding his hand over mine, pressing it onto the table. 'To new beginnings.'

They lift their glasses and look at me expectantly. I raise my own and smile, thinking: *What is happening here?*

'You fired Frankie,' I say as I open the menu.

Marco nods, adjusting his tie.

'You were right to,' Jackie says, eyes gleaming. She is already halfway through her wine. 'If he's lying about one thing who's to say he's not lying about everything?'

I stare at my drink, amber-coloured, frosted with condensation.

'What if it wasn't him?' I say suddenly. I feel Marco stiffen in his seat.

'But you said—'

'I need to talk to you about Joey Fraser.'

'What about him?'

'He's been coming to the café. Asking about me. Calling me at the house. He wants to do a *Marigold!* reunion.'

Marco is turning his glass by the base. He fixes me with a stare. 'How much is he offering you?'

'It's not the money—'

'Yes, but how much?'

'He said he'd been offered twenty thousand.'

Marco whistles. Jackie looks shocked and sits back in her seat. 'I hope you've said yes.'

'Well, no, I—'

Jackie and Marco share a look as though they've made a bet. *Tenner says she's lost her mind. Twenty says she'll be institutionalised before December.* I take a sip of my apple juice, so cold it hurts my teeth.

Marco takes my hand, squeezing it. 'You should rethink. It's money for nothing, honey.'

'I don't want to see him again. He was a horrible kid, and he's turned into a horrible man. Did you know he told me my mother was the reason for all the cast changes, all my lines? He's still bitter twenty years later. He's pathetic.'

Jackie looks down into her drink. She doesn't lift her head when she next speaks.

'Your father put up with a lot from your mother, Stella. We used to wonder who your career was really for.'

'What?' I snap.

Marco is moving his hand beneath the table, creeping up my thigh towards the warmth of me. He squeezes painfully and I gasp, eyes wide. He leans back in his chair.

'Listen, Stella. Jackie and I have been talking . . .' They exchange a glance full of conspiracy and I feel my pulse quickening. I try to smile.

'We both think you're going to need a little more time.'

'Time for what?'

'To work on yourself, love,' Jackie says, stretching over the table to put her hand over mine. *Ugh*, I think. She says stuff like this all the time, since she married the tennis coach. 'Chase Happiness', 'Be Your Own Guru'. There is a sticker on her car that says 'The only "BS" I need is Bags and Shoes'.

'I don't want to work on myself, Jackie. I want to go back to London.'

'What would you do there, sweetie?'

'Well,' I say, suddenly enthused, 'I've been looking at interning in a gallery for a while, just to find my feet. And Marco, your PA, Alice? She knows a lot about art, she might have some contacts she can—'

I see their faces. First one then the other. The good humour, falling away like ice melting. Beneath it a stone-cold impasse.

Jackie's eyes switch to Marco behind me. When she talks it's as if I'm not there.

'I thought you said she understood?'

'I thought she did,' he says quietly, before turning in his seat to face me. 'Stella, do you remember what Doctor Wilson said?'

I look at them both, their wide-open eyes as smooth as pebbles.

'You had a breakdown, Stella. That's why you're here.'

'But I'm better now!'

'Honey. Honey, no, just listen to me. Last night you stabbed me in the arm.'

'I didn't know it was you!'

'Okay then – what about this person that you say has been coming into the house? Have you seen them? Have they taken anything? Do you remember what you did to Carmel? To me?'

'Marco—'

'I can't—' He looks pleadingly at Jackie, rubbing the side of his head. 'I thought you understood. There's nothing for you in London anymore. Except pain. Regret.'

'What Marco's offering you, Stella, is a rent-free house in a beautiful part of the country. Have you any idea how much properties cost down here? And you could go to St Ives or Newlyn if you want galleries so much.'

The way she says it is so dismissive it hurts me.

'But I don't want to live down here. I don't want to live in that cottage. It isn't mine.'

'But it will be when you're married,' Jackie says, smiling. 'And then you never have to leave.'

I stand up. I can't listen to any more of this.

Jackie nods drunkenly, as though this is what she expects. 'There you go, running off. It's your answer to everything, isn't it? Just like your mother.'

Outside, black clouds scud overhead like the sails of a doomed boat. I stand in the darkness blinking back tears. God. I pull Marco's cigarettes from my pocket and light one. I'd swiped them from the table while Jackie had been talking, my chest suddenly aching for nicotine. That kick to the back of the throat is still as sweet as it was when I was fifteen. I hear the door of the pub open, and I don't look up. Hear the noise spilling out, the warm amber light on the pavement. Still I don't look up. The heavy tread of footsteps in the mist. A shape, a figure approaching. I don't look up because I don't need to. I know who it is.

'I didn't know you smoked.'

'I don't.'

'Ah,' Frankie says. There is the click of a lighter and a long, slow exhalation.

'I didn't know *you* smoked.'

'I smoke when I drink and when I have sex. So I'm a – heh – I'm a forty-a-day man.'

I smile weakly.

'I didn't see you in there.'

'I was at the bar. I saw you. I saw Marco.'

'You don't like him, do you?' I say.

Another inhale.

'Nope.'

He continues to look flatly at me, one hand stroking his beard thoughtfully. I realise he is drunk, just a little. He has reached what I think of as the tipping point. I drag sharply on my cigarette.

'Why did you lie about Mr Kennecker, Frankie? That's why you lost your job, not because of Marco. Don't blame him.'

'Mr Kennecker didn't want to do that job because Mr Kennecker doesn't want to work at that house any more. Mr Kennecker doesn't want to work for your boyfriend – sorry, sorry, fiancé – anymore. He's afraid of him.'

'It's still a lie. You could have told me the truth. I thought we were friends.'

'Yup. I lied because I'm an asshole. But unlike Marco, I don't try to hide it. I don't make people do things they don't want to do.'

I blink at him. I am getting angry.

'Do you mean me? You know nothing about me and what I want to do.'

'No, I don't. But I've got him pretty square though, haven't I? So my question remains. Why do you stand for it, Stella?'

He is standing in front of me now, arms folded.

'You're drunk.'

'Ah, come on. I just told you I was an asshole, what did you expect? For what it's worth I'm sorry I lost my job too. Mostly I'm sorry we won't get to hang out anymore.'

I blink back sudden, frustrated tears.

He throws his cigarette away in a shower of amber sparks, walking back into the pub. Before he reaches the door he turns back to me.

'I've been digging on your fiancé, Stella. It isn't nice. He's going to sink you like a stone.'

Chapter 25

It is the dead of night, and I am awake. My sleep recently has been like tumbling down stairs; fits and jolts and breathlessness. When I wake up I don't know where I am. Marco is asleep beside me, his breathing steady. I swing my legs out of bed and creep across the room. I do not want him to wake up. I have to see it again.

Downstairs in the darkness I turn on the computer. Alice had emailed me earlier, a brief, concise message – *Hope this is what you are looking for* – with the picture attached.

I open up the first image, full-screen. My ears are pricked up, listening, alert to Marco stirring or Jackie creeping down the stairs.

The photo is the one I'd seen on the slideshow that day in the office, a day that feels like a thousand years ago. It shows Marco, tanned and handsome, standing in front of a fountain, his arms around a woman. He is smiling, his hair slightly longer than I recognise and a few days' worth of stubble built up on his jaw. It doesn't look too old although it's hard to place his age. Maybe five, six years ago.

The woman is only half in the picture, as though she had turned away at the last moment to look over her shoulder. Her profile is visible though, and her slim shoulders. I check the darkened stairwell but the night is very still and quiet.

I hold the photograph of the beaten woman up next to the screen. Alongside each other the comparison is clear. It's her. I'm sure of it. I can just make out Marco's hand around her tiny waist. I swallow, massaging my throat. The second message arrived tonight while we were at the pub. Another photo, one I haven't seen before. There is a little postscript from Alice: *P.S Thought this one would interest you too.*

The photo is definitely older. Marco I recognise right away. Even in school uniform with his dated Flock of Seagulls haircut and the slightly oversized blazer. He looks exactly as I would have pictured him. Cocky. Knowing. That smirk which lifted just one corner of his mouth. Next to him is another boy about the same age, same navy uniform, a straw boater tipped back on his head. It's the smile that gets me, the lifted, defiant chin. It's Doctor Wilson.

I'm frowning in the glow of the screen. *They went to school together?* That means they've known each other – I'm working it out on my fingers – over thirty years. Why hadn't he told me? I am seized with the idea of going upstairs and shaking him awake, demanding to know why he kept this information from me, but I am gripped by a horrible certainty that his answer will be: 'I *did* tell you, Stella. Don't you remember?'

And weirdly then it isn't Marco I think of, it's Frankie. I remember the night we had dinner and talked and talked and how happy I had been – how substantial I had felt, how real – and then I remember how he'd lied about Jim Kennecker, the nasty way he'd talked to me outside the pub – and my heart sinks.

A sound then in the kitchen. Through the dark doorway behind me, a low scratching as though of claws on wood.

Mice, I think. No. Too big for mice. Rats then. I listen as I hear it again, a scratching, louder this time, and closer. I slowly walk across the kitchen.

Now there is a clicking sound, and I think immediately (and horribly) of bones knitting together. When I reach the pantry on the far side of the kitchen it stops. I put my ear to the closed door. The pantry is a windowless, narrow room in perpetual shadow. Frankie had told me with naked admiration that it was probably 'the oldest, most authentic thing about this building'. I had gone in there once and been struck by the dank chill, sour and ancient, the stone walls clammy to the touch. I had not gone back in there again. I stand there awhile, but there is no further sound, so I cross to the sink and pour a glass of water. When I glance back I see the pantry door is standing open.

I am acutely aware of the feeling in the room, a buzz like electricity, enough to lift the hairs on my arms. The pantry has a heavy oak door, the handle blackened with age. It has swung inwards about nine inches, exposing a thick slice of darkness.

I feel a horrible certainty that something is moving in there. Something is inside, looking out. There is a flash of movement and what appears to be the impression of a face peering out from the darkness. Pale and translucent like a jellyfish. In my chest something cold shifts, like ice falling from an Arctic shelf. Slowly, I put down my glass. I can hear more scuffling and have a horrifying mental image of a shrouded figure, stooped with decay, long, horny toenails yellowed with age. As I approach I feel the draught coming through the gap in the doorway. It is cold and smells stagnant. There is something moving in the darkness, just behind the door. Then, unmistakably, a wet sigh, like someone at the end of a long pneumonic illness. From within the pantry a dripping noise, a burst pipe leaking, a sound like pattering rain. I reach out a hand and grip the door handle. As I do so there is a whisper from inside, so close to me that I gasp and grip the handle with both hands.

'Pay Attention!'

I find my strength and pull hard at the door. An inch or so before it closes I meet with some resistance, as though it is being pulled open from the other side. I groan and redouble my efforts, arms trembling with the strain. I tilt my head back and shriek for help. Suddenly the door slams shut. I back away, expecting at any moment to see the handle begin to jitter and tremble as bloodless fingers manipulate it from that dark, airless space. The door shudders in the frame, just once, and I watch and I wait. My fingers are in my hair, and I am sweating. Behind me, a clatter on the stairs as Jackie comes at a run. Marco's voice down the hallway asking what time is it, what's the problem?

'Stella, love, are you all right?' Jackie has a glass of water. She presses it into my trembling hands.

'There's something in there. In the pantry. I heard it moving around.'

'An animal?'

'Too big. Oh God, it was horrible. Can't you smell it?'

She sniffs and glances over my shoulder as Marco comes into the kitchen in his old T-shirt and boxers, rubbing his arms.

'It's cold in here. What's going on?'

'Stella thinks there's someone in there.' She points at the closed door.

I stare at Marco with big, round eyes. 'I heard it breathing.'

They exchange another of those looks.

'I did!'

'Okay, honey, we believe you. You want me to check?'

'Yes. No. I don't know.'

Marco approaches the door and presses his palms against it. I am holding my breath, expecting at any moment to see the handles start to move, the door shaking in the frame. When nothing happens Marco pushes the latch, and it swings inwards, revealing that thick darkness.

'Careful!' I call out. I am remembering the way the smell had bloomed from in there. Marco steps inside and for a moment it is silent. When he reappears he looks puzzled, wiping his hands on his T-shirt.

'It's damp, and cold. But it's empty, kitten. Come and see.'

At first I don't move, but then I feel Jackie's palm in the small of my back urging me forward. I step up to the door and look inside, careful not to cross the threshold. The smell has disappeared, the darkness a grainy grey instead of the smothering black I'd seen. There is nothing in there.

Marco takes my arms and says, 'Maybe you were dreaming.'

His eyes drift over my shoulder towards the sitting room. I have left the computer on.

'Stella?' he is saying, moving away from me, looking at the screen. 'Stella, what have you been doing? It's the middle of the night.'

Horrified, I slowly turn, wondering how I will explain the photograph of him and Doctor Wilson which Alice has sent me, how I can make it look like anything other than a betrayal. But it is just the screensaver, the starfield as though you are flying through space. Marco crosses the room and stands before it, his hands on his hips. If he presses just one button he will see the emails from Alice and the photo of him and Doctor Wilson as teenagers. I swallow, my throat very dry.

'Marco,' I say, and he turns, his two fingers poised over the keypad. 'Can we just – let's go to bed, yeah?'

I am willing him to not move, to not hit the keyboard. I have to try very hard to keep the pleading note out of my voice. There is so much gravity to Marco, I can't stop looking at him. He draws you in, like a black hole. And what was it they said about black holes? Not even light escapes.

'I wonder, Stella—'

He looks at me, head tilted as though listening to a faraway sound. *What the hell is this?* is what he'd say as the photo appeared, him as a boy. *What have you been doing?*

'Please.' I hold my hands out to him. His face is concealed in the shadows, my man. My good man. Then he moves his hand and very slowly, without taking his eyes from mine, closes the lid of the laptop.

Chapter 26

The damp has come back. It appears the same day Marco and Jackie leave to go back to London. Some of the black spots are migrating, appearing around the window frames. They speckle the skirting boards and the grouting about the bathtub, stain the corner of the bedroom in a shape like a horned beast, a Minotaur. I press my hands to it and they come away chalky with plaster.

The miserable weather of the last few days has given way to a mellow morning of butter-coloured sunshine. On the kitchen table in the fruit bowl there is a satsuma slowly turning green with putrid, sunken flesh. No food in the fridge. I *have* to go to town.

As I cross the beach car park I see Frankie. Immediately I remember the sting of our argument, as intimate as a secret kiss. He waves and I lift my hand in response but do not smile. Halfway up the hill I hear him calling to me and I turn to see him barefoot in a wetsuit.

'Can I give you a lift anywhere?'

'It's fine. It's a nice day. I'll walk.'

'Stella, listen. I owe you an apology for being a drunk asshole. I shouldn't have said the things I did. It was nice to be your friend.'

We look at each other and I can see him itching to smile. I swallow. I need the company, God knows. I miss having a friend too.

'Sure, okay. A lift would be nice. Thank you.'

At his van he peels the wetsuit away from his damp skin and I can't help but look at him. He isn't as out of shape as I'd suspected. I am so familiar with the lean and hungry body of Marco, with his personal trainer and high-protein diet, crunches and pull-ups, that I can't help but look at Frankie with his rounded stomach, the line of hair bisecting it a curved black feather. His arms are roped with muscles and his chest broad. I notice another tattoo on his pectoral muscle and when he sees me looking he touches it briefly with his fingers. A series of three fat black lines stacked atop one another. The simplicity appeals to me and I tell him so. Frankie nods.

'I like it too. I forget what it means now but at the time you can be sure that there was some deep philosophical junk I'd attached to it. At that age everything is heartbreaking. One thing I'll teach my kids is that you grow out of it. You always grow out of it. Love? You grow out of it. Grief? You grow out of it. Heartbreak? Scandal? Your first pair of shoes? You grow out of it, baby.'

'Do you want kids?'

Frankie shrugs, pulling a towel around his middle and removing his shorts, sitting down on the floor of the van. Uncomfortably aware of the thin towel concealing his nakedness, I turn away from him, very deliberately.

'I don't know. Depends what mood you catch me in. Some days I'll tell you that it's a cruel world and overpopulated and other times I'll tell you that I can't imagine not being a father. I thought I would know by now, but I'm still waiting to see. Do you?'

'Want children?' I shake my head. 'No. I'll never be rich enough or free enough or well-travelled enough. That perfect time doesn't exist, at least not for me.'

'Not for you right now,' he corrects me. 'You and Marco are still young, and he makes good money. Your position could be a lot worse.'

I blink. I hadn't even been thinking about Marco. I turn to face Frankie but he isn't looking at me, he is standing and buttoning his jeans.

'Anyway,' he continues, throwing his towel into the back of the van. 'Let's get going.'

◆ ◆ ◆

We drive in silence, Blue panting noisily in the back. The light casts long shadows across the curve of the valley, through the atrophied trees, branches swept eastward by the winds. Here and there granite boulders thrust up through the ground like the exposed bones of the old land, and buzzards and gulls float on warm updrafts. Finally, we turn into the lane which leads to Chy an Mor. I am thinking of the way the contents of the cupboard had been piled on the floor, the way the voice had spoken to me from the darkness. I think of Heidi saying that the chemicals released when you fall in love are close cousins to those responsible for mental illness.

Frankie switches off the engine. He is looking at me curiously, arms crossed over the steering wheel.

'What was it?'

'Hmmm?' he says. His eyes are narrow, smiling.

'You said you found something out about Marco. What was it?'

He sighs. 'When I first came to Tyrlaze, I didn't know who Marco Nilsen was. I didn't know about this house. I didn't know anything. I took this job on because the money was good. I did it as favour to Jim Kennecker but anytime I mentioned it to anyone it got the same reaction. Can you guess what it was?'

I shake my head.

'You don't see it? Didn't notice when he walked into the pub last night? How people look at him or try to get out of his way?'

'No.' But then again I hadn't been paying attention, had I?

224

'People are scared of Marco. The ones who live here in this town, especially the ones with long memories. Not one of them will say why. That's the kind of fear it is, the kind which shuts you up. Remember what Jim Kennecker told me when I took the job?'

I do. '"Keep her warm and keep her safe."'

'Uh-huh.'

'But that's just gossip,' I say, folding my arms. 'It's the way all small towns are. And he's not like them, is he? He's—'

I hesitate. What is he? There is a word on the tip of my tongue and I don't like it. *Cruel.*

'Do I need to be worried about you, Stella?'

Of course I'm going to tell him that it is all fine. I will tell him that everything's just peachy, thank you, just dandy. So what comes out surprises me more than Frankie.

'There are two possibilities and each one scares me. The first is that I'm losing my mind.'

'What's the other?'

'The other is that this house is haunted.'

We both look towards the house, so like a witch's cottage in a fairy tale, one of the cold ones, the Brothers Grimm, in which the children are tricked and eaten. In the half-light we peer at the cracked and flaking paintwork, the slightly tilted aspect it has, the tarnished brass knocker in the shape of a fox. In the silence I tell him about the footsteps and the noises in the night which sound so much like weary sighs. I mention the smell that lingers in some of the rooms after dark, seeming to draw in like an ancient rising tide.

Frankie listens stoically. When I finish he cracks his knuckles.

'Are you taking your medication?'

'I poured it away, into the toilet. Sleepwalking. I'm aware of how all this sounds, by the way. You don't need to look at me like that.'

'How am I looking at you?'

225

'I believe the word is "sceptical".'

Frankie sighs, running his fingers over the cracked leather of the steering wheel. He dips his head momentarily, letting the dark mess of his hair fall over his face.

'When my wife died I went into shock. I felt nothing for a long time. The last time I saw her she was standing in the kitchen, telling me how I'd made the pancakes wrong. She was laughing, framed in sunlight. That's how I remember her, like an Egyptian goddess. She had a way of teasing me which made her eyes gleam. So that was then, and five hours later there is a call from the hospital, which makes all the saliva in my mouth dry up. She's gone by the time I get to her bedside but really she was gone before her poor body had hit the floor. No warning. Just a bit of faulty wiring up here.' Frankie taps his temple. His eyes are cold and troubled. 'That's all. Just that and nothing more. Like a bulb fizzling and blowing out. And in the months which followed part of me got lost. I became convinced that she was trying to talk to me. I thought that she would be scared and confused, not knowing what had happened to her. I thought maybe if I could just talk to her I could stop – I could stop her being so lonely. Her loneliness was killing me. So I hired mediums and went to spiritualist churches. I played with Ouija boards and I tried automatic writing and sound recording and magic mushrooms and ayahuasca and tarot cards. I cried my throat raw.'

He takes my hand in his, interlocking our fingers tightly together. His profile like a charcoal sketch in the growing dusk.

'Stella, she never came back, not once. So I will ask you once more. Do I need to worry about you?'

'Yes.'

Frankie smiles weakly. 'Who should I call first? The doctor or the priest?'

'I feel like my mind is slipping away. Everyone keeps telling me I'm losing control.'

He bends towards me. Our faces almost touch in the inky twilight.

'Say that again. The last bit, say it again.'

'Everyone keeps telling me I'm losing control.'

'Yes, Stella. Now we're getting somewhere.'

As we walk towards the house the shadows swell and grow fat, black as cartoon holes. The moon is rising, the pole star glittering like a hard frost. Frankie looks up at the house, then back to me.

'Who's that?'

I look to where he is pointing over my shoulder. A movement, in the garden. Someone small and slightly built hurrying away from the house, hood drawn up, shielding their face.

'Hey!' I shout, and the figure begins to run towards the road. Frankie brushes past me, moving with that slippery grace which Heidi had spoken of. The diminutive figure, now only a sketch in black against the tall hedgerow and violet sky, is pulling something from the ground. I am running too, and distantly I hear Blue barking from the cab of the van. I run forward over the rocky uneven ground. In the spring the fields here will be carpeted with pink thrift and yellow vetch, veined with blue spring squill and heather. Now it is just the yellowing sea grass and outcrops of rock finely laced with lichen. I hear Frankie shout, and then a shot rings out, sudden and violent, the amplified sound of a branch snapping. A clamour of rooks lifts off from the trees, startled. They rise like pieces of burned paper into the air.

'Frankie!'

'It's okay.' His voice. 'It's okay.'

He is still standing, one hand pressed to his shoulder. I stop, just feet away. I can see the gun in the hands of the hooded figure.

'Have you been shot?' My voice is high with panic.

'Air pistol. Stings. But I won't lose my arm.'

'Who are you?'

I move forward, and the figure moves back a pace. I can hear my pulse throbbing, blood ringing in my ears, Blue barking: woof, woof, woof.

The figure pulls back his hood. A boy, no older than thirteen. His face is a waxy-white circle, his eyes round and terrified.

'I'm sorry,' he says, voice cracking. 'I was just trying to scare him off. I didn't mean to hit you, Frankie, swear to God. Please don't call the police.'

'Mickey? Mickey Tallack?'

Frankie steps forward, hand outstretched, palm facing outwards. Mickey wipes a hand across his eyes.

'I'm sorry, Frankie mate. I didn't know it was you, I swear.'

'What are you doing out here?' I am so angry, my whole body vibrates. My fists are open, closed, open, closed. Frankie looks at me.

'Why have you got a gun?'

'I'm Mickey Tallack,' the boy is saying. 'I'm twelve years old. I live on Polperro Rise, number seven. Frankie knows my dad, don't you, Frankie?'

Frankie nods solemnly. There is a hole in his jacket where the pellet hit, no bigger than a penny. He winces when he touches it.

'I'm calling the police.'

'Stella. I know this kid. He's not dangerous.'

'I don't mean to state the obvious, but he's just shot you.'

There is a bike lying in the grass a metre or so away. Mickey must have cycled all the way up here in the inky twilight, all the way down those dark, leafy lanes. Why?

'I'm not trying to hurt no one. Someone asked me to come up and give you this. They gave me twenty quid and told me to leave it on the door.'

He holds out an envelope, small and white. There is no writing on it.

'I hid in your garden but then you got out the van and I ran for it. I didn't mean to hit you, Frankie, I'm so sorry.'

His voice is becoming tarry and thick. He is about to cry. *Good,* I think. *Good. Cry, you little shit.* His eyes switch between Frankie and me, pleading.

'An air rifle though? Why are you even carrying that thing?'

'Mrs Dalton told me to. She said it was dangerous to be here. That I should protect myself.'

'From me?' I'm shocked.

'No, from the other fella. Marco Nilsen. She said if he caught me he'd kill me.'

There is something here. A thickening as of strangers pressing close together, a feeling of feverish anticipation. It is almost tangible, like the smell of cordite or blood in the air, heavy and slow-moving.

I take the envelope from Mickey Tallack and tell him to go home.

'Tell your friend Mrs Dalton to expect a visit from me very soon,' I add as he climbs onto his bike. 'Tell her I don't like playing these sorts of stupid games.'

Inside the cottage it is cold, almost dank, and there is a smell like the water at the bottom of a ditch. The pendant light which hangs over the dining table is a glass globe in a delicate shade of rose-pink. As we walk into the room the light stutters once, twice. I can hear the bulb fizzing. In the hallway the telephone pings as though a storm is approaching.

Frankie takes off his top, inspecting his shoulder. There will be a bruise, he says, but there's no blood. I turn the envelope over between shaking fingers.

'It's cold in here. Is there a window open?'

I shake my head. He is right, it is cold, dank and heavy like the chill of a cave.

'I can smell the sea.' Frankie walks to the back door and moves his hand over the frame. 'No, more than that. It's like the water at the bottom of a vase of old flowers. Something rotting.'

I move to the table. 'I found a stone in my bed on my first night. Only small. A small speckled stone, still wet. Sometimes I find others, balanced on things. I see things out of the corner of my eye, just shadows, really. But there have been moments when those shadows have looked like figures, and faces.'

Frankie looks across the room at me, frowning. 'Look. Whatever is happening here, it isn't Mickey Tallack. He's a good kid. Well – generally a good kid. He's young and dumb and his family are – uh – feckless, I suppose is the word. Sounds to me like he just found a way to make some money. But he hasn't been breaking into your house, I'd put money on it.'

I cross the room and open the back door. The night air is sharp. I feel as though it could blow me away like powder.

'Who is Mrs Dalton?' I ask, and just as quickly I remember. 'It's Penelope, isn't it? Penelope Dalton. She lives in the house in town, the one with all the chickens. She's been funny with me since I first saw her. Her mother-in-law has dementia, and I suppose she's unhappy. It can't be much of a life, waiting for someone to remember you.'

'I know her.' He chooses his words with care. 'She's eccentric, lonely. But not malicious. I'm certain this is a misunderstanding.'

I open the envelope carefully with a strange impending feeling. Not a letter, as I had first thought, but a page, lined and torn from an exercise book. The paper has a soft quality as though it has been folded and refolded over a long time. At the top, underlined:

Ellie

The writing is rounded, the dot over the 'i' a big comic love heart. It is girly and charming and at the same time so insufferably babyish it makes my teeth itch.

'What is it?' Frankie asks. I pass it to him.

'Nothing. Numbers – phone numbers, by the looks of it. Don't recognise any of them.'

However, a dread is forming in me, a vault of ice melting to reveal a terrible knowledge, fossilised. Something seismic, shifting. Frankie stares at the paper, smoothing his fingertips over the words. He is reading aloud.

'"Mum and Dad", "Laura" – who are these people? "Marcella", "Claudia"? Do these names mean anything to you?'

I fill the kettle, trembling slightly. It is full dark out there now.

'No. It's just numbers,' I repeat. 'It doesn't mean anything.'

'Okay,' Frankie says, passing it back to me. 'Why don't we call one?'

'Are you mad?' I laugh, but Frankie isn't joking. He has taken a packet of frozen peas from the freezer – years old, by the looks of things – and wrapped them in a tea towel before pressing them to the welt on his shoulder. It is a livid red.

'Call one, find out. Tell them who you are, ask if there is a reason you've been given their numbers. If not, then' – he shrugs – 'at least we know that Penny is just losing it.'

'Okay,' I say more quietly, looking at the numbers in that childish hand. The network of creases remind me of writing Mr Kennecker's number in tiny digits and slipping it into my bra so Marco wouldn't see. Hiding it. There is something there, isn't there? Something about to drop into place like the spring on a mousetrap swiftly closing or mental locks tumbling.

'Which one? I'm not calling "Mum and Dad" – I have a nasty feeling about this and I don't want to upset them.'

'Call Claudia. See the way her name's been written there? It's bigger than all the others, plus there's a landline *and* a mobile. Call her and just ask.'

'She's going to think I'm a nutcase,' I say, dialling. After a few rings I get a recorded message thanking me for calling Blades hairdressers in Falmouth, would I like to leave a message? Relieved, I hang up.

'Well, that's that.'

'Call her mobile.'

Frankie is leaning forward. He has such a clarity about him; his warmth, his weight, the smell of him, like something solid and resinous.

I dial the mobile with shaking fingers and when Claudia picks up she sounds annoyed. I think I can hear a TV in the background. I'd been told when making cold calls that you need to say something of interest in the first five seconds so they don't hang up. Once they hang up, you've lost them.

'Claudia, my name is Stella and I have been given your number by someone who knew Ellie. Why do you think that is?'

I can almost hear the frown in her voice. 'Sorry, what? Who is this?'

'My name is Stella. I've been given your number by someone who knows Ellie.'

A sharp intake of breath. Frankie is looking at me across the table.

'Please don't hang up,' I continue. 'I'm just trying to figure out what's going on.'

'Where are you calling from, Stella?'

'Cornwall. A cottage near Tyrlaze. It's called Chy an Mor.'

This time I thought she'd gone. The silence goes on and on.

'Hello?' I say. 'Hello?'

'I'm here. This had better not be a joke.'

'It's not, I promise. I'm just trying to understand.'

'Ellie was my best friend. Before it all happened I was closer to her than anyone in my whole life.'

'Before what happened?'

'Before she died, stupid.'

I'd been expecting it, but even so I sit back in my chair, stunned.

'You know what? She was dead when she reached the cottage, that's what I think. She was dead when she met Marco fucking Nilsen.'

I look at Frankie, who is watching me carefully. He raises an eyebrow. *Are you all right?* I nod.

Claudia is still talking. 'He didn't want her. That's what gets me. He could've just left her alone because it was never her he wanted.'

I can hear in her voice that she is about to cry.

I say, 'Please can we meet? I want to hear more about this.'

'I don't think so, Stella, it was a very bad time for all of us.' She hangs up.

I clatter the phone to the table and put my head in my hands, groaning.

Frankie stays quiet. Finally, I look at him. 'What you said, the other night—'

'I was rude and I was drunk and I am sorry.'

I wave him away.

'Marco lied to me.'

'Oh yeah?'

'I showed him the photo of the woman – the one, you know, where she's all beaten up. Marco said he didn't know her; said he'd never seen her before. But he had.'

'Maybe he didn't recognise her? She was in a bad way.'

'No. No. I don't believe that. I managed to get hold of a photo of the two of them together. He knows her. He's just not telling me why.'

'Why didn't you ask him about it?'

'Because I'm frightened.'

He smiles unhappily, his hands dangling between his legs as he leans forward. 'What do your friends make of him, of Marco?'

I shake my head. Whenever I think of my friends, of Martha and James and Carmel and all the ones left behind in my old life, a hard little lump rises in my throat. Most of all it is Carmel I think of with a sorrow as sharp as grief. Carmel stretching on the pitted and scarred velvet sofa, asking me how my day was. Interested. We could start talking at eight, and a bottle of wine or two later it was two in the morning, and we still weren't done. I can remember Carmel returning home one sunny Saturday morning and taking off her long coat to reveal nothing but a gold G-string. When she saw me raise my eyebrows, she had snarled, 'That idiot told me he didn't want me to leave so he hid my clothes. Ha! As if that was going to stop me.'

And even though it had been nearing the end of our friendship, we had laughed and laughed, and the flat had been sunlit and beautiful. That was before, just before, I think. Before she had turned cold and jealous and unhappy.

Chapter 27

That night sees a hard, driving rain attack the cottage like artillery fire. I drowse in the big rose-patterned armchair and my dreams are all the same; the clifftop, a moon as waxy and round as cheese, a woman, skin marbled white. Her smile exposes rotted stumps of teeth.

The woman whispers, her words snagged in the rising wind, 'Pay attention, Stella. Pay attention.'

I snatch for her just as she jumps into the abyss without a backward glance, hair fluttering out behind her like the tails of a kite.

An electronic chirping wakes me. I reach for my phone, still half dreaming.

'Hello?'

Nothing. Wind on the line. A fizz of static.

'Hello?' I say again, sitting slowly upright. I am afraid. I can hear them breathing.

'Leave me alone,' I tell the silence. I am about to hang up when I realise I can hear, very distantly, a song. My theme song.

'There's Bonnie and there's Eddie and there's Mum and Mikey too, Daddy, Lucy, Frisky, we'll never forget you!'

Someone is watching the show. I shiver. I can hear breathing now, as though they are standing too close to the mouthpiece. Slow, laboured breathing. The song ends, and I hear the programme start, my voice as clear as a bell.

'Aw, Frisky, I wish I had some friends to play with!'

'Leave me alone,' I say as I hang up.

I sit mute for a few moments before releasing a long, shuddering breath. Through the doorway into the kitchen I can see the back door standing open. Outside the rain has stopped and the sky cleared, revealing an arch of stars in the vault of the sky. At the back of my mind something is stirring. An awareness, flexing its muscles. I both welcome and fear it, knowing that it means a change is coming. Something seismic. I have made a decision.

I call Frankie early the next morning. I have no one else.

'I'm going to see her.'

'Who?'

'The hairdresser. Claudia. I've made an appointment. See if she'll talk to me.'

'Stella, I—'

'Don't try to talk me out of it.'

'I was going to ask if you wanted a lift.'

We drive to Falmouth later that morning. The rain has stopped but the sky is still dull and heavy. We park in the town and walk to the hairdresser's in a shrill wind which whips at the hem of my dress. By the time we get there I am flushed and nervous, fingers raw with cold. Frankie points to a coffee shop a little further up the road.

'I'll be in there. Call me if you need me.'

Inside, the hairdresser's is warm, a comforting smell of shampoo and soap, strong artificial perfumes. At the front desk a young woman, no older than nineteen with poker-straight hair down to her waist, looks at me expectantly. I ask for Claudia. She checks the book in front of her and points to a couch.

'She'll be with you in a minute,' she tells me. Pink lips the colour of bubblegum. I envy her lineless face, the knowing arrogance. I flick through a magazine I can barely see. Nerves have made me shaky. I need a drink. I don't hear Claudia saying my name because I haven't given my real one. I don't look up when she asks 'Maria?' and only realise she is there when she puts a hand on my arm.

'Maria? You awake, love? Do you want to come with me? We'll get you washed.'

I stand and face her. She is smaller than me by at least a foot, with a rounded face and large, heavy breasts. She is holding a towel out to me but when I turn to face her it falls from her hands and folds to the floor. It's the same look Jim Kennecker gave me that first day. Her eyes, claggy with thick, dark make-up, widen. It is the expression I imagine you'd have if a family member pulled a gun on you.

'Is this your idea of a joke?' she hisses.

'No – I – I'm sorry, Claudia, I didn't know what else to do.'

She flashes me a look of real anger. I see her hands ball into fists. I wonder if she will hit me.

'We spoke on the phone.'

'I told you already I don't want to see you.'

'Please. Just five minutes, that's all. I need to know – is this her, is this Ellie?'

I pull the photo from my pocket, hold it out to her. She looks at it stiffly, a muscle twitching in her eye.

'Don't you see it?' Claudia asks me, and her fierceness has softened a little. Just a little. 'Don't you see the resemblance?'

I nod. I had, of course. It was difficult to tell under all the bruising in the photo but it was there all right. Even her posture was familiar to me, that coquettish way of looking up from beneath her lashes even though it was clear her nose was broken. My stomach rolled sickly.

'This isn't how I remember her,' Claudia tells me. 'She used to be so beautiful before.'

'Listen, Claudia. I'm sorry to have misled you, and I know this is painful. But I've paid for an hour of your time, and I don't need a haircut.'

'You do.' She nods at my hair, unsmiling. I don't think she means to be so blunt but who knows?

'Okay, yes. But today I just want to speak to you about Ellie.' I lick my lips. 'Marco too.'

'That prick.'

The anger again. Corrosive.

'Come on,' Claudia says finally. 'I'll give you ten minutes.'

We walk across the road to a café in silence. Claudia orders us both drinks without checking what I want.

'You're paying, right?' is all she says as we find seats. Her handbag, her nails, her lips, everything about her is glossy and dark. She looks at me expectantly over the table.

'So you want to hear about Marco, do you?'

I nod.

'I can't look at you. You're so like her. At the end, I mean. When he'd finished with her.'

'How was she before?'

'Happy,' Claudia says immediately. 'You ever seen the way a room can change just by someone being in it? Like, how happiness is catching? That's her. Everywhere she went. At school everyone loved her, even the teachers. She was just one of those people, you know?'

I nod.

'And then she met Marco. Probably when he was down here in that house of his. She'd just set up her own business, and he offered some investment.'

Our drinks arrive. She pulls the sugar bowl towards her and starts to lift the sachets, shaking them with pinched fingers.

'She came to me because she wanted hair extensions. Right the way down to her waist, like yours. That was the first time I thought that maybe something was going on. She'd always looked so beautiful with short hair – Ellie always said it was easy to look after, one less thing for her to worry about. Marco paid for them – the extensions, I mean. And she never outright *said* it was his idea. It was just a feeling I got. Then she started to lose weight. I think they had moved in together at this point. Last time I saw her she was frantic. Called me up out of the blue and told me she'd lost her keys. Couldn't remember when she'd last had them or where. I drove over there and . . .'

Claudia swallows. She looks desperately uncomfortable. 'I wish we could still smoke in these places. Anyway, when I got there I couldn't believe what she looked like. She didn't look like Ellie at all. She looked like a little doll. Like she should have been under glass. And all those bruises. Her face was so swollen she could hardly speak. She'd been locked out of the house for three hours. Five minutes after I get there, guess who arrives?'

I guess. Claudia nods.

'Course. Marco. Prince Charming. He had her keys. Said they must have fallen out of her bag into his car. She cried when he handed them back to her. Told him he'd saved her life. They were only keys, but she thought he was God Almighty.'

'Did you talk to him? To Marco?'

Claudia shrugs. 'I tried. Asked him about the injuries she had. He said she'd fallen in the night. Sleepwalking.'

I shiver then. Just a little. Claudia doesn't notice.

'I wasn't being dramatic on the phone, you know. I really do think he killed her, whatever the papers say.'

'Do you know Penelope Dalton? Penny, maybe. She lives in Tyrlaze.'

She nods. 'That's Ellie's mother. Surprised to hear she's still alive, to be honest. She had a problem, you know?'

She makes a motion with her hand, tipping a drink into her mouth.

'She gave me your number. Any idea why?'

I hold out the piece of paper.

Claudia scans it. 'This is Ellie's writing. I don't know why Penelope had it. Ellie changed her number about a week before she jumped. I couldn't get hold of her anymore, just a recorded message saying that number no longer existed. She called me once, about three days before she died, but I was too busy to talk to her.'

Claudia pulls a napkin out of the dispenser and blows her nose. I think of my new phone at the cottage, the one with only three numbers in it, the ones Marco had put in there. He said it was because I'd lost my phone, but I don't remember losing it. So I'd taken his phone and copied Mr Kennecker's number down, hadn't I? Hidden the piece of paper in my bra where he wouldn't find it. Had Ellie done the same with her friends and family? Tucked this little note somewhere to keep it safe, in case of an emergency? But then why did Penelope Dalton give it to me?

'I have to go.' She's standing, pushing her hair from her face with her fingers. 'I can't say it's been a pleasure to meet you, but I hope you got the answers you were looking for.'

'You know we're engaged, don't you? Me and Marco.'

She gives me a look of such abject pity I want to shrivel up. 'I bet you are. You're just his type.'

I ask Frankie for one more favour. We are sitting in the garden on the sun-warmed stone bench.

'Upstairs there are two bottles of pills in the drawer beside my bed. I want you to take them away, and not give them back to me no matter how much I ask you, no matter how upset I get. You think you can do that?'

'Sure, I've done much worse.'

'Will you destroy them?'

'Yup.'

I lean closer to him. Over our heads the gulls circle like vultures.

Marco fires Alice. The first I hear about it is when I receive a call from her while I am sitting on the sofa, watching TV. I almost don't answer. I've had three calls in the last twenty-four hours, each one almost silent except for the wet rattle of breathing and, just audible in the background, the playing of old *Marigold!* tapes.

'Stella, it's Alice.'

I'm puzzled. 'Is everything okay? Is Marco okay? Are you at the office?'

She surprises me by laughing. 'Didn't Marco tell you? I got fired yesterday.'

'No. No, he didn't mention it.'

'It's no drama, Stella. Just time for me to move on.'

'But – but why?'

'He found out that I sent you those photos for your "collage".'

I want to think I'm imagining the inverted commas around the word 'collage'. She sounds bitter and angry. I feel immediately guilty.

'Oh no. Oh, Alice. I'll talk to him. I'll tell him I pressured y—'

'I don't want that job back. I don't want to work for Marco Nilsen anymore. Do you know how he found out? He'd had keystroke software installed on my computer. You know what that is?'

I tell her I do not.

'It's a way to monitor what I'm typing. It records everything. It's spying, in layman's terms. I'm not even sure it's legal. You know, it's funny, looking through all those old photos of his. It felt like trespassing, in a way. I felt bad doing it. I don't now.'

I have a feeling I'm not going to like what comes next but I can't stop listening, can't end the call. A part of you always wants to know the worst. It's the darkest part of you, where the abyss deepens to a pitch-black.

'When I checked his hard drive I found a site he'd been visiting. Willowvale. You know what that is, Stella?'

'Well, Willowvale is the name of the village in the show—'

'Yup. You been on that site, Stella?'

'I've never even heard of it.'

'It's weird. I'm not going to lie to you. It's for some of the more . . . fanatical enthusiasts of *Marigold!*, I guess. There's photos, of course. Mainly of you as Katie Marigold. Looks like they were taken on set – they're what I suppose you'd call "candid". You look like one of those kids at the American beauty pageants. All hair and make-up and big frilly dresses. He was *infatuated* with your hair.'

That expression you hear, 'my blood ran cold'. I understand it in that instant. I am chilled with a slow and creeping horror.

'You want to look it up. That's what I think. Oh, and Stella?'

'What?'

'If he knows that you asked for those photos, you're going to need a better cover story.'

Chapter 28

As soon as I hang up I type 'Willowvale' into my browser. I click on the first result. It's a chatroom, fairly innocuous-looking except there are pictures of the *Marigold!* family as the header across the top of the page. It's all very twee, and I'm loath to go further, but Alice had sounded so insistent that I click on a thread headed 'Joey Fraser AKA Eddie interview The Times 03/04'. There are a few commentators on this but it is brief and runs out fairly quickly. I scroll to the next heading, 'UR favourite Marigold! MOMENTS1', which is considerably longer and populated with users with names such as 'Bill501' and 'FriskyTheDog' and 'HoneyPot64'. I don't read the posts, just scroll quickly through. I've no desire to reminisce over my past. I hadn't liked it all that much at the time. In fact, I'm about to close the screen when I see something which pulls me up short. It's a user called 'Uncle'. A line of text and no more: *I think you'll find that the catapult only featured in series one. They removed it for the remaining episodes as it was considered too dangerous.*

He's right, I think faintly. There was an episode in which Eddie Marigold had fired rocks from a catapult, but it had been deemed too violent to be shown at teatime. It's not something widely known, I don't think, at least not to people who weren't involved with the show. I click on the name Uncle and immediately see the vast quantity of posts that user has made. Photos, some of them years old, of me in make-up, still with gaps in my teeth. Photos of me signing autographs aged ten. Here's me in my 'Here Comes Katie Marigold' dress with the ruffled sleeves. And my hair. So many photos of my long, wavy golden hair. It leads to a memory then, of my mother, brushing my hair in front of the mirror. She had called it my 'asset'. I hadn't known what she'd meant. Later I would overhear her and my father arguing about money, the money he'd gambled away. We were going to lose the house. My mother had had some loony idea of cutting off locks of my hair and selling them to fans.

'People will buy it, David,' she was saying. I could tell by how ragged her voice was that she was done shouting. It sounded like my father was only just gearing up, however.

'You think that's the answer? Selling Stella's hair? You think that's what's going to save this family? She's not bloody Rapunzel!'

'There are people out there—'

'Say what you mean, for crying out loud, Marion. There are perverts out there. Sick perverts who want to buy a little girl's hair. Why don't you just throw her to the wolves?'

'Oh, now you're saying—'

'This is what I'm talking about—'

'I only want the best—'

And on. And on. Worst thing is I would have done it too. I would have hacked all of my hair off in a heartbeat if it had meant keeping our family together.

When my phone rings I jolt upright, slamming my computer closed with a snap. Of course, I realise as I pick up my mobile, if Marco has installed the same software on my laptop as he did on Alice's, he'll already know what I've been doing.

'Hello?'

'Stella? Stella? Is that you? It's Joey again, Joey Fraser.'

I cradle the phone beneath my chin.

'I'm here.'

I smooth my hand over the table surface, feeling the years of it, the chips and knocks and bumps.

'I need to see you, Stella.'

'Where are you?'

'You know where I am. Don't you read the news?'

I roll my eyes. He'll never change. 'Can't say I've seen mention of you.'

'For the last few weeks I've been staying in St Ives. The Portmoir. Five-star. On the seafront. Jack Nicholson stayed here in the eighties. Hold on.' I hear rustling, the sound of pages turning. 'Here we are: "*Hollywood Actor Joey Fraser Enjoys the Beach Life*". Page nine. There's a photo of me in the sea, one of me having an ice cream. It's cute, I'm loveable. Bringing glamour to your dingy town.'

I laugh, I can't help it. I can hear the smile in his voice, the knowing wryness.

'Please can I see you, Stella?'

'Why? I'm not doing a reunion, Joey. I'm not.'

'No, I suppose not. In California if you don't see your face in the papers three times a week you're downgraded to a civilian.'

'Is that so?'

'You wouldn't last five minutes out there with this attitude.'

'So what *do* you want from me?'

'I think we need to talk. About what happened.'

I prickle with cold. Distantly an alarm bell is ringing at the back of my skull. 'Joey—'

'Please, Stella. Please let me move on.'

I hesitate. I can hear him watching the television in the background of his hotel room. It immediately makes me think of the silent calls I've been getting. I am so tired of being afraid.

'All right,' I tell him. 'All right. Come on over.'

◆ ◆ ◆

Less than twenty minutes later Joey Fraser arrives at the cottage in a rented Prius. As he steps out of the car, I notice his mirrored aviators, his oak-coloured tan. He is alone, and my nerves are singing. I shouldn't have let him come here alone, I should have called Frankie. That day in the trailer. I can still remember the burning pain, the shock. The way my mouth had tasted metallic and sticky. I open the door as he walks up the path. I've made an effort with myself – showered, brushed my hair, changed my clothes – but all the same I notice the slight hesitation as he looks up and sees me, the ghost of a double take.

'Stella?' It's almost a question, as though he can't believe it. I know I don't look well.

'Hi, Joey. You look great.'

He nods, as if this is the least he expects. He's toned and lean and has shaved at least ten years off his age. His teeth are bright and white and strong and unnerving. I hold out my hand and he shakes it, waits to be invited in.

'I should have done this years ago,' he tells me, as he drinks his iced water (*Any jasmine tea? How about oat milk? Any coconut water?*). He picks up an earthenware bowl and puts it down again. 'This is a nice place.'

'You should know,' I tell him. I feel hyped up, jumpy. 'You're the one that's been creeping in here when I've been asleep.'

His face creases with confusion and I laugh at him airily. 'I was thinking about you the other day. You ostracised me. You and all the other kids. You cut me out. A seven-year-old girl. You made me feel like the loneliest person in the world. You wouldn't even let me join in your games, for Christ's sake!'

246

Where's your muzzle, Katie Marigold? I can hear it now. That high, girlish voice ringing out, the muffled sniggers, the way my cheeks had flushed and burned with shame.

'You ever wonder why we behaved like that? You ever stop and think that there might have been a reason – a pretty good reason – why no one wanted to go near you?'

'You going to tell me I was some kind of monster, are you? Is that what you're here for?'

'No, Stella. No, you weren't. It wasn't your fault you were the way you were. I know that now.'

We stare at each other in silence. Joey adjusts his shirt cuffs and sips his drink as though he wishes it were something stronger.

'Hey, do you remember the Christmas episode with the fake snowman we made?' he says. 'I've still got it. I bid for it at auction.'

'Why?'

'Something to remember the show by.'

'You hated the show.'

We are both silent for a beat.

When he next speaks his voice is level and quiet. 'It wasn't just me, Stella. It was all of us.'

'Well, I'm glad you were all united in your hatred of me.'

'You know, I've kept in touch with most of the old *Marigold!* crew – Christmas cards, occasional emails. Sometimes we meet when I come to London.'

I feel that familiar envy spike, and I am seven years old again, wanting so desperately to be included. *Put your muzzle on, Katie Marigold.*

'You didn't keep in touch with me,' I say petulantly.

'No. I didn't. You must know why.' He leans forward in his chair. 'Lesley would always ask about you though. Anne too. She would always say it wasn't your fault. It was her idea I contact you to get some – heh – closure.'

247

Why weren't you invited to these meet-ups? I think in my mother's sour, shrill voice. *You were the star of the show!*

'Well, go on then.'

He looks up at me. The back door is propped open with the heavy black doorstop and a cooling breeze is blowing through. I sit on the arm of the sofa, my legs crossed serpentine around my thighs and ankles.

'Go on. Say it.'

Joey looks genuinely confused. He scratches the back of his head.

'That's why you're here, isn't it? To be forgiven?'

He tips his head back and laughs. Slaps his palm against his thigh. 'That's a good one, Stella,' he says, and then he sees that I am serious and the smile drops away like a landslide.

'Oh, Jesus. You're not even joking.'

Now it's my turn to be confused. He smiles at me again. It is not a nice smile. It is loaded.

'Okay then. I'm sorry, Stella. I'm sorry for hurting you.' Pause. 'You were just a kid.' Another pause. 'A spoiled, horrible little kid who always got her own way no matter what.'

I stare at him, heat building in my chest. Somewhere in the house my phone is ringing and ringing.

'But like I said, it wasn't your fault. Not really. I knew that even as a thirteen-year-old boy.'

He leans closer, lacing his fingers over his knee. 'Your mother was a bitch, and I'm not sorry she's dead. Not a bit.'

'You can't say that.'

'She had a way, didn't she, of getting what she wanted? A way of twisting things so they always turned in her favour – in *your* favour. Why did you think the show changed so dramatically? Because you were talented? Irreplaceable?'

248

He laughs again, a strangled, sick sound. 'No, no. Of course not.' He lowers his voice, careful to keep it level. 'Even your dad knew. Your poor dad. Sidelined by his daughter's career and his promiscuous, fame-hungry wife.'

My past is a tapestry unravelling at frightening speed. I keep picturing my mother climbing the stairs of the multi-storey car park, the darkened stairwell smelling of piss and oil, the way the wind would have buffeted her at the very top where she would have climbed over the railing to stand on the ledge. That plunge onto the hard concrete.

'That's not true. It's not true.'

'Everyone knew. Everyone. And it was so unfair on the rest of us. But she didn't care, and why would she when you were pulling in three, four times as much money as the other kids? I mean – do you want to get that phone?'

I wave it away.

'I guess I went a bit overboard. We all did. We were mean to you and could see you were cracking under the pressure of it all. Too much going on in here, you know?' He waves a vague hand at his temple and then his voice at that awful high pitch which makes the hairs on the back of my neck stand up. 'I got a lot of thinks in my brain, Katie Marigold!'

I flinch, visibly. I remember now. That day in the trailer. He'd been nearly thirteen years old, me only seven. We'd been in costume – navy-blue bell bottoms, sailor collars, anchor motifs stitched onto our chests – and he'd come to the door, stuck his head round it, all freckles and jug ears, that horrible high voice.

'Your mama's in the room with Terry,' he said to me. 'Heard 'em talking.'

Terry was one of the producers on the show. I'd been introduced to them all, and they all looked the same; interchangeable, Terry, Barry, Gerry.

He made a ring with his thumb and forefinger and slid his index finger in and out of it, leering at me.

'Your mama sure likes "talking", Stella, I suppose that's why she does it all the time.'

I stared at him. In my stomach, fury, white-hot. My eyes filled with tears.

'Aw, is baby upset? Does baby want a dummy?'

I'd let the tears roll down my face, thick as treacle. His expression changed, his mouth pulling downwards into a moue.

'Oh, hey, listen, don't cry. I'm sorry, I'm sorry.' He was looking around nervously, frightened of being caught. He came in, pulling the door closed behind him. 'Come on, Stella, don't cry.'

He walked towards me and my breath was coming in gasps. He could see the sobbing coming, swelling in my chest, and he was so desperate to stop me that he put his arm around me and that's when I bit down on his arm, hard. He had forgotten the rules about not getting too close to me. There had been a memo sent out. His skin broke and my mouth filled with blood. I was only seven years old, and I hung on as he tried to pull away, shouting, wailing. I had done this before. It was why people tended to avoid me. I pulled away, my teeth snapping as he planted a hand on my chest to keep me back. He was trying to get out but I wouldn't let him. I sank my teeth into his shoulder and wrist and he howled with pain. Then he slapped me, hard across the face. The air rang with the sound. For a moment there was a fine, brittle silence. He was cowering and the thing he was holding out of my reach was his arm, his injured, bleeding arm, staring at me with horror and suddenly I was screaming and screaming. Then they finally came to the door, my mother pulling her shirt around her, just the top two buttons undone (*Your mama's 'talking' with Terry in the room, Stella*), and she was saying, 'What happened, what the hell happened?', and I told them all: 'He hit me.'

Later, my mother and I in my trailer, and two women from the Social Services dressed in corduroy and polyester shirts, both smelling of cigarettes, and my mother saying, 'Tell them, Stella, tell them what you told me. Tell them he touched you, he's always had a funny way about him, he's always been a creep', and I don't think I said a word, she did it all for me. All I had to do was point.

'You said I molested you.'

'I know.'

'I had to leave the show. Move house. My parents got hate mail for twenty years. You know someone put a firework through the letterbox? The whole place nearly burned down. I didn't work again for ten years.'

'I know.'

'Why did you do it, Stella?'

'I don't know.'

'You know it's on my Wikipedia page? It gets brought up in interviews every goddamn time.' His hand makes a fist and he thumps the arm of the chair he's sitting on. 'It's followed me my whole life. It's a curse.'

'You slapped me.'

'You were hysterical.'

'I know.'

He toys with the cuffs of his shirt, won't look at me. 'I suppose you saw the story in the papers?'

I think back. I have a vague memory of Marco showing me an article on Joey Fraser when he'd first come back to England. Was that in the spring? What had it said?

'Sexual harassment.'

He nods. His lips are set in a grim, bloodless line.

'She was a make-up artist. I met her on set. She liked me – or she had seemed to. I thought she did. Guess I misread the signals, huh? That's not a crime, is it? To ask a woman out?'

I shake my head.

'You can't even— I mean, I never touched her, Stella, I swear. Not once.'

'Okay.'

'Anyway. She's dropped the charges.'

'Oh yeah?' I don't know where this is going.

'Yeah. It's a relief, I'm not going to lie to you. Even my lawyer said as much. Because with what's been said about me in the past – about what you and your mum claimed I did – well, it wasn't going to look good for me. Makes me look like a predator.'

We look at each other across the room.

'And I'm not. And you know I'm not, don't you? Don't you?'

I nod.

'Say it. Please, Stella. It's been over twenty years, and I've never stopped thinking about this. For a long time, I thought maybe I did do it, maybe I did and I just don't remember. Why else would you say I had? And it went round and round in my head, until I believed that I'd assaulted you. What other explanation was there?'

'I'm sorry, Joey.'

'Just tell me. Just this one thing.'

He fixes me with his pellucid eyes.

'You – you didn't do it. You were mean and you were unbearable and a bully, but you never did the things my mother accused you of.'

I can see something cross his face, a ripple over dark water. Is it relief? Happiness? I don't think so. Not quite. But all the same I see the way he inhales, eyes closed. I step towards him and he says, 'Christ, please get that phone, it's driving me crazy.'

I stumble into the kitchen, my head reeling. I snatch my phone from the table, not looking at the caller ID.

'Hello?'

'It's Marco, Stella. I just don't know what to do to help you anymore.'

I am silent.

'You've been going behind my back. I know about the photos you were sent. The ones you lied to get. I can't stand it. I can't bear dishonesty.'

I snap then. 'Dishonesty? When were you going to tell me about Ellie, Marco? When you moved down here? After the wedding? When? Don't you talk to me about deception, Marco, don't you fu—'

'Don't swear at me. Don't raise your voice.'

'Why did you do it, Marco? Just tell me that. Why?'

Silence. I can hear the huff of his breath. Then: 'You've been so on edge. Unpredictable. I haven't wanted to upset you. I don't think you have any idea how hard this is for me.'

My heart twists in my chest because deep down, of course, I believe him. I swallow, fighting back tears.

'Stella? Stella?'

'I'm here.'

Through the window the sea is glassy and green and cold. I wonder what it would be like to walk into it and just keep on walking.

'I'm sorry too,' I say. 'I shouldn't have lied about the photos. I was just interested, I suppose. But you should have told me. You should have told me about Ellie.'

'Ellie isn't important anymore. I've got you now. So you need to hold on, Katie. Just hold on. I'll be there soon. I'll be there.'

I heard it. My heart is pounding as he hangs up the phone. He called me Katie. I don't think he even realised he was doing it.

Chapter 29

As I am walking back into the sitting room I remember a party Marco had taken me to last year. It had been a hazy day, stiflingly hot. We had driven out to an affluent suburb in Essex and the dress I had been wearing made me itch and sweat. It had rustled when I'd walked, prickly beneath the fabric. I'd been nervous that day. Anxiety spreading through me like the roots of a tree. The party was boring – Carmel would have described it as the Whitest Party In The World – and I'd found myself wandering through the land-scaped gardens. At one point I'd caught sight of my reflection in the kidney-shaped swimming pool. *She looks familiar*, I'd thought. I'd leaned out over the cobalt-blue water to get a better look at myself. You ever peered into the mirror and seen someone you don't recognise? I have. It's terrifying. I'd looked in the water, and I hadn't seen Stella Wiseman. I'd seen Katie Marigold. Marco had found me there, kneeling over the lip of the water. He had been black-suited, scissor-legged and stiff as the Reaper. I'd done something, I think, to make him angry. And then, olfactory memory, that smell of burning, roasted meat.

My God.

I lean against the doorframe, and Joey stands as though to catch me.

'I'm fine,' I tell him, 'but you have to go.'

The Reaper is coming. And I have to be ready.

◆ ◆ ◆

I walk the narrow lane which threads like an artery through the landscape towards Tyrlaze. I walk in the places where the pavement disappears and the hedgerow crowds in. I walk past silvery cobwebs like garlands, heavy purple fruits just turning rotten. My hair snags on brambles, pulling at my scalp like ghost fingers as I approach the house, the one with the eggs outside it.

I am not expecting her to answer the door, beady eyes looking me up and down, taking in every detail. The hallway floor behind her is littered with feathers, white and delicately speckled brown.

'You again.'

'Hello, Beverley.' I speak slowly, so she can understand. 'I'm looking for Penelope. Is she here?'

She looks at me blankly. I notice she is wearing lipstick, bright red. It bleeds into the cracks at the edges of her lips. Her cheeks are rouged, her hair pinned. It looks like she is getting ready to go somewhere. I wonder what it is like to be in her head.

'Penelope has sent me some quite disturbing things in the post. I'd very much like to speak with her about it.'

'Penelope didn't do that. I did that.'

For a moment I am silent, my breath caught.

'But the boy said—'

'Oh, that boy, that troublemaker. All the Tallacks are trouble-makers. He told you Mrs Dalton, did he? You should have asked him which one. You should have been more specific.' She drops me a wink. 'My daughter-in-law is in Plymouth for the day. On a date. It's a wonder she found a man willing, but life is full of mystery, is it not? Meanwhile, in her absence I am enjoying the peace and the box of truffles she thinks I don't know about under her bed.'

'Why did you send me those things?'

Her smile broadens to reveal yellowing dentures.

'You'd better come in, Stella.'

We walk together into a little room nearest the front door. Inside it is astonishing. Velvet-draped curtains of a deep fungal red hang beneath a gilded chandelier. A series of oil paintings positioned along the far wall. I recognise 'A Bar at the Folies-Bergère' by Édouard Manet in a gilt frame. There is a daybed in the corner, piled high with blankets, quilts and throws against a mound of cushions. I realise this is where she sleeps. The room has a chemical smell, like a hospital. Sickness.

'I think we need to talk . . .' I begin, watching as Beverley moves to a roll-top desk of chestnut wood. She peels back the lid to reveal a kettle, sugar bowl and a quarter-pint of milk in a glass bottle. Beside the desk is a sink cluttered with toiletries, above it a shelf piled with plates, cutlery and condiments. I can count five different types of mustard. A dressing table is littered with perfume bottles and powdery cosmetics, bags of medicine, syringes. From the mirror hang long strings of pearls and brightly coloured silk scarves. She notices me staring and smiles.

'It's a big house.' Beverley is pouring water into the cups. 'And like me it's falling apart. Far better to move everything I need into the one place I like best of all in the whole house and let the rest of it rot. Besides, I have much better things to do with my time than clean it. God knows I did enough of that when I was married.'

'When were you married?'

'For about ten days in the sixties. Terrible idea. Terrible choice of husband.'

'Did it not end well?'

'I shot him,' she says mildly, easing herself into the daybed.

I pause for a moment before picking up a teaspoon and stirring the tea.

'I don't mean I killed him, of course,' Beverley continues. 'Two sugars for me, Stella, dear. I just injured him enough to know not to come crawling back if the mood took him. He was a terrible crawler.'

I pass Beverley her cup, noticing the oxygen mask hanging on the bed post.

'He died in the end. His next wife ran him over with her car, a big one. Killed him outright.'

'Did she go to prison?'

'Pah! Not a jury in the world would convict her of murdering that bastard. They should have given her a medal. Couldn't get away with it nowadays, of course, more's the pity.'

Beverley looks over the rim of her cup with a mischievous smile. She is having what Penelope would describe as a very good day. I remember seeing it in my own grandparents, the mental decline, the confusion which comes in waves. Some days my grandmother would call me by her dead daughter's name, asking me over and over where the best china was kept, why I thought I was better than anybody else, even though we all knew I was a little bitch. Other days she was lucid and generous, charming even, but those days shrunk very fast and soon she barely had any of those days at all.

But there the similarity between Beverley and my grandmother ends. Beverley is small and fierce-looking, like a little bullet. Today her eyes are luminous, looking me up and down with plain curiosity.

'I'm sick,' she says. 'I suppose you know that. But I'm glad you finally came to me. It's been so hard to get your attention.'

She laughs, and it rapidly turns into a fit of coughing. I hear the rattle of phlegm in her chest and wonder how much longer Beverley has to live. She hunches into the cushions with her ashtray balanced on her bony knees, holding a handkerchief to her lips.

When she pulls it away it is spotted with blood. She folds it up her sleeve and fixes me with her watery eyes.

'Would you murder him if you thought you could get away with it?'

'No!'

'I don't believe you.' She is talking in a sing-song voice, teasing me. 'Or maybe you just haven't reached your limit yet. Not like Ellie. She reached her limit, and' – her hand lifts and drops like a stone, miming a great descent. I stare at her.

'She put up with a lot, my granddaughter. But the pain, I think it was one step too far. Pass me that.'

She is pointing to a silver picture frame behind me, propped on the dressing table. I do so, careful not to knock over the rest of the clutter on the table's surface.

'This is her, back in the days before Marco. When my son was still alive. That's what did for her, I think. Losing her dad like that.'

'How did he die?'

'He got sick. Cancer. He was only a young man. It broke my heart.'

'God, I'm sorry.'

'And he left these two behind him and they both fell apart in their way. Here.'

She passes me the frame. In it is an old photograph taken just outside the front door of this house. The man is tanned, his shirt sleeves rolled up to the elbow. He has one arm draped around a dark-haired woman – Penelope, I see now – who is flashing a smile at the camera. And standing in front of them both . . .

'Is this her? Is this Ellie?' I ask, peering at the glass. 'She looks so different.'

'Of course she does. This was before. I mean' – a fly buzzes by her hair and she swats it absently away – 'you saw the photo I sent you? Marco Nilsen packed her off to Prague to see a plastic surgeon – a *butcher*, more like – to correct all the things he found wrong with her. He told everyone she'd been in a car crash – that's how bad she looked when she came home. All that bruising and broken bones.'

Something clicks into place. 'He wasn't beating her up?'

'Just because he didn't use his fists doesn't mean he didn't hurt her. Between that fat-fingered surgeon and that shady doctor in London I'm amazed she lasted as long as she did.'

Beverley must see something in my expression – a wince maybe, a tightness – because she looks at me with narrowed eyes. 'You saw him too, didn't you? That sham "doctor".' She spits the word. 'And of course then there was the gaslighting—'

'The what?'

'Oh dear girl, you have to listen to what I've got to say because if you don't know what gaslighting is you don't know the first thing about what he's doing to you. He's been undermining you – he wants you to think you're going mad. To doubt yourself, to lose it. Until, at the very end, you can't get by without him.'

She leans closer. I can smell the cigarettes she is smoking, like pepper and cloves.

'Death follows that man around.'

'I don't understand.'

'We tried, Penelope and me. Just once. We tried to get her away from him. This was after the plastic surgery, the day after I'd taken that awful photo of her. We drove up to the house, Chy an Mor, two desperate women thinking we could reason with him. Appeal to his better nature, Penelope had said. Ha! We were dreaming. We had no idea of the hold he had on her. He wouldn't even let us into the house, kept us right out there on the doorstep.

'When I realised pleading with him wasn't working I got mad and poked him in the chest. He didn't like that. He doesn't like women standing up to him. He started talking about how sad it was when old people lose their faculties. How they often can't cope and have to go into care homes. How dreadful he thought it was when they had to sell their own houses to pay for it. Penelope had gone pale by this point. This is my house, you see, and if I went into a home it would need to be sold to pay the fees and she'd have nowhere to go. Remember she'd already lost her husband. Being made homeless at sixty would have finished her off. Marco carried right on talking, telling me a story that had been in the news about a care home which had left residents lying in their own waste for days on end. He came right up close to me, barely blinking, like one of those snakes you see that just lie in the long grass, and he said, "I'd hate for Ellie to have to sign her dearest grandmother into one of those places to die alone."'

My throat has constricted to a thin pipe. It is the smell in here, I think. The medicines and the sting of disinfectant, the stink of illness. Something else too, lower than that, lower than the chemical air fresheners dotted about the room, cloying jasmine and lavender, synthetic. It is a dead smell, rising from her in waves.

'My granddaughter was an adult. She made her own decisions. We tried to warn her. But what else could we do?'

She leans so close to me that I can smell her breath. 'You should know. After all, *your* friends tried. Didn't they?'

I stare at her.

She gives me another sick smile. 'That list of phone numbers was the last thing Ellie ever gave me. She'd hidden it in her locket because she was so afraid of him finding it. She gave it to me to keep it safe. We were friends, Ellie and I. Closer than she and her mother were. She was a Daddy's girl you see, and after he was gone I was the next best thing. But I had to watch what Marco was doing to her, making her sick, making her think she was losing her mind.'

She is tapping her temple. I am heady, dizzy. I steady myself on the table. She is asking me a question.

'Are you all right?' Beverley asks, her face creasing with concern. 'You've gone very pale.'

'Dizzy spell.'

'Ellie got those too. She got them a lot. He eroded her, starting with her friendships and her online accounts and finishing with her going into the sea like a rock.'

Something pitch-dark, like grey wings enfolding me. I sway slightly in my seat. Without thinking, my hand has gone to the back of my neck. There is a patch of tender skin there, perfectly circular. When I touch it my nerve endings light up. Beverley sees it, her eyes narrowed against the smoke.

'You too? Ellie was the same, although I think – now I can't be sure – but I think hers was a little further towards her left ear.'

Another sick swooping sensation. The ground beneath me heaves violently as though on the deck of a ship, a galleon plummeting down the side of a long, dark wave. I grip my knees with hands which seem very white, very distant.

'I think I may need some fresh air. I'm feeling very faint.'

'You don't look well. Tell me, did he use one of his big cigars on you? He got Ellie with a cigar, you know, because she wouldn't tie his shoelaces. And when she did, when she stopped refusing and caved in – which she always did eventually – he stubbed it out on the back of her neck as she bent over his shoes. It left a scar as big as a two-pound coin. She always wore her hair down after that, just like you. He likes it long, doesn't he, your hair? To hide the marks.'

I hang my head between my knees. *Shut up*, I think, *shut up. Leave me alone.* Something is coming. I can feel it. It is in the set of my shoulders, bracing for impact. Because that's how it feels, when you get right down to it. An impact.

Something is coming.

'You been into the loft yet, Stella? You seen what he's keeping up there?'

I lift my head. Beverley seems very dim, very far away.

'That's where you need to start looking, if you want to see the kind of man you're really dealing with.'

I gulp and a watery bile rises up my throat. 'Please stop,' I say plaintively. 'Please stop.'

The edges of my vision bleed into soft greys and blacks. Blooms of midnight like Rorschach blots are rising and, just before my eyes roll up to the whites, I remember, and the memory is cruel and ravenous.

◆ ◆ ◆

It had been the day of the Essex garden party – the one Carmel would have called the Whitest In The World. The tail-end of summer had been filled with a squalid heat which had seemed oppressive; hot, stagnant air. 'Migraine Fuel', my mother had called days like that in her sour way.

I had angered him and I can't remember why. Only that I'd asked to be taken home. My stupid dress itched, and my make-up looked wrong.

'I don't look like me,' I'd told him, when he'd found me kneeling by the pool. 'I look like her, and I don't like it.'

Marco had climbed silently into the car, his rage almost tangible. There was a rapid pulse beating in the crook of his jaw like something trapped beneath the skin. I had pushed myself back into the warm leather seat. Dread was building in the hot, airless car and I began to bite my nails with quick, sharp attacks, flaying the skin. He had not spoken to me until we were back in London and had pulled up outside my flat.

'Marco, please talk to me. Please.'

He leaned back in his seat, hands folded over his chest, eyes closed.

'Get out of the car.'

I was crying, thick syrupy tears. There was a sound in my throat – *wheeeeowahh* – that I was barely aware I was making. I was saying please, and I was saying just listen Marco, but he would not look at me. I was gulping air, hiccupping with sobs.

'I can't do this anymore, Stella,' he'd said evenly. The calmer he sounded the more agitated I became. I'd always been this way, even as a kid. A biter, a pusher. 'You're so ungrateful,' he continued. 'I bought you the clothes you wanted, the shoes. You're still not happy.'

I looked down at my ruffled dress and rounded patent-leather shoes. They were not very 'me'. I didn't remember wanting them. But he was looking at me with such weary anger I suppose I must have done. I scratched at my scalp. The hair extensions itched. My hair was longer, blonder. It was almost all the way to my hips. I was barely recognisable. I was *her*.

'Get out, Stella. I'm done with you.'

I stumbled out onto the hot pavement, sticky in the heat. I could smell tar. Our road was quiet – middle-of-the-day quiet, the absence of people quiet – and as I stood, brushing myself down, tears dripping from my chin, I wished Carmel was there. She was in Brighton with someone for the weekend. A friend? I hadn't listened when she'd told me. I'd been struggling. I'd been sick.

It was Marco who caught my hand as I unlocked the front door. I did not hear him coming up behind me. He circled my wrist with his long fingers and half pulled, half dragged me inside. His face was a slack mask, terrifying. In contrast my fear was as sharp and shiny as a new pin.

'What are you doing?' He clutched my cheeks in one of his large hands, pushing my lips together into a surprised 'O'. He leaned his body against me until I was crushed into the wall. His erection pressed against my thigh. I was frightened. The flat was still and dark, the curtains drawn. There was a lit cigar in his hand. He told me I am spoilt, that my parents ruined me, always letting me get my own way. I could smell whisky and his aftershave, and beneath it something musky and sour, my sweat, my fright.

'What did I tell you, Stella? What did I ask you explicitly not to do?'

'Embarrassh oo.' My voice was soft and pulpy.

'It's a simple request, isn't it? You can follow instructions, can't you?'

'Yesh.'

'Okay, great. Well, here's an instruction for you. Turn around.'

His breath was boiling out of him in hot gasps, as it did when he was aroused. I shook my head.

He nodded in response. 'Yes. Turn around.'

His hand tightened on my face. Later I would look in the mirror and see broad strips of scarlet there as though my flesh had been seared.

I shuffled myself around so that I was facing the wall. My legs were watery and weak. He pressed up against the length of my spine, the cigar smoke thick and toxic. It was right by my left ear. His mouth bent to my right, pressing up against the soft fleshy lobe.

'I want you to remember this,' he said, and then a searing pain just below my hairline, the nape of my neck. There was a moment of intense heat followed by the rich smell of burning. My skin was burning. It smelt like crisped pork.

I screamed, but I had no strength, and he was pressing against me and, oh God, it hurt, it hurt. When he pulled away, I put my hands there and felt a raised welt where the skin was scorched and tender, weeping a light fluid.

Marco was looking at me like a man awakening from anaesthetic, his eyes seeming to focus and lose their hazy, frightening blur. He crushed the cigar out beneath his foot and clawed for me, pulling me to his chest. I did not resist. The smell of burned skin and hair made my stomach roll. Marco was whispering apologies, stroking my shoulders.

'I'm so sorry, Stella. Look what I did to you, my beautiful girl. My favourite thing. Look what I did to you. I'm so sorry.'

I let myself be stroked and after some time – surely only a few minutes – I returned his apology, telling him that it had been me, I had provoked him, telling him not to be upset, not to cry. I kissed him and told him we would seek help together. 'Yes,' he agreed, 'we will both get help. I'm so sorry—'

'No, I'm sorry.'

'You complete me,' he'd said, taking my hand, stroking my hair, 'you complete me.' Over and over and over and over. And then, like magic, with the swallowing of each little grey pill I had forgotten the crawling, prickling fear, just like I had forgotten the way my flesh had smelled like roast meat as it burned. A week or so later I would lose my own phone, misplace it, just like he told me I had. All these things I had forgotten.

When I come round, one of the windows has been opened and the air is clearer, less pungent. I apologise as Beverley hands me a glass of water. I sip it, hands shaking. '*You complete me.*' Oh, I have heard that before all right, always delivered softly into my ear as we lay, hands entwining each other, on his bed or on the couch. 'You complete me,' he would whisper, and I would feel a heat somewhere behind my ribs, a slow-burning furnace. 'You complete me.' My mouth tasting of red wine and semen. 'You complete me.' Singed hair and burning flesh. 'You complete me', as he stripped me of my friends one by one.

My phone is ringing again. I can't face it. I can't face anything. Tremors beneath the surface of my skin. Something inside is beginning to split wide open, and there will be pain that comes with it.

'I have to go, Beverley.'

Beverley nods and waves a hand in the air. 'I shan't get up. It's too much effort and my bones are weak. You seem a lovely girl, Stella. I know it must be hard work to live in the shadow of a work of fiction. You mind and pay attention.'

Chapter 30

Outside the light is bright and clear, the day magnified as though through a lens. In the dappled shade of the trees I smell wood smoke and earth, the effluvious dank smell of ditch water and wet leaves. Everything about me seems to have an extraordinary clarity but inside my thoughts buzz and collide like flies shaken in a jar. I am walking too fast, head down, thin stem of my neck drooping. Soon the sky will darken; funeral clothes for the dying day. I pull my phone from my pocket and call Frankie.

'I need to get into the loft,' I say breathlessly.

Frankie hesitates and I wonder if he is regretting getting involved in this.

'The loft.' I'm breathless, sweating. 'The loft has a lock on it, a big one. I need to get in there. I need to see what he's hiding. Can you come over? Reckon you can break it?'

'Well – sure, I suppose so. I mean, there won't be any finesse to it, it won't be my finest piece of work – but I reckon I can smash it open with something heavy unless it's one of those industrial ones.'

'I don't think so. Can you come now? Right now?'

'Yeah, course. You okay?'

'I just need to know – I need to see it for myself. Who he is.'

'Okay. I hear you.' A pause. 'You know what? You're incredibly brave.'

I stop, panting. I have never thought of myself as brave before. I am struck by it. I am brave. I am a brave woman. But inside something is moving, some new knowledge as lethal as a blood clot.

Chapter 31

When I get back to the cottage there is someone sitting on my front porch. Long legs drawn up to their chest, head resting on their knees. A dark globe of hair. An Erinys. A Fury.

'Carmel,' I say.

She stands awkwardly in the kitchen, her coat folded in her arms. She won't have a cup of tea, and she can't stay long, she tells me. When she looks at me, right at me, my eyes slide away from her gaze. I feel almost delirious. I haven't forgotten what I did to her, you see. At the end. I'd believed Marco when he'd told me that she wasn't going to press charges, that I'd never see her again. I want to reach out and touch her.

'You look well,' I tell her. She looks better than that. Vital. Even with no make-up on and her hair growing out from her buzz cut in weird kinks. She is wearing a white shirt, neatly pressed. The sleeves are rolled up to her forearms. There are still marks there, in the places that my teeth had broken the skin. Marco had said she'd probably be scarred for life. He'd laughed when he'd told me that, and said it was about time. 'Bitch got her comeuppance,' he'd said with that same wide smile.

Carmel lifts her chin, her jaw set. Her eyes are flat and cool and dark and I miss her so much I am aching as if with fever.

'I found your bag.'

'I know. Alice had it sent here.'

'No. Not that one. Your handbag.'

I blink.

She tilts her head slightly. 'It had your phone in it, your keys, bank cards. Everything.'

'It was stolen. I was drunk. Marco sa—'

'Ask me where I found it.'

I don't want to. Suddenly I want her to go, to leave before she does some real damage. I turn away from her and pour myself a glass of water from the tap with slightly shaking hands. When I lift the glass to the light it is tinted brown like nicotine. There are bits floating in there, black flecks.

'It was in the meter cupboard in the hall. It had been shoved right to the back, behind the pipework.'

I shrug. *So?*

'It wasn't stolen. It was hidden from you. Did Marco give you a new phone?'

I don't answer that, so she comes around the table and stands in front of me, arms folded.

'Do you remember what happened, Stella?'

I force myself to look at her. Her face is stone, granite. She does not smile but something softens, I think, in her eyes.

'You lost your parents' wedding rings. Do you remember?'

'Yes.'

'And you thought I'd taken them. Sold them. Because I was flat broke. Or because I was pissed off that you'd given my birthday party a swerve. Or because I was jealous of you and Marco.'

I'd said those things, all of them. I'd been looking for a fight, muggy-headed and restless. It was just a couple of days after her birthday party and her boxes were stacked in the hall, waiting for the shipping company to spirit them away. I'd gone to my room and upended my jewellery box onto the bed. My parents' rings hadn't been there. I'd grown hysterical, started pulling my room apart. I'd overturned my mattress and dismantled my bookshelf. Then I'd turned to the boxes in the hallway, the ones Carmel had carefully packed and labelled. Pulled out the contents blindly, scattering them on the floor; her clothes, her make-up, the bottle of her favourite perfume which smashed and filled the room with a dark and mossy fragrance. When she'd come home I'd been wild-eyed, shrieking. She hadn't been able to calm me down. I'd called her a thief and worse than that I'd called her a shit friend, a parasite. I'd asked her how much she'd got for selling the story about my overdose.

'I bit you.'

'You did. You did. All up my arm. My cheek. I had to have seventeen stitches. When I was triaged they thought I'd been attacked by a dog. They gave me a tetanus shot.'

Of course, I remember. I called Marco. 'Help me,' I said, 'help me.' I'd been scrubbing blood out of the carpet, almost hysterical.

'We'll fix this, Stella,' he told me. 'Don't worry. The best thing you ever did was jettison that bitch.'

'Why are you here, Carmel?'

'How much weight have you lost? Christ, there's nothing to you. Sit down.' And then more gently, 'Sit down, Stella.'

I let her lead me to a chair. Carmel moves around the kitchen, opening cupboards.

'Haven't you got any alcohol here? Vodka or something? You must have something stashed away. I thought you were meant to be an alcoholic.'

I laugh, and she brightens a little. She goes to her bag and pulls out a half-bottle of brandy. Pours us a glass each, healthy measures. She clinks her glass against mine.

'You're no more an alcoholic than I am the Pope. Have a proper drink. I know I've given you a hell of a shock, and you're about to have another, I'm afraid.'

I love the smell of alcohol, the hit at the back of the throat, the warmth blooming in your chest. I drink it in three quick swallows, and it is delicious. She pours me another, slightly smaller.

'Do you want to do this now?' she asks me, taking her iPad from her bag. I meet her eyes for the first time since I saw her outside.

'I don't know. Do I?'

She thinks for a moment. 'Yes,' she says.

The small screen fills with a grainy black-and-white image. It is a yard, seen from slightly overhead. A car is parked there, the back end of it just visible in the left-hand corner. It is Sadie, I know, and then the image falls into place the way an optical illusion does. It is outside our old Lewisham flat, mine and Carmel's. There is no date or time stamp, but I don't need one. It was the morning we left for Cornwall. Here I come into the frame, head bent, carrying my suitcase. The sun had only just begun to rise to a watery grey dawn, and my breath is visible. Here is Tonto, the neighbour's cat, coiling round my knees, tail curved. I watch myself bend and run a hand along its spine. There's me walking to the car and putting my case in the boot, going back through the open doorway. Moments later Marco comes out. He crosses to the car quickly, removes my case and goes back inside. It is just a moment. The entire footage is less than a minute long.

I watch it all again from beginning to end.

'Where did you get this?'

'The guys upstairs – their names are Drew and Ben, by the way – the cyclists. You remember they told us there had been a lot of break-ins last summer?'

'Yes.'

We had been on the balcony, Carmel and I. Drinking wine from tumblers. The air had been dusky and smoky and just right.

'Those bikes of theirs are expensive. They had CCTV fitted from their bedroom window. I remembered them doing it.'

She takes my hand and presses it gently between her own. 'On the day Alice came to collect your luggage I was at the flat packing up the last of my things. I must have looked a state because I'd been crying and I was still all stitched up. Alice was very kind. Very polite. Not pushy. But she knew. She said, "Has she gone with him?"

'"Yes," I told her. "Looks like she forgot her luggage."

'"No," Alice said, "I doubt that she did."

'And that was all. After she'd left I started to wonder what she meant by that. She worked for Marco, after all; she knew him better than all of us. Even you.'

There are tears standing in my eyes, shivering there. If I move they will fall, so I stay completely still and let Carmel finish.

'After I found the CCTV, I called Alice up at work. She told me you'd been looking for photos of Marco, and, I'll never forget it, Stella, she said, "Perhaps she is not in the dark anymore."'

'I'm so sorry, Carmel.' The tears come. Thick, syrupy. I feel them drop heavily into my lap. It is as though something has fractured, some internal fault line finally shaken apart by wave after wave of shock. 'I didn't listen.'

'You didn't know. How could you? He's a monster. Him and that quack doctor. They get off on it. Power. Control. They are very selective with their targets. They like vulnerable women.'

I wipe my nose with my sleeve.

Carmel squeezes my hand. 'Let me tell you what Alice told me. When Marco and Doctor Wilson were at university in the eighties, two women died on their campus within a year of each other. Suicide, according to the post-mortems. One of them overdosed on Quaaludes, of all things. The other hanged herself in the basement. Both women had been involved with Marco, at least one of them romantically. Funny, huh? Funny how tragedy seems to follow him around.'

'There's someone else too. Ellie. An old girlfriend. She died.'

Carmel's eyes widen.

'Here, at the house. Jumped off a cliff into the sea. She'd been taking the pills too.'

There is something unravelling within me, like a thread drawn rapidly from a spool. The more I talk the faster it comes loose. And what will happen when it does? What then?

'Just after your dad died I had a job offer in New York. I didn't tell you about it because I didn't take it. I was so worried about you; you couldn't be left alone. I didn't mind the sleepwalking, or the crying, or the melancholy. I expected that, I think. I didn't even mind that you were stealing my Valium because I could see how upset you were, how raw. But after the overdose something changed. It was Marco, the way he looked at me when I was leaning over you on the sofa, trying to wake you. He looked so angry, like he might hit me. He wanted to be the one to find you, Stella, to save you. Then you would be indebted to him. Bound to him.'

'I didn't take an overdose.'

'I know that now. He'd put something in your drinks. He was doing it to you for months.'

I remember the night of her party. How I'd woken disorientated and naked and sad. It had ruptured things between us,

Carmel and me. Not irreversibly, that was still a little way off. But the damage was deep.

'I'm going to take you home now, Stella,' Carmel says softly, squeezing my forearms with her long fingers. 'You can come with me to Paris and live in the cupboard under the sink.'

I laugh. She grins at me.

'You know I've met someone?'

'No! Who? What's his name?'

'*Her* name is Zita and she's been showing me all the most beautiful parts of Paris. You're going to love it there, Stella.'

'You look happy.'

'I am.'

We look at each other in that moment with something akin to wonder, as if we can't really believe we're sitting opposite one another, as if it's been years rather than weeks.

'You didn't sell the stories? The photos?'

She shakes her head slowly. 'Never. And I'm betting the same person who did also hid your bag and took your parents' wedding rings. All the better to turn the screw, am I right?'

I nod miserably and look down at my ring finger. I'm still wearing his ring, the one he said had belonged to his grandmother. I slide it over my knuckle and place it on the tabletop. *It comes from Penang*, he'd said. *That's in Malaysia*. I know where Penang is, dickhead.

'Now I want you to listen to me. Get your things. You need to get away from here. It's poi—'

The knock at the door is loud enough to startle us. We exchange glances, wary, frightened, and then I remember. Frankie. I am filled with a mixture of thrill and treachery, my heart rising into my throat, blood hot and restless. Once we have broken the lock we cannot go back. I will have to go up into that dark, airless space and reveal what he has been hiding from me. All this time.

'It's Frankie,' I tell Carmel. 'He's going to help me get into the room upstairs.'

'You know the tale of Bluebeard's wife, Stella?' Carmel is asking me as I am hurrying towards the door. I don't answer and later I will wish I had. It will be the last thing she ever says to me.

Chapter 32

Just before I open the door I turn and look over my shoulder. I cannot shake the feeling that something is creeping up on me. I unlatch the front door. 'What took you so long?' But it is not Frankie.

'Hello, Stella.'

Marco. He stares at me flatly. His knuckles are bloodied and raw-looking, his nose a bright-red pulp. A bib of blood stains his shirt. I can't speak. I feel like my throat is plugged with cotton.

'Say something.' He spits on the ground; it is foamy and red.

'What happened to you?'

'Smashed the car. Can I get a drink?'

'Christ, Marco. You're hurt.'

'Yeah.' He pulls down his lip. 'Lost a tooth, see? Maybe I could put it under my pillow, see what I get.'

I shiver with revulsion. Something has spoiled, curdled inside him. He even smells sour as he pushes past me, into the hallway. Outside, the mist is thickening, reducing everything to shadow.

'We need to get you an ambulance. You're hurt.'

'You should see the other guy.'

'What?'

'You should see the other guy.'

I run into the garden and down the path. Up ahead I can hear the tick of cooling metal, the hiss of escaping steam. One ghostly light winking on and off in the gloom. A hazard light.

'Frankie!'

There, on the lane. A shape, dark lines growing clearer as I run towards it. I can see Sadie, skewed across the stony track at an angle, slammed into one of the hawthorn trees which line the road. There is steam coming from beneath the crumpled bonnet, a spider-web crack in the glass of the windscreen running from one corner to the other. The *ding*, *ding*, *ding* of the seatbelt alarm. I listen for a moment, and I hear something else. A faint groan, almost spirited away in the fog. I press my face up to the glass but there is no one in the car. The seatbelt alarm is chiming quietly, and there is blood pooled on the passenger seat. Chunks of safety glass stud it like glittering diamonds. Then I see him, lying in the road a little further away. He has crawled there on his hands and knees. Now he is lying face up to the sky, the mist crawling all over him, in the places where the blood has seeped through his clothes.

'Frankie!' I shout, unable to stop myself. 'Frankie!'

His head lolls, his eyes rolled up to the whites. For a moment he is horribly still. Then his chest jerks and I hear him cough weakly, and with considerable pain.

'Frankie.' I kneel beside him, wanting to touch him, not wanting to move him, resting my hands against his face. He is cold.

'Frankie, let me call an ambulance. I'm going to call someone for you so hold tight, okay?'

I don't think I am crying, but when I try to speak again a lump fills my throat like soft dough. His hand lifts and drops onto his chest, on top of mine. It squeezes, just once. I lower my head to him, next to his cheek where the stubble grows thickest, the curls of his hair meeting his neck. I breathe him in, crying and choking and unable to move. I tell him I'm sorry, I tell him I will get help. He opens his eyes and gives me a pained smile.

'Get out of here. Run.'

'Frankie—'

'Run, Stella, please run. I so want you to live.'

I find his lips – they are so cold – and plant a kiss there, soft and warm and tender. I am acutely aware of his taste, the firmness of his mouth, the way his hand lifts a little to stroke my hair. My eyes are bright with unshed tears.

'Don't leave me,' I tell him and then—

'Stella!'

Marco's voice, sharp and flat like a gunshot. I jump, scrambling to my feet.

'Stella!'

I stare into the fog. I can't risk running along the cliff in this, not with the crumbling, unsafe ground. I can run to town along the road, maybe make it as far as the Daltons' before Frankie dies. I don't like the whistling sound his breathing is making, and I don't like the sticky pool of blood slowly spreading beneath him. I can call an ambulance if I lock myself in the bathroom, but my phone is in the house and to reach it I will have to get past Marco. And what about Carmel? I can't leave her. She has come here to help me.

'Stella!'

'Hold on, Frankie, hold on.' His eyes have closed again. I lean forward, kiss him on his forehead. 'Hold on.'

Marco is waiting at the house, standing in the doorway. He is very pale, his eyes hooded pools of ink. He is singing, I can hear it more clearly as I get closer. The theme tune to *Marigold!*, the one I've always hated.

'There's Bonnie and there's Eddie and there's Mum and Mikey too,
Daddy, Lucy, Frisky, we'll never forget you!
But who is coming out to play to say how do you do?
It's little Katie Marigold, with eyes of sparkling blue!'

I'm standing in front of him and now he reaches for me, pulls me towards him. I am limp, in shock. Real love is glacial, hard and cold. It is not this love, this meteorite, this fiery comet, obliterating. Marco has scarred me, the force of his impact. I am shaken by it.

'Frankie's hurt.'

'He's dying,' he tells me flatly. 'I saw him hit the dashboard. Made a sound like you wouldn't believe. Still, when you're that fat, perhaps it's like wearing an airbag.' He smirks at me. 'I thought you wanted to see what was in the loft. Isn't that why you called Frankie to come and visit you with his enormous tool?' He laughs at his own innuendo. 'Well, Stella? You must have figured it out by now.'

'I don't kn—'

'Oh, come on, honey. Come on, baby girl. You were never that great an actress. In 1989 *Smash Hits* described you as wooden as a plank in a wig. Did you know that?'

'No.' I'm telling the truth. My mother kept all the bad press away from me, every negative review, every insult. I can see why now, because it still stings.

'You know what I did?' Marco has guided me into the house, closing the door softly on the mist, on Frankie. 'I bought every single issue of that magazine from eleven different newsagents, and I burned them all in the garden.'

He is looking at me, deadly serious. I look down at what he is holding. It is the doorstop, the cast-iron one which props open the back door. There is something stuck to it. Is it hair? Is it *hair*?

'Every single one. No one says that about Katie Marigold. Not about my girl.'

'We need to call an ambulance, Marco. For Frankie. He could die.'

'Could he? Yes, I suppose he could. Get one for Carmel too.' Marco doesn't move. 'Light me a cigarette, would you?'

Wait.

'What do you mean, Carmel too?'

He doesn't answer, and I run towards the doorway, calling her name. My legs feel like rotten wood, as though they are going to splinter and give way under me.

'Carmel!'

I can see blood. That is the first thing. Spatters of it, coin-sized, leading from the kitchen to the sitting room. A smear of blood on the doorpost there, jewel-red. Something flips in my stomach. I walk slowly, but I don't say her name again. She is lying on the floor of the sitting room, parallel to the couch, as if she had crawled the last few feet and not quite made it. I swallow the gorge which is rising in me. She is face down, surrounded by a halo of blood so glossy I can see the reflection of the window in it. I approach her, put my hand on her back. There is no rise and fall of breath. One of her shoes hangs off her feet, exposing a heel, her dainty toes. I want to cry.

'Don't turn her over.'

It's Marco in the doorway. I try to inhale but my chest is painful and tight. Her hand is curled above her head. He has struck her a violent blow, but she can't be dead, I tell myself. *But look. Look at all that blood.*

'Don't, honey. You don't want to see that.'

'What did you do to her?'

'Knocked a little sense into her. Come away. Come on. It's for your own good.'

'You— You've killed her.'

'I was defending you.'

282

I look up at him, confused. He is holding out his hand to pull me up. I don't know what to do, should I take it? I don't know. I look down at Carmel again. She can't be really dead, can she? Not *really*, really. But I've never seen so much blood and still it is growing as some vital artery pumps out the last of her. I close my eyes and see stars and then Marco is pulling me up onto my feet.

'Can you walk?'

'You killed her.'

'She was trying to attack me. It was self-defence.'

I look at him aghast as he walks to the window, bending down to look outside. We are back in the dining room now, and I have to lean on the mantelpiece for support.

'Why was Frankie in the car with you?'

'Bumped into him turning into the lane, right at the top. Looked like he'd been running to get here, like he was about to have a heart attack. Fat men shouldn't run. I told him that. It's dangerous, I said. You want to know something funny? He didn't want to get into the car. Kept walking, head down. "Do you want a lift, Frankie? Do you want to get in here with me?" Just shook his head. Then I saw what he was holding.'

'What?'

'A hammer.'

Marco puts the doorstopper down gently on the polished surface of the table.

'I had a bad feeling, Stella. Like he meant to hurt you. After everything you said about him, and then here he is, in thick fog, alone, with a weapon, heading to the cottage. I couldn't let that happen. So I told him to get into the car, that I needed him to help me – to help you. Told him you'd finally lost the plot, that I was worried about you. That convinced him.'

'You've as good as killed him. Both of them.'

'Accidents happen, honey. In the mist, on twisting lanes, driving too fast. Recipe for disaster.'

My stomach knots itself slickly. I have to get to my phone. It is on the table. I can see it from where I'm standing. If I am careful I might be able to slide it into my pocket or up my sleeve without him noticing. Marco looks at me carefully, his mouth twitching in a barely concealed smile. That's the thing about Marco. He always could read me.

'It's just us now. As it should be.'

He walks to the table, picks up my phone and slides it into his coat pocket. When he smiles at me my skin crawls.

'Tell you what, Stella, here's what we'll do. I'll take you up to the loft, because I'm the only one with the key and your pal Frankie would've taken off his fingers trying to break through that padlock – and if you're a good girl – if you behave – you can make a call, get a doctor or whatever. Okay?'

He's lying, of course. He has no intention of giving me my phone back or letting me call an ambulance. I feel like screaming but instead I just say okay because my friend is dead, my friend who lit up a room like Oxford Street at Christmas, she's dead, and so what else is there?

'I don't trust you when it comes to doctors.'

He laughs. It is rich and warm and pleasant, as though the woman who taught me how to roll a joint isn't lying in a pool of blood next door. I have to keep my head. I have to think clearly.

We're standing in the hallway. The light is diffuse and grainy. I am trying not to shiver, not to think about Frankie bleeding out alone on a dirty, unpaved road. I choke a sob and Marco looks at me, just once, his eyes crawling over me like searchlights. He is holding up a key, small in his large hand. One look at his eyes confirms all I have feared. There is nothing there at all. The mask has slipped, revealing a simple cold fury.

He unlocks the door and opens the hatch, drawing down an aluminium stepladder. He stands aside so I can go up first and I am suddenly sure that this is the place where I will die. About us that strange smell that has haunted all my days here is rising, rising like the mist. Like rolling dunes at the bottom of the ocean where a body may be buffeted by the tide for long months, flesh stripped from bones, seaweed threaded through empty eye sockets.

I start to climb up into the darkness. I can hear him below, telling me there is a light switch to my right, and I grope for it with fast, frightened breath. I find the switch. I turn it on, cry out. There is someone up here with me. A woman.

'Marco!'

'Isn't it great?' He is smiling, delighted. 'Do you like it?'

It's a mannequin. I can see that now that my eyes have adjusted to the thin light. She wears a wig, softly curled at the edges, and a dress of sickly jade-green with a long sash wound about the waist. Marco pulls himself up through the hatch and closes it quietly behind him. Now it is the two of us, here in this tiny low-ceilinged room. I look around. There are boxes and an old vacuum cleaner shoved into the far corner, thick with dust. To my left are several bulky shapes shrouded in dust sheets. A low futon, the mattress old and fusty-looking, sunken in the middle, has been pushed against the wall. It is dappled with stains. I can't imagine sleeping there, where the roof meets the eaves. In the thick darkness it must be like being in a coffin.

'You know what it is, right?' He is looking at me eagerly. 'Come and see it. Come and feel it. It's silk.'

I walk forward stiffly and dutifully stroke the fabric. 'Soft.'

'It's perfect, isn't it? Look at the buttons, the detail is amazing.'

I look at them and it drops into place with such gravity my stomach rolls. The buttons are round and golden and big as coins. The shoulders puff at the sleeves where little ribbons are knotted in oversized bows. There are Chinese dragons stitched onto the hem. I have to put out a hand to steady myself. The room pinholes as though I might faint.

'"Katie Marigold and the Chinaman", right?'

'Right,' I manage, and then because he expects more, 'It's my dress.'

'That's right! It's a perfect copy, just a little bigger. You did the song in this one, do you remember?'

'Uh-huh.'

The wig on the mannequin is a carbon copy of my hairstyle all those years ago, Regency ringlets in a dark treacle colour. I touch it, moving it gently with my fingers.

'Careful,' Marco tells me, 'that's human hair.'

I pull my hand back as though stung and he laughs.

'Silly. It's from Russia. I had to pay a lot of money for that.'

He has pulled the dust sheet away from the object in the centre of the room and now I see it is a clothes rail, at least fifty dresses: ruffles and prints, crinoline and taffeta and stiff cotton. My head is spinning. I wish I could breathe properly. Marco is almost giddy with excitement, pulling out a red-and-white candy-striped smock and turning it on the hanger, holding it up to the light.

'"In Your Dreams, Katie Marigold",' I say. 'God, Marco. How did you make all of these?'

'I don't make them, Katie. I have a lady in Kent, a seamstress. She is very, very talented. Has been doing this for years. She thinks I'm a cross-dresser and that suits me fine if it gets the clothes made.'

'You're not?'

He pulls a face. 'Of course not. What kind of question is that? These aren't for me to wear. They're for you.'

I have to be very careful here, I tell myself. 'Marc-oh.' I am speaking very carefully, very slowly, the way I had with Beverley Dalton at first. '"Uncle". That's you, isn't it?'

He laughs jerkily – heh, heh – it doesn't sound like him at all. Then he exhales, just once, and there it is. That phlegmy, wet rattle. I feel sick.

He looks up at me. 'You're so funny on the phone. I can hear the way your voice trembles. It's exciting.' He has been rummaging beneath the futon and now he finds what he is looking for. 'Ah – here it is!'

Marco pulls out a box and places it on the floor. Inside, shoes. Little buckled-up Mary-Janes, in patent black and red. Just like the ones he'd given me to wear to the party in Essex. My pulse throbs just once, hot jets of blood.

'I have to get out of here. I can't breathe.'

'God, you are spoilt, aren't you? Even now. Joey Fraser said it and your Aunt Jackie said it and Daddy Marigold called you a high-handed little bitch to the *Daily Mirror* in 1988 and that was the end of his career. You know what? They're right. Every one of them. Look around you. Have you any idea of the amount of effort I've gone to for you? Each sequin is individually sewn. Every fabric swatch was sent for my approval. One dress took ten months to get right. All for you, Katie.'

'What about Ellie?'

His face changes suddenly, becoming a cold fury which frightens me. His eyes glitter in the darkness. 'What about her?'

'I mean, did she wear these clothes too? Was she Katie Marigold, at least for a little while?'

'She tried her best. She was a poor imitation. You though, you're the real thing.'

He is grinning at me, exposing gums the colour of liver. Outside I can imagine the fog pressing close to the house, isolating us, turning the cottage into an island on which I am marooned with my past, and a little further away the wreck of the car and the body of Frankie, breathing in that slow, rapturous way. How long does he have? How long do I have, stranded up here with someone whose love is a poisoned arrow? I can see the shape it has burned into him, all those years of pining and wanting, the fierceness of it.

'I need to get out. Please, Marco, please. I can't breathe in here.'

'You'll get used to it.'

His voice is clipped and cold and he doesn't look at me as he opens the hatch. I see that he means to leave me up here and I open my mouth to scream but the only sound which comes out is a reedy whisper, something choked. No, no. Then it closes with a soft thunk and the scraping sound of the padlock being fixed into place and that's when my knees give way.

A little later, perhaps, I don't know how long. I have been shouting for a long time and banging the palms of my hands on the floor. Now my throat is raw and my eyes sting. The darkness up here is thick and pressing, even with the light bulb overhead. It smells too, something musty and slightly spoiled, like milk left too long in the sun. I am sitting on the edge of the futon with my knees drawn up to my chest. I found a box beneath the bed, an old-fashioned wooden one with a brass clasp. Inside it is make-up – some face powder and a creamy blusher and a little bottle of perfume which smells of grit and violets. I can't stop thinking I can't afford the luxury of waiting too long. I wonder if it is getting dark out there yet. I wonder if Frankie is afraid.

I dress slowly, carefully, ignoring the horror crawling up my throat. I leave my crumpled jeans and bra on the bed and slip the green dress over my head. It rustles like dry leaves. At the side a series of hook-and-eye fasteners draws the material together although it is still a little loose at the hips. I tie the sash as I was shown all those years ago, on set on Hastings Pier, the wind teasing my skirts, the smell of face powder and hairspray and the sea. The sea. I can smell it here as I slip the wig over my hair, securing it with pins from the make-up box. Sea mist and cool air, a dank perfume, rising, rising. I think, just for a moment, that I see something moving in the dark, just ahead. A shadow seeming to detach from the gloom. It is cold in here, and the air is close. Like before a storm.

I am gulping back tears, trying to ignore the weight of sadness on my chest like a concrete block. I can't think about Carmel. Can't afford the tears it will cost me. I apply the make-up with hands which tremble slightly, making sure to get the cheeks pink and rosy, almost flushed. That was the thing with Katie Marigold, there was so much make-up, especially as I got older. By the time I was ten they were painting on my freckles with watercolour paint and a cotton bud, masking the onset of my adolescent acne with thick unguents. I press the powder to my face, turning my skin a rich, creamy colour. Even the smell is the same. I don't know how he found out what make-up we'd used but then I remember Willowvale. He must have asked a lot of questions, must have tracked down the right people. What was the word? *Fanatical.*

Finally, I am ready. I feel ridiculous. The wig itches and sits too high on my head, the blusher staining my cheeks like a pink fever. The skirts whisper as I walk across the floor and knock carefully on the hatch. I need to sound calm. I need to sound normal. Lucky I've had so much practice.

'Marco? Marco, can you hear me?'

Silence. I know he's there though. Sitting close by, waiting. The idea of it – the image of him sitting motionless in the gathering darkness still stained with blood, waiting, waiting with his jaw clenched, is so horrible that I catch my breath.

'Marco. I've made up my mind. Please open the hatch. Please.'

I don't like the way my voice is softening, becoming girlish, buttery. Katie Marigold spoke like that, careful with her words.

Hesitating when the script said *pause for laughter*. I knock again. 'Marco.'

Finally, the rattling sound of the padlock, the click. A frame of light appears around the square shape of the hatch in the floor and then a moment later it opens inwards and he lifts his head, squinting into the near darkness.

'Baby,' he says softly, his breath hitching, 'you've done a beautiful job. Come here so I can look at you.'

I step a little closer, turning slowly when he indicates I do so. He laughs and runs his hands through his hair.

'I – oh, wow – I've waited for this moment for so long. I can't believe it, it's you, it's really, really you.'

'It's me.'

I wonder what comes next. I don't think he wants to have sex with me; his fascination is less shallow than that, less carnal.

'I need a dog.'

He pulls a face. 'No. No dogs. Didn't Frisky bite you once in 1992?'

Yes, he did. Had to be put down after that. A danger to the kids, they'd said. What I hadn't told anyone is that I'd bitten him first. My mother always said I'd been an angry child, gnashing my teeth and grinding my jaw until my gums bled. The biting came later, not long after I'd put on the Katie Marigold costume for the first time and I'd bitten the wardrobe assistant on the arm. Her eyes had widened and the look of shock on her face had made me feel powerful and excited. She'd bled. That had excited me too. The purple marks of my teeth on her skin.

'When I found out Frisky bit you I felt pretty angry. There was a picture of you and your mum in the *Mirror* and you had a bandage on your arm.'

'Is that why you did it?'

'Huh?'

'Poisoned them. The other dogs.'

'Oh. Yeah. I got three of them, right before they locked security down on the set. You wouldn't believe how easy it was to walk in and out of there. I told them I was the tea boy, and they let me go anywhere. Even made me a pass. After the third time though they got a bit suspicious with all these dead animals piling up.'

I'm remembering Alice telling me how she had found those photos on his hard drive. What was it she had said? They look like they were taken on set. Candid, she meant. A hidden camera.

'So you know what I did? I hid rat poison in the locker of that cleaner. Rat poison and slug pellets. He cried when they arrested him. Told them he loved the show. I bet he bloody did. They found all those things he'd stolen in his dingy little hovel, didn't they? Photos and props and stuff. He'd been stealing it and selling it to fans. He was wrong in the head. I did you a favour there. They never tracked me down, of course. I knew my limits, Katie.'

'I'm not Katie.'

'You never thanked me, you know. For all the things I sent you. All the things I made you.'

'Thank you.'

'My pleasure.'

I have to get out of this room, out onto the road. I'm worried about what the futon means, the little tray beside the hatch. I think he means to keep me up here, keep me prisoner. He lifts himself up, sitting with his legs dangling into the empty space beneath him.

'I promised you something, didn't I, if you were my good girl?'

I nod. He holds out his hand. On his palm are my pills, more pills, four of them. Unmarked, unbranded. I could take them and drift away, forget everything. It was a wonderful feeling. I'd like it back.

'Take them. I've got you some water. Are you hungry?'

I shake my head and he tips the pills into my outstretched hand.

'I've made you a sandwich. I'll leave it up here for you, it's nearly teatime. You can have it when you get hungry.'

I can't cry. I can't protest. I nod, smiling weakly.

'You know you were right,' I manage. 'This does feel good after all this time. Safe.'

'Exactly. I knew you'd get it. I knew you'd understand.'

I say his name as he begins to climb back down the ladder.

'Marco, I just want one thing.'

His features are clouded with a frown of suspicion. I've asked him wrong. I need to be careful. I am Katie Marigold now, and she wouldn't talk that way. I try to keep my voice light.

'Can I ask for something? Something little?' *Liddle*, something *liddle*.

'Sure.'

'I want my mummy's jar. The one with the pennies in. It's all I have of her.'

'You brought it all the way down here with you, that stupid jar? Honey, really?'

'Really truly absol-ully.' Another Marigoldism. The whole sickening family said it.

Marco brightens, smiling again. 'Where is it?'

'On the windowsill by the sink.' Where I could see it every morning when I woke up, filled the kettle. All I had of the woman who had forged my career from her flesh and sweat and sex.

'I'll get it for you if you take those pills. Do we have a deal?'

'You bet!'

'Okey-dokey.'

I stare at the pills as he closes the hatch and carefully, carefully, slips the padlock closed. Marco is not taking any chances, but chances are all I have. Overhead, only a centimetre or so above my scalp, are the rafters of the house. I wonder if I can hide the pills up there, if I can convince him that I am swallowing them with a closed hand. With a sinking heart I realise Marco will not allow that. And if he finds out I'm trying to deceive him? I don't know. I just don't know. I think Ellie had the right idea, when she jumped. I wonder how she got down from here and then realise he wouldn't have been using a padlock then. That would have come after, after she escaped. She was off her head in the last days, too spaced out to move, to speak out. I wonder what her breaking point was. Was she wearing one of these dresses, specially made to Marco's specifications? Probably. Heavy, dense silk maybe, weighing her down in the water. If the fall hadn't killed her first, the dress would have. It comes down to a choice, I realise. A choice. *Do I want to live?*

Marco is back with the jar. He places it carefully on the edge of the hatch and I have to stop myself from grabbing it, from snatching it away. I kneel in front of him, and he passes me the water. All these will knock me out; my tolerance is low, and they are very strong. *Do I want to live*, I ask myself as Marco puts them carefully on my outstretched tongue one after the other. *Do I want to live?*

'Drink it all, Katie,' he tells me, and I do, and down they go. Now I have very little time before they wipe me out. I wonder if I will do it. My chances are not good. Still, I am careful not to shatter the illusion. I take his hand in my clammy, damp one.

'Thank you for showing me this, Marco.'

He breathes me in, holding his face close to mine. His face is so happy beneath all the blood. My hand moves slowly, finds the place where the jar is, lifts it carefully. All I have of her, airtight, untouched. I have to be careful, and I have to be quick. I let out all the breath I am holding, force my shoulders down. My fingers tighten around the jar, just a little. I move quickly, lifting my arm over my head. He sees, but too late, drawing his arm up protectively. The jar shatters with the impact, the full force of me. It slices into my soft palm, against Marco's temple. He makes a nasty, strangled noise, knocked backwards where his head rocks against the baseboard with a sharp snap. The coins fall to the floor musically, bouncing and spinning, and all I have left in my hand is a jagged shard no more than four inches long. I slam it against him, cutting into his cheek, which wells blood thickly. Breathless, I slide my body down the hole, feel his fingers grasping for me, circling around my wrist, tugging. There is an awful pain in my shoulder as something gives, as I am jerked just short of the floor. I look up and see his bloodied, awful face leering down at me, his lips drawn back in a snarl. He has his hand around my thin wrist, squeezing it so the bones grind together painfully. I yelp, stabbing at him with the glittering blade, puncturing the soft web of flesh between his thumb and forefinger. Then he lets me go, and I stagger and fall, pitching forward towards the stairs. A thud behind me tells me he is already through, landing on his feet the way he always does, moving towards me as I gather these stupid skirts in both hands and run.

He catches me at the top of the stairs. I hear his grunt of exertion as he lunges forward, feel the air shifting behind me. I'm okay, I'm doing all right, and then I have one of those sickening lurches that reminds me I have just taken four sedatives and the floor shifts and it slows me just a fraction, and then he is on me, pinning me down, a knee in my kidneys. I bite my tongue, see stars. His hand like a manacle, clutching my calf and the other plunging into my hair, grasping. He pulls my head back, grunting with satisfaction. I can feel the rage seething off him like a heat.

'Shouldn't run,' he is saying, and he lifts my head by the roots, slamming my face into the floor. I see stars. My scalp is full of needles. There is a sense of wetness and when I look down there is a steady trickle of blood, a crushing pressure in my sinuses. I swallow, try to roll over. He smothers me with his weight, pulling his face close to my ear. His breathing is harsh and ragged.

'I didn't want to do this, Katie. You should have kept taking the pills. I'm not even sure you're worth all this trouble.'

A sound, then. The clicking of a latch. So simple it startles us both. We look up.

'There's someone in the house,' he mutters.

I feel his weight lift away from me. I want to call out but I have no breath left, my words won't come. Marco is smoothing down his shirt, fixing his hair. He looks troubled and I don't blame him. There is a dead body downstairs and blood all over him. Again, that smell, that feeling of coldness to the bone.

'It's Ellie,' I tell him, using the wall to help myself to stand. I have another dizzying rush to the head, the pills are starting to kick in. My nose feels plugged, my throat too. There is blood in my mouth. Marco does not turn round. He walks to the top of the stairs, peering down into the blue shadows.

'She's come back for you.'

He puts his foot on the top stair, not looking back at me. The air has grown dense and cold and frightening and I am short of time. I draw myself up from the soles of my feet and run at him, hands outstretched, shoving him in the back.

You ever pushed someone down the stairs? It's harder than you think. First, they don't tumble end over end. That's for stunt men and cartoons. Second, you need a lot of force and although I take Marco by surprise I am weak and injured, and I think I have dislocated my shoulder in the fall. The shove I give him only makes him lose his balance for a moment, long enough to grapple for the banister, snatching at the air, teetering. He almost had it. Almost. I step closer to him. So hot, it is almost unbearable. A raging fury in the pit of him, where it is blackest. Behind him a figure is climbing the stairs. I see it and do not. Every time I try to focus my eye simply slips away like butter in a hot pan. A thin shape, long hair which she always wore down to hide the scar on the back of her neck, the one as big as a Cuban cigar. There is a film over Ellie's eyes, gummy and translucent, and water running from her pale fingers, rivulets flowing like tributaries from the soles of her feet. Her mouth is open, and she snatches for him and down he goes.

Toppling forward, his descent marked by a series of unhappy slapping sounds, the clatter as he connects with the banister, the crack which rings like a shot in the empty house. *That is a bone*, my horrified brain insists on telling me. *That is one of Marco's bones breaking. Maybe even his neck. Are you happy now?*

Then. Silence.

I have to lean on the rail for support, swaying slightly. There is a darkness at the edge of my vision but worse than that the pills are making me care less. Not careless. I'm just losing interest, the way I had before. Suddenly this doesn't seem so important. Easier just to sink. I try to fix on Frankie, the way the blood had pooled beneath him, his eyes rolled back. I am still holding that shard of glass and now as I make my way down the steps saying Marco's name in a small voice I grind it into my palm, squeezing my fingers around it, letting the pain sharpen me. A gout of blood spatters onto the floor.

I draw a thin breath, then another. It feels as though I will never be able to inflate my lungs. In the thick silence I wonder if I have killed him. I think of that sharp cracking sound again. From here I can see the tangle of his legs where he landed a good foot or two away from the last step. Listening. No one down here but Ellie and Carmel. No one down here but us dead folks.

'Marco?'

I begin to edge down the stairs.

'Marco?'

I can see him more clearly now, face down on the floor, legs sprawled beneath him. Only one arm is visible, the other pinned beneath his body at a terrible angle.

I am halfway down and can feel a cold draught. The back door has been thrown open hard enough to knock a chunk of plaster from the wall. There are wet footprints leading to the foot of the stairs.

I approach the body of the man who used to be my lover and crouch down next to his face. The ends of my hair brush against his cheek.

'Marco?' I whisper. There is no response. I cannot see the rise and fall of his chest.

'Marco?'

I put two fingers to his neck and almost scream when he groans and spits out a long web of bloody phlegm.

'You bitch,' he slurs, and plants the palms of his hands on the floor, trying to lever himself up. 'Pushed me. You bitch.'

'No, no, Marco, I—'

'I think you've broken my ribs.'

He lies still for a moment, breathing heavily into the crook of one arm. I stare about the room wildly. I tried to kill him. I'm going to prison.

'Come here.'

I lean in. The room lurches, expands like a bubble. Soon I will pass out, I think. My mouth is dry.

Marco lifts his fingers to his mouth and says, 'Look at all this blood.'

He holds his fingers out to me.

'Look at it. You did this. You did this to me. You're going to hell, Katie Marigold.'

His voice is flat, uncurious. I can feel the draught against my ankles, a cold drift of sea air. The smell too, salt and blood and the ocean, thickening.

'Here.' He holds his bloodied fingers up to my face. 'Closer.'

I do as he asks, closing my eyes. Now we are barely inches apart. I can see his bloodied fingers glistening. He strokes lines down my cheekbones with unbearable tenderness.

'Warpaint.'

Marco's eyes have a hard, flat shine. He presses his fingers to his swollen, bleeding lips and smiles. There is no kindness in that smile, only a cold malice, an unsheathed blade.

'Open your mouth.'

I shake my head.

'Open your mouth.'

'No, I don't want—'

He sighs. 'Open your fucking mouth.'

Sullenly I open my mouth a little way. He reaches forward, grips my lower jaw and forces it open until I hear the bones click. His fingers slide into my mouth. I can taste his blood on them, metallic. He smears them over my teeth, my gums, the roof of my mouth. Some horrors are nameless; I know that now. They lie still as sediment, and they wait. I close my eyes, my mouth is full of Marco's blood, his fingers painting my lips. I think of Frankie. It was a good kiss. I want to remember it well.

I jolt myself, squeezing my injured hand into a fist again. The pain flares like heat, as though my palm is full of smoking embers. My vision clears. I was nearly asleep. Marco is crawling to the fireplace, one arm across his stomach. He uses the mantelpiece to haul himself up. I watch horrified as he turns to face me. His skin is taut and shiny, his lips raw meat, his eyes sunken into puffy purple flesh like rotting plums.

He beckons me. I shake my head. I say, 'Please, Marco.' He grins and there is nothing in it but a hate, black and rich and subterranean. I wonder how I could ever have believed he loved me. I'm going to die here. I can't defend myself against this man. He will always have this power over me.

He stoops and draws a poker from the fireplace as I walk towards him. It is brass and heavy and still I am walking as though through a swamp, slowly, just one foot in front of the other. The pills are sinking me and the headlines will read '*Miserable Death of Tragic Child Star*'.

'You. You don't deserve to win.'

'Always a competition with you, isn't it? Always about you. Daddy Marigold said the same in' – he turns his head and spits blood onto the floor. We both regard it solemnly for a moment. The room gives another of those lurches and I stagger slightly. I have to stay focused. – 'in the newspapers. Said you were a horrible child who was going to be a horrible adult. He's dead now. But guess what? He was right.'

'He was an actor. It was just a show. We all hated it by the end. All hated each other.'

Marco is holding on to the mantelpiece so tightly his knuckles are white. His pallor is a ghostly grey, sweating. He looks very bad. I tighten my grip on the glass and a fresh wave of pain swells in my arm all the way to the elbow. My brain jolts. I stiffen.

'That show killed your mother and now it's going to kill you too. You should have just listened to me. Why couldn't you listen? Why couldn't you just take the pills?'

I step closer towards him. I don't know if he has enough strength in him to swing that poker but if he does he could kill me from here.

'You're shaking.'

'I'm scared,' I reply truthfully. 'I've never been so scared. I think you're going to kill me.'

He does not reassure me that he will not. Instead, he nods as though he understands. His expression has calcified, it's terrifying.

'What was I saying?'

'The pills,' I whisper.

'That's right.'

'You need an ambulance, Marco.'

'No, no. No. But we will need painkillers. A lot of painkillers. I'm going to bite you till you bleed. See how you like it.'

He smiles, and it is hideous, and I want to run but my legs are leaden and so here I stand after all, despite everything. I am too late for Frankie. I am too late for me.

'You planted the knife. That night you came down here with Jackie. You put it on the counter because you knew I'd pick it up, that I'd be frightened. You – you *made* me stab you – you were trying to make me look mad.'

'Honey, I didn't need to try too hard.'

'That night in the taxi, back in London. I didn't attack you. I fell asleep. You did it to yourself, and it was awful. And the car. Sadie, outside. You drove it off the road. You injured yourself, and you killed Frankie. Do you think this is normal, Marco? To hurt yourself like this over and over till your skin bruises and your bones break?'

'I did it for you!' he shouts suddenly, the tendons on his neck standing out like cords. 'You'd forgotten who you were! You needed to be reminded!'

He spits, a white foam bubbling at the corners of his mouth. He smells like spoiled meat and his hand is flexing on the poker. I step a little closer. The room moves around me. I don't know how much time I have left but not long till I go under. Not long.

'You were drugging me. I lost my mind. It's called gaslighting, the things that you do. Did you know that?'

'They were dragging you down, Katie. All those monstrous friends, that boring little life you had. You should be thanking me. You should be on your knees thanking me.'

I am close enough now to see that one of his eyes is filled with blood. I squeeze the glass in my palm to remind myself. This is who he is, this pain.

'What did you do with my parents' wedding rings?'

'In the canal they went. It's not healthy to hold on to sentimental things. You, you should know that.' He wipes his lips and his ghastly red eye fixes on me. 'I'm going to knock that gap back into your teeth. Stand back, honey. This is going to hurt a lot.'

He is lifting the poker, and I turn to run, tripping over the stupid ruffled skirts, sending myself sprawling. I roll, amazed at my agility, and he brings the poker down, splintering the floorboards. I know what I have to do. I have to get him outside. I have to stay together long enough to get him onto the cliff and then Ellie will help me. I start to crawl and I hear him behind me, coming forward, the rush of air as he lifts that poker, and so I pull myself beneath the dining table, hear the crash overhead as something breaks, the fruit bowl perhaps, a thud as the strike leaves a long gash in the beautiful polished oak. The back door is open, and even though I am floaty, floaty, I scramble towards it stiff-legged on all fours like a bear. Outside the mist has thickened to a dense, glittering fog. I can hear Marco behind me, the crash of an overturned chair, I can't believe how fast he is after losing all that blood. It's the madness, boiling in him, galvanising him.

I push through the back door and hear the frame fracture as he swings the poker sideways into it, missing me by a hair. The coolness of the outside wakes me immediately, and I run into the curtain of mist without looking back, hoping he can hear my footsteps. He mustn't lose me. If he does, then he will just go back to the house and wait for the mist to clear. I will collapse on the clifftop if I'm lucky, maybe ten, fifteen minutes from now. He will drag me back before nightfall. So he has to be able to see me. He has to be close.

I turn around, see him struggling with the poker, which is embedded in the plaster. He finally jerks it free and turns, squinting into the gloom. I move, and he spots me, lurching forward, face twisted into a sneer.

'Marco!' I call him and he walks forward, slashing at the fog with the poker, the *whicking* sound it makes flat and horrible. His breathing is ragged, focused. I call him again, a little ahead of him, and to my shock and surprise he runs, almost grabs me, appearing out of the grey like a phantom. I pitch at the last minute, turning sharply, the glass grinding into my palm, my throat tight. All the sounds are like underwater, seven minutes, maybe less, and I will be so unsteady I will need to hide. I stumble along the cliff path, trying to be careful, trying to be fast. I hear him behind me, clumsy, spitting, and the *whick, whick, whick* of the poker as though he might get lucky.

'Marco!'

I have moved a little to the right, a little too far from the path, and now I realise I am dangerously close to the edge. I try to move further along and I see him, shadowy and bent over, coming towards me when I have nowhere to back in to. Behind me, the drop and the Atlantic. I can hear the deep booming of the waves in the caves below. For a moment my world balloons horribly, throwing me off balance.

'Marco!'

He spins on his heel, listening. That was not my voice. Was it? It was another woman.

'Marco!'

Now it is slightly behind us, back the way we have come. Someone with a thin, lonely voice calling to him.

'Marco! Over here!'

He staggers off and slowly, I follow. We are both responding to her words, but I know something he doesn't. The direction of her

302

voice is where the cliff ends. I wonder if Marco knows that. I hope not. *Whick. Whick.*

'High-handed little bitch,' he growls.

Whick, whick.

Then, again, 'Marco!'

Laughing, merry. It infuriates him. He moves faster, heading down the slope where the wild grass and gorse grow thickest. I can just see him there in the gloom but I daren't go any further. I know how deep that drop is.

'Marc-oh.' He has become a thin sketch, a shadow figure. I cup my hands together and blow on them. It is very cold up here and the light is bad. Marco has stopped moving, seems suddenly unsure of himself. Perhaps he can hear the sea just below him, sense that vast emptiness. If the fall doesn't kill you the cold will. Good. I hope it is miserable and lingering. There is someone else there too, moving towards him. Another figure in the dark. She is very close to him now, and he sees her. I hear his voice just barely. I think he is saying, 'Not you, not you', and then he moves as if to run, pinwheels his arms as the ground gives way, crumbling. I am glad I do not see his face as he falls.

Epilogue

The sky is overcast, threatening rain. Although it is not yet late afternoon the day is darkening, and many of the cars already have their headlights on. I am walking towards Abney Park Cemetery near Stoke Newington. It's where Carmel grew up and where we used to come when we were teenage Goths, drinking snakebite and black and smoking Embassy down to the filters. She was cremated, but we planted a tree here, her mother and I. It's a rowan tree, said to protect against evil.

I pass someone, and they do a double take. It happens a lot, even now, although it's nothing to do with *Marigold!* anymore. It's the story they printed in the papers. Afterwards.

It is nearly two years since Marco went missing. A patch of his blood was found very close to the cliff edge and less than a foot away they found one of his shoes. Italian, hand-stitched leather. What a waste.

By the time I got back to the cottage that day I could barely stand. My dress was trailing on the ground behind me, my wig lost, my nails split and torn. As I pushed open the back door I saw a figure in the kitchen and staggered, sure it was somehow Marco, with those pills and a cigarette and that poker in his hand, *whick, whick.*

But it wasn't. It was Frankie. He was leaning on the table, his face grey. When he saw me his jaw fell open and his hands moved as if to catch me.

'I thought you were dead,' I told him.

'Stella. Oh my God. Come here.'

I started to walk towards him, but I didn't make it. I went down, down.

A list of my injuries as reported in the papers: broken nose, dislocated collarbone, soft tissue damage, various abrasions. The level of barbiturates in my system was exaggerated, but not by much. Attempted suicide, the papers said, just like her mother. Tragic.

Carmel's death was recorded as blunt force trauma. Marco had felled her like a tree, denting the smooth bone of her skull in the process. My wonderful friend, who had lain in a pool of tacky blood as I'd placed her hand in my lap and waited for the police to arrive. They'd found his fingerprints on the doorstop along with traces of Carmel's blood and strands of her hair.

I spent nine days in hospital and several hours under police interrogation. It was only Alice giving evidence against Marco which means I am no longer under suspicion for murder. Alice calls me now and then. Tells me she thinks of me often. Sometimes we meet for coffee. It is good to have a friend again.

Frankie had a punctured lung and at least two broken ribs, a fractured jaw and elbow as well as scrapes and injuries to the side which bore the brunt of the impact. Later he would tell me that Marco accelerated almost immediately after he got in the car, before he could put on his seatbelt. He still walks with a limp, leaning heavily on his left side. The car almost overturned up the bank before hitting the tree. In the boot of the car police found a hunting knife, cable ties and rope, a bottle of ether and wads of gauze. The knife had an eight-inch blade and, I was told later, was used for gutting deer. Any idea why Marco would have these in the car, they asked me. No, I said. No idea.

Except, of course, I did. I'd been so sure he was going to keep me prisoner, that he wanted to preserve me like a little doll, that it hadn't occurred to me that he was going to kill me. High-handed bitch, he'd called me, and I still thought he'd wanted me to live. A man who, as a boy, had sent those strange little packages to a ten-year-old girl: crushed-out cigarettes, nail clippings, tissues still gummy with semen. All that time. All that time. Talk about a life sentence.

Doctor Wilson was arrested only days later at his home for three counts of practising medicine without a licence; two counts of practice of gynaecological examination without a licence; three counts of forgery; two counts of theft; and three counts of fraudulent use of personal identification information. 'I deal with a lot of addicts, Stella,' he'd told me, and in a way I suppose that was true, wasn't it? He'd been a dealer of sorts. In the cupboard beneath his desk was found a large quantity of opioids and stimulants, mainly morphine. He liked to dabble, and he's known to have spiked a number of his patients, mostly young women. I'm hoping they too will testify.

Sometimes the fall is more frightening than the impact. That's what I keep telling myself. Ten months of therapy and a wedding and a funeral and all it took was the phone call I received yesterday morning to shake me to my bones. There is only one person I want to see to share this news with and I have come a long way to see her. The sky in London is flat grey chrome. I am wearing a plain blue dress and I have lost my brittle, fragile shell, cutting my hair short, allowing it to lighten in the summer sun. I have been married a little over a month and the wedding ring still shocks me when I see it on my finger.

Frankie and I were wed in a church in the far south of Cornwall, a long way from Tyrlaze, and even further from Chy an Mor. It was a bright spring morning, bitterly cold with the first few flurries of snow falling amongst the yellow daffodils growing in the church-yard. It was a small ceremony, very informal. I wore yellow and carried primroses in my posy. Aunt Jackie wept in the front pew, her face shiny with happiness. She'd come to see me in the days after Marco's disappearance, hugging me tightly to her with a jangle of charm bracelets and rosaries.

'He told me you weren't coming back,' she said.

'I know.'

Martha and James had also sat in the front pew, in the space my parents would have occupied. Baby Oskar had been cradled in Martha's arms, his skin downy-soft and peach-coloured. Earlier that morning Martha had helped me get ready, smoothing my skin with her beautiful, expensive face serums and dusting me with soft perfume. She had reached into her bag and pulled out a liquid eye-liner – a bright, vibrant blue colour – that I recognised immediately as the one Carmel used to wear.

'Your "something blue",' she had said, her hand only slightly trembling as she'd applied it to the line of my lashes.

I take a right and then another right down a long street of houses stacked like crooked teeth. Deep breath. The London air curdles my lungs. A cat lies on a windowsill watching me, tail switching, half asleep.

I'd taken flowers to the spot on the cliff where she jumped. Ellie. I wonder how it would feel to plummet that far; would there be a lightness, a liberation? Would the air rushing past your ears sound like voices in the dark? I'd closed my eyes and seen the rain dimpling the surface of the water, and Ellie jack-knifing into it like a blade, over and over on a loop. A descending horror, down where the thoughts bury themselves like reclusive creatures of the deep. I had stood until the wind had made my eyes stream and then I walked back the way I had come, up from Tyrlaze, around the coastal path. I did not look over my shoulder. I did not look at Chy an Mor.

I don't take flowers to Carmel's tree. I take wine and cigarettes and something bright to hang in it. Neon-pink fishnet, a vivid green taffeta, ribbons in electric blue. In the winter I string fairy lights through the branches. Last year a robin nested in the Y-shaped bough. Her mother had been pleased. They're said to be good omens, she'd told me. A symbol of dead loved ones. Then she'd hooked her arm through mine and said she would buy me tea in the café in the park. That was then, last time. I'm here alone now. Some nights I wake and think I see someone standing in the corner of our bedroom where the eaves dip the lowest. A shape, slightly blurred. Like moving smoke. I think it may be Carmel, come back to me in the still hours of the night. I jerk awake as though she is standing over me and I can never tell if my heart is beating too fast because I am hopeful or because I am frightened. And so I come here, and I bring her things, and I tell her I am sorry.

I still have her gift, the inscribed bracelet, but I have not been able to bring myself to wear it. I haven't felt worthy. Not till yesterday. Not till I got the call.

They found his body. After all this time. The phone had rung yesterday morning, startling me from a dreamless sleep. The skeletal remains of Marco Nilsen – a man also known as 'Uncle' – had been washed ashore at high tide in a bay thirteen miles away. He was still wearing the remaining shoe. He had been missing his lower jaw and his right hand. I like to think of crabs nesting behind his ribs, barnacles clotting his spine.

I am nearly at Carmel's tree now. I'll sit there awhile. The crocuses are bursting through the earth and my silver bracelet winks as it catches the sunlight. It is a good day. A warm day.

I will enjoy this day and all the ones after it.

And I will make scar tissue of my memories.

And I will heal.

I will heal.

ACKNOWLEDGMENTS

I owe heartfelt thanks to so many people for helping me to write this book.

My agent Catherine Cho at Curtis Brown for her enthusiasm, her ideas and her determination. This would not be happening without you.

To my editor Jane Snelgrove for your boundless belief and the help you've given me. Wishing you many great things ahead. Thanks also to Ian Pinder for your patience and assistance and to Hatty for her creativity. Extremely grateful to all at Thomas & Mercer for their hard work!

I am lucky enough to have some wonderful family and friends who supported me while this book was written, in particular my sister Simone Franklin for her insights, my pal OJ Murrell for his patience, Erica Morgan for the loan of the laptop and the shove to get going, Mary Torjussen, a brilliant writer who has been so much help, and of course to Anne Booty, for her friendship and constant, unwavering belief in me. To these original readers, thank you.

Also special mentions to Writers HQ in Brighton, New Writing South and the Literary Consultancy as well as Bill Griffin from Crowdwish, who all helped me keep going. Many, many shout-outs to Pleasant Cafe in Lewes (RIP) for all the coffee and to Amy Murrell for making a photoshoot fun even when I'm dying inside.

To my family, especially my mum and Steve, to Berwyn and Dominic and Simone, I promise I'll never write about the old days (I will write about the old days). And to my wonderful daughter Poppy, a force of good and happiness in my life. I love you, darling.

Lastly, thanks to Stephen King. I love you, man.

ABOUT THE AUTHOR

Photo © 2019 A. Murrell

Daisy Pearce was born in Cornwall and grew up on a smallholding surrounded by hippies. She read Stephen King's *Cujo* and *The Hamlyn Book of Horror* far too young and has been fascinated with the macabre ever since.

She began writing short stories as a teenager and dropped out of a fashion journalism course at university when she realised it wasn't anywhere near as fun as making stuff up. After spells living in London and Brighton, Daisy had her short story 'The Black Prince' published in *One Eye Grey* magazine. Another short story, 'The Brook Witch', was performed on stage at the Small Story Cabaret in Lewes in 2016. She has also written articles about mental health online. In 2015, *The Silence* won a bursary with The Literary Consultancy, and later that year Daisy also won the Chindi Authors

Competition with her short story 'Worm Food'. Her second novel was longlisted for the Mslexia Novel Award.

Daisy currently works in the library at the University of Sussex, where she shelves books and listens to podcasts on true crime and folklore. She lives in Lewes with a one-eyed Siamese cat and a nine-year-old daughter who occasionally needs reminding that ghosts and monsters aren't real.

Sometimes she almost believes it herself.

Printed in Great Britain
by Amazon